GW00471303

FURY

A Collection of F/F - M/M Fight Stories

Liz Edon

WARNING

This book contains explicit content, including scenes of violence, mature themes, tobacco use, strong language, and potentially triggering scenarios. Reader discretion is advised. Suitable for mature audiences only.

TABLE OF CONTENTS

CORPORATE CATFIGHT

The ultra-modern boardroom was awash with the sterile gleam of chrome and glass, every surface polished to a mirror finish. The late afternoon sun pierced through the floor-to-ceiling windows, casting long, ominous shadows across the vast conference table. At one end of it, sat Marianne, a statuesque brunette with a gaze as sharp as the tailored lines of her charcoal power suit. At the opposite end, her counterpart, Grace - a fiery redhead, her presence like a shock of electricity in her crimson blazer and pencil skirt. Their feud had been simmering for months, a poisonous cocktail of professional jealousy and personal disdain. But it was today's merger decision that was the spark to their tinderbox of hostility. Rejection hung heavily in the air, the proposed deal shot down, a victory for Marianne and a stinging defeat for Grace.

As the last of their co-workers filed out, the tension between them was as tangible as the cold marble under their feet. When the door clicked shut, their steely gazes locked, and in an unspoken agreement, the boardroom became their battlefield. Marianne was the first to move, striding across the room in swift, predatory steps, her stilettos clicking like warning shots on the floor. Grace held her ground, her emerald eyes sparking defiance. The collision was swift and brutal, a tangle of silk blouses and biting words, their fury echoing in the hollow expanse of the room. Their catfight was a dance of power and dominance. Fingers tangled in glossy hair, nails leaving a trail of marks on unblemished skin. Each blow was punctuated by a harsh grunt or a hissed insult, an embodiment of their burning rivalry. The thud of bodies against the cold, unyielding conference table echoed ominously, papers fluttering to the floor like defeated white flags.

Marianne, using her height to her advantage, attempted to pin Grace against the polished mahogany, but the fiery redhead was nimble, slipping out of her grip and retaliating with a swift knee to the midriff. The brunette doubled over, winded, but her retaliation was swift - a calculated punch that sent Grace sprawling across the table. Grace, sprawled across the table, momentarily dazed, quickly regained her bearings. Her chest heaved, each breath a gasping intake of the frigid, air-conditioned atmosphere. She pushed herself off the table, her eyes meeting Marianne's, each pair reflecting a potent mix of animosity and resilience. Marianne straightened her posture, the pain from the earlier blow receding into a dull throb. She crossed the distance between them once again, her every muscle coiled, ready to strike. Grace mirrored her stance, her emerald eyes sparking with determined fury.

Their second clash was just as brutal as the first. Fingers clenched in expensive silk; elbows jabbed into toned midriffs. Sharp gasps and stifled grunts filled the silent room, punctuating the clicking of the wall clock and the distant hum of the city. Marianne, attempting to regain her previous advantage, landed a calculated blow on Grace's belly. Grace stumbled back, her back hitting the icy glass of the floor-to-ceiling window. A shocked gasp left her lips as the cold seeped through her blouse, a stark contrast to her heated skin. Not one to be caught off guard for long, Grace recovered quickly. She retaliated with a sharp jab to Marianne's cheek, using her leverage against the window to send the brunette reeling backward. Marianne stumbled but quickly regained her footing, her dark eyes blazing with renewed defiance. They circled each other like predators, both nursing their injuries, their breaths coming out in ragged pants.

They lunged for each other again, their movements now somewhat sluggish but still filled with determination. The echoes of their struggle grew harsher, the room bearing silent witness to their grueling catfight. Their feud, once confined to snide remarks and icy glares, had now become a physical manifestation of their fierce rivalry. Despite the pain and exhaustion that were starting to set in, neither showed any signs of backing down. Each blow, each grapple, only served to fuel their determination further. Marianne's sharp nails found Grace's arm, leaving behind bright red streaks that stood out starkly against her pale skin. A wince flashed across Grace's face but was quickly replaced by a defiant smirk. She retaliated with a swift punch to Marianne's abdomen, the surprise impact sending the brunette sprawling onto the cold, hard floor.

Marianne grunted as she hit the floor, the shock momentarily knocking the wind out of her. Grace, taking advantage of her rival's fall, lunged for her. But Marianne was quick to recover, rolling away just in time, leaving

Grace to stumble awkwardly over empty space. In the dim light, their silhouettes were a whirl of activity. Marianne rose, advancing on Grace with renewed vigor. Their fingers tangled once again, a brutal tug of war. Grace took a swift step back, pulling Marianne with her. In a quick, calculated move, Grace spun, using Marianne's momentum against her, and sent her crashing into the glass window. The impact was jarring, the sound echoing through the silent boardroom. Marianne slid to the floor, stunned. Grace, breathing heavily, stood her ground, waiting for Marianne to rise. But the brunette remained down, her chest heaving, her spirit finally worn down.

As Grace stood over Marianne, her victory was not one of joy, but of survival. She had proved herself in the most primal way, her triumph echoing in the silent room, etched into the battered surfaces of the corporate battlefield. Outside, the city came alive with the sparkle of night lights, oblivious to the epic showdown that had taken place. Grace straightened her crumpled blazer, smoothed her disheveled hair, and walked away from the scene, leaving behind the remnants of the intense 'Corporate Catfight'. The echoes of their battle gradually faded, swallowed by the serene silence of the night.

HEAVY HITTERS ON THE HIGHWAY

In the dusty, forgotten corner of a truck stop, the usual clinks of mugs and murmur of idle chatter were replaced with a tense silence. The patrons, a motley crew of grizzled truckers, held their breath as two women stepped into a makeshift ring, outlined by the semicircle of parked rigs. These weren't the lithe, young fighters of the professional circuit. They were middle-aged, robust, and as tough as the 18-wheelers they drove. They were called 'Mama Bear', a burly woman with a booming laugh, and 'Big Betty', a woman whose size was rivaled only by her reputation. This would be a brawl where no punch was off-limits. Mama Bear and Big Betty were not strangers to physical confrontations. Living a hard life on the road, they had had their fair share of fights. But this face-off was different. There was a personal score to settle, an old grudge that had turned the friends into rivals. And tonight, they would settle it with their fists.

Dressed in their usual trucking gear, jeans, and worn-out t-shirts, they eyed each other across the ring. Mama Bear, her auburn hair pulled back into a messy bun, cracked her knuckles, her usual jovial demeanor replaced with a steely determination. Big Betty, her strong features hardened into a glare, responded with a flex of her powerful arms, a silent declaration of her readiness. The referee, a wiry old trucker who had seen his share of fights, signaled the start of the match. Mama Bear and Big Betty advanced towards each other, their heavy steps echoing through the silent truck stop. Mama Bear was the first to throw a punch, her fist flying towards Big Betty's face with a thud. Betty was quick to retaliate, her own fist thrown with a powerful jab that connected with Mama Bear's cheek, drawing a gasp from the crowd.

The fight was on, and it was brutal. There were no fancy moves or calculated strategies, just raw, unadulterated power. Their punches landed with a force that shook their robust bodies, the impact resonating through the silent truck stop. Mama Bear, despite the brutal punch she had taken, retaliated with a swift jab to Betty's stomach, her powerful fist making the larger woman stagger. Betty, however, was quick to recover, her punch landing square on Mama Bear's jaw, a grimace of pain flashing across the burly woman's face. Their fight was a brutal showcase of raw power, their punches landing with an intensity that left the spectators on edge. Despite their size, or perhaps because of it, their movements were swift, their punches deadly. There was no holding back, no mercy, only the relentless pursuit of victory.

The fight between Mama Bear and Big Betty raged on, their grunts of exertion punctuating the silent night. Their powerful blows echoed through the truck stop, their grimaces of pain a testament to the brutality of their face-off. They traded blows, their powerful punches landing with a force that had the crowd wincing in sympathy.

Despite the brutal punches and the growing fatigue, neither woman was willing to back down. Their rivalry, their personal grudge, fueled their determination, pushing them to fight with everything they had. Their fight was as much a battle of wills as it was of strength, their resolve as powerful as their punches. Mama Bear, her face beginning to bruise, landed a powerful hook on Betty's face, her fist connecting with a force that staggered the larger woman. Betty, however, was not one to be easily taken down. With a swift uppercut, she retaliated, her punch landing squarely on Mama Bear's chin, sending the burly woman stumbling back. The spectators, a tough crowd of truckers who had seen their share of fights, watched with bated breath. Their usual boisterous demeanor replaced with a tense anticipation; their eyes glued to the brutal face-off taking place in front of them. Mama Bear and Big Betty, their bodies bruised and sweating, their breaths labored, fought with a relentless determination. Their punches, brutal and unforgiving, were a testament to their toughness, their will to win unwavering despite the brutal nature of their confrontation. Finally, after a grueling battle, Big Betty landed a powerful punch that sent Mama Bear crashing to the ground, her burly body kicking up a cloud of dust. The crowd let out a collective gasp, their tense anticipation giving way to surprised silence. Big Betty, panting heavily and nursing her own injuries, delivered a couple of powerful kicks to Mama Bear's side. Leaning down to face her opponent, Big Betty delivered one last punch to the side of Mama Bear's face. The fight was over. Big Betty's victory was evident in her hardened gaze. The fight was a brutal testament to their toughness. Their personal grudge settled with their fists.

BOUND BY THE BRAWL

In the damp basement of an abandoned warehouse, a peculiar fight was about to take place. The participants: two women, fierce and fiery, with a shared history of rivalry. The twist: one woman's left wrist was handcuffed to the other's right, a restriction that promised to make their confrontation even more challenging. They were Sally, a tenacious bartender known for her scrappy fighting style, and Rita, a tough mechanic who earned a reputation of unyielding determination. The onlookers, a small group of locals who thrived on the thrill of these underground fights, watched with bated breath as Sally and Rita stepped into the makeshift ring. The metallic clink of the handcuff echoed through the silent basement, a grim reminder of the challenging conditions of their brawl.

Sally, her blond hair pulled back in a messy ponytail, sized up her opponent, her emerald eyes flashing with determination. Rita, her strong features set into a stern glare, flexed her free hand, her dark eyes fixed on her handcuffed rival. The match began with a loud cheer from the crowd. Immediately, the limitations of their bound wrists became evident. Every punch thrown was a risky move, opening the opportunity for the other to retaliate. Their confrontation was as much about strategy as it was about strength, their moves calculated and precise. Sally, with her scrappy fighting style, aimed to land quick, successive punches. Her strikes were swift and accurate, but Rita was quick to retaliate. With a solid punch, Rita landed a hard belly punch that made Sally wince, the impact reverberating up their connected arms. The match was brutal and relentless. The confines of the handcuff made their fight even more challenging, each punch thrown a dangerous gamble. Their fight was not just a physical confrontation, but a battle of wits, their moves calculated to exploit the vulnerability of their opponent.

As the match progressed, the physical toll of their brutal face-off began to show. Sally, despite her agile moves, sported a swelling right eye, a testament to Rita's powerful punches. Rita, despite her solid defense, was panting heavily, the relentless pace of the fight pushing her endurance to the limit. Rita's nose was bloody from Sally's repeated punches. Not to the extent of Sally's near swollen shut eye, Rita was sporting a colorful shiner. In the end, it was Rita who claimed victory. With a final, powerful punch, she caught Sally off guard, sending the tenacious bartender crashing to the ground, with Rita falling with her. As the crowd erupted into cheers, the cuffs were removed and Rita stood victorious, her dark eyes shining with the thrill of victory. Their rivalry had been settled in a fight that was as unique as it was challenging. Rita's victory claimed not just with their fists, but with her relentless will to win.

ASHES OF ENDURANCE

In the mysterious underbelly of Houston's underground fight club, a unique contest was about to take place. The participants: three women, each fierce and formidable in their own right. The rules: one woman holds the opponent while the second lands the punches. The challenge: if the victim can remain standing until the puncher's lit cigarette, clenched between her teeth, burns out, she wins. But if she drops to her knees at any point, she loses. The contenders were Marla, a bouncer with a reputation as formidable as her physique, Gina, a fiery waitress known for her relentless punches, and their chosen victim, Ivy, a yoga instructor known for her incredible endurance. As the crowd, a rowdy mix of fight enthusiasts and thrill-seekers, watched in anticipation, Marla, Gina, and Ivy entered the ring. The dingy underground club was alight with excitement, the grimy walls echoing with the hum of expectation.

Marla, with her hulking frame and powerful arms, stood behind Ivy, ready to restrain her as per the rules. Gina, a lithe figure in contrast, stood in front of Ivy. She held a long cigarette, its end glowing ominously. Once it was nestled between her clenched teeth, the contest would begin. And then, with a quick flick of a lighter,

Gina ignited the end of her cigarette. The club went silent, the burning ember at the end of Gina's cigarette marking the beginning of their brutal contest. As soon as the cigarette was lit, Marla took hold of Ivy, her powerful arms effectively restraining the slender yoga instructor. Ivy's eyes, usually serene and calm, flickered with a hint of determination. She was ready to face whatever Gina had in store for her.

Gina, her eyes narrowed into a hardened gaze, pulled her arm back, ready to throw the first punch. The orange glow of the cigarette, clenched tightly between her teeth, cast an ominous glow on her stern features. This was the start of a contest that promised to be as brutal as it was unique. With a swift, practiced move, Gina threw her first punch. It landed squarely on Ivy's stomach, the force making the slender woman wince. But Ivy, with her extraordinary endurance, remained standing, her feet firmly planted on the ground. The crowd, watching in tense anticipation, let out a collective gasp, the thrill of the contest only beginning to unfold.

The room echoed with the brutal sound of Gina's fist colliding with Ivy's midsection, the crowd holding their collective breath as they watched the unusual contest unfold. Ivy grimaced but remained on her feet, her resolve evident in her clenched fists and stern gaze. Marla, maintaining her hold on Ivy, watched the proceedings with a cold detachment. She was there to hold, to restrain, not to intervene. The grim set of her jaw was the only testament to the brutal nature of their contest. Gina, her cigarette still burning between her teeth, prepared to throw another punch, the fiery ember casting an ominous glow on the scene. With a swift, precise movement, Gina landed another punch. This time, her fist collided with Ivy's side, the force of the blow making the restrained woman gasp. Yet, Ivy remained standing, her face pale but her eyes resolute. The onlookers watched in tense anticipation, the brutal contest unfolding in front of them a unique spectacle. The hum of conversation had long since died down, replaced with a tense silence, punctuated only by the sharp thuds of Gina's punches and the labored breaths of their victim. Gina, her punches powerful and relentless, continued her assault. Ivy, despite the brutal onslaught, stood her ground. Her body swayed with the impact of each punch, her breathing became labored, but her determination was unwavering. The glowing end of Gina's cigarette continued to burn, the thin trail of smoke curling upwards a grim reminder of Ivy's challenge. The glowing ember inched closer to its end, the ashes falling to the floor a silent testament to the passing time. Marla, her hold on Ivy unwavering, watched the spectacle with an unreadable expression. Her role was not an easy one, but she performed it with a stoic determination, holding Ivy as Gina continued her relentless assault. As the contest continued, Gina alternated between landing her brutal punches and taking deep drags from her cigarette. The glowing ember reduced with each puff, the resulting smoke curling upwards and disappearing into the dim lighting of the underground club.

Ivy, despite the onslaught, remained standing. Her breathing was labored, her body visibly strained, yet her eyes remained resolute. Each punch was a challenge she met head-on; each draw Gina took from her cigarette a reminder of the time ticking away. Gina landed another punch, this time targeting Ivy's ribs. The sound of the impact echoed through the silent club, a stark reminder of the brutality of their contest. But Ivy, despite the pain, stood her ground, her legs shaking but refusing to buckle. In between the brutal punches, Gina took deep, deliberate puffs from her cigarette. The smoke, thick and heavy, hung in the air, adding to the intense atmosphere of the club. With each puff, the ember at the end of the cigarette grew smaller, the ashes falling to the floor marking the passage of time.

Marla's hold on Ivy was unwavering. Despite the visible strain on the yoga instructor's face, the burly woman didn't loosen her grip. Her role, though passive, was a crucial part of their brutal contest. The crowd watched in silent anticipation as the contest unfolded. Their expressions ranged from awe to shock, the brutal spectacle unfolding in front of them unlike anything they had seen before. With a final, powerful punch, Gina aimed for Ivy's belly button. The impact was brutal, causing Ivy to gasp and sway. Yet, she remained standing, her body trembling but her resolve unbroken. Gina took a final drag from her cigarette, the ember at the end flickering before it died out. As the last wisps of smoke curled up and disappeared, the underground club erupted into cheers. Ivy had done it. She had remained standing until the end of Gina's cigarette, earning her a hard-fought victory.

BRUTAL MISMATCH

In a secluded location away from the prying eyes of the public, a highly unequal match was about to take place. The participants: two women, one obese and towering, named Mary, and one slim and petite, named Lily. The setting: a private fight, away from the roaring crowds of an underground fight club, destined to be a one-sided beatdown. Mary, with her hulking frame and raw strength, was an intimidating figure. In contrast, Lily, with her slender figure and delicate features, seemed almost fragile. Yet, in the brutal world of underground fights, appearances could be deceiving. The cause of the fight was simple, and as old as time, Lily's constant badgering on Mary's size.

As the fight started, Mary's raw strength quickly came into play. Her punches were powerful and brutal, each one landing with a thud that echoed in the secluded room. Lily, despite her nimble movements, was unable to dodge Mary's relentless onslaught. The brutality of the fight was hard to watch. Lily's attempts to retaliate were futile against Mary's superior strength. Each punch Lily threw was easily deflected, each attempt to dodge met with another brutal hit. Despite the uneven odds, Lily didn't back down. Her face was a mask of determination, her green eyes flashing with a fierce resolve. Yet, as the fight progressed, it became increasingly clear that Mary's strength was overpowering. Mary appeared almost untouched. Lily, on the other hand, was bruised and bloody. Lily's left eye was quickly swelling shut and blood flowing from her nose and lips.

Mary's final blow sent Lily crashing to the ground, her slender frame no match for the powerful woman's strength. As Lily laid on the ground, Mary stood victorious, her large frame casting a shadow over her defeated opponent. The fight had been as brutal as it was one-sided, a stark reminder of the harsh reality of their world. The aftermath of the fight proved grimmer. Mary, as part of her victory, straddled Lily's face, forcing Lily to satisfy Mary's sexual desires. The brutal act emphasized the harsh reality of verbal abuse Mary had routinely received. From this moment on, Lily never made fun of Mary again.

KITCHEN RECKONING

The atmosphere inside Emily's kitchen was charged with tension. Emily, a 30-year-old woman with a toned physique and an aura of confidence, was about to face a confrontation she never expected. Opposite her stood Martha and Gloria, two 60ish-year-old women with a shared history, both harboring a long-standing grudge against the younger woman. With swift precision, Martha moved in, using her surprising agility to get behind Emily. With a tight grip, she executed a full Nelson restraint, locking Emily's arms behind her and leaving her vulnerable. Gloria, seizing the opportunity, lunged forward and grabbed two handfuls of Emily's silky brown hair, ensuring that her head was held firmly in place. Emily's eyes widened in shock and panic as Gloria began her assault. Her fingers were nimble as they tore open Emily's blouse, exposing her black lace bra. With a swift yank, she pulled the bra upwards, revealing Emily's full breasts. Now completely vulnerable, Emily tried to break free, but the combined strength of the two grandmothers held her in place.

Taking a deep breath, Gloria began her methodical assault. Her first punch was directed at Emily's ribcage, making the younger woman gasp in pain. "That's for the disrespect," Gloria sneered. Her next punch landed squarely on Emily's left side, right below her armpit. "Remember the time you lied to us?" Gloria spat, her eyes cold and unyielding. Martha tightened her grip on Emily, ensuring she couldn't escape. Emily's face was a mixture of pain and disbelief as she struggled against her restraints. Gloria's fists moved with precision, connecting with Emily's belly just below the belly button. Emily's body convulsed with each hit; her face contorted in pain. "You thought you could get away with it, didn't you?" Gloria taunted, her voice dripping with venom.

The rhythmic thudding of Gloria's fists against Emily's flesh filled the kitchen. Each punch was a testament to the older woman's strength and determination. Despite her age, Gloria's blows were powerful, each one leaving its mark on the younger woman's body. A particularly hard punch to Emily's side made her cry out. Tears streamed down her face, but she was unable to break free. "Please, stop," she gasped, but her pleas fell on deaf ears. Gloria's favorite target was Emily's midsection, just below the belly button. She landed punch after punch in that spot, enjoying the younger woman's cries of pain. "You deserve every bit of this," Gloria growled, her eyes filled with rage.

With every hit, Emily's body buckled and shook. The pain was overwhelming, but the humiliation was even worse. Held in place by two women old enough to be her grandmothers, she was completely powerless. The kitchen, once a place of warmth and comfort, had become a battleground. The sound of fists connecting with flesh, the cries of pain, and the cold, harsh taunts from the grandmothers filled the room. It was a confrontation that would leave a lasting mark, both physically and emotionally. Martha's grip never wavered, her fingers digging into Emily's arms, ensuring she remained an easy target for Gloria. With each hit, she spoke words of encouragement to Gloria, further fueling the older woman's fury.

Gloria, taking a moment to catch her breath, looked into Emily's tear-filled eyes. "Did you really think you could betray us and not face the consequences?" She hissed; her voice laced with contempt. With that, she delivered a powerful punch to Emily's cheek, causing her head to snap to the side, only to be held in place by the tight grip on her hair. With Emily's face now an open target, Gloria focused her attention there. She landed a series of hard slaps across Emily's cheeks, turning them a bright shade of red. Each slap was accompanied by a biting comment. "That's for the lies," *slap*, "That's for the deceit," *slap*, "And that's for simply being a Bitch," *slap*. Emily's face stung from the force of the blows, her skin burning from the repeated assaults. Her vision blurred with tears, and her breaths came in ragged gasps. The pain was unbearable, but it was the betrayal she felt that hurt even more. She had never imagined that the two women she had grown up respecting would be capable of such brutality.

As Gloria continued her relentless assault, focusing again on Emily's exposed midsection, Martha leaned in closer, her voice low and menacing. "You brought this on yourself, dear. We had to teach you a lesson. No one crosses us and gets away with it." The ferocity of the blows to Emily's stomach was relentless. Each punch seemed harder than the last, forcing the air out of her lungs and leaving her gasping for breath. The tender spot just below her belly button bore the brunt of Gloria's fury, the skin there turning a deep shade of purple from the repeated impacts. After what felt like an eternity, Gloria finally stepped back, her fists red and swollen from the force of her blows. Martha released her grip on Emily, who crumpled to the floor, her body wracked with sobs.

The two grandmothers looked down at their handiwork, a mix of satisfaction and regret in their eyes. They had made their point, but at what cost? As they left the kitchen, the silence was deafening. Emily lay on the floor, her body bruised and battered, the weight of the confrontation heavy on her heart. The aftermath of the brutal confrontation was a stark reminder of the fragile bonds that tie us together and the lengths some will go to protect their honor and pride.

INTERVIEW WITH A CAT FIGHTER

Meg interviews Mara for a podcast on aggressive women in the porn industry. Mara has a website and is infamous for her fight videos, among other things.

Meg: "Can you tell us your name?"

Mara: "It's Mara, Mara Callahan. Everyone in the scene knows me by that."

Meg: "Do you mind me ask you how old you are?"

Mara: "I'm 51, though I reckon I can still hold my own better than most of these younger girls coming up."

Meg: "How old were you when you had your first fight?"

Mara: "Ah, I was just a kid. 'Bout 22. Young, reckless, and thinkin' I could take on the world. Guess I never really grew out of that mindset, huh?"

Meg: "How did it turn out?"

Mara: "That first fight? Ha! It was a mess, to be honest. I went up against a girl, Becca, I think was her name. She had a bit more experience than me. I landed some good shots, but she got me good too. Ended up with a black eye and bruised ego, but I learned a lot from that scrap. Made me realize how much I loved the thrill of it all."

Meg: "Would you say you won or lost?"

Mara: "Heh, if we're being blunt? I lost that one. Physically, she got the better of me. But mentally? It lit a fire in me. So, I might've lost the battle, but it set me on a path to win many more wars, if ya get what I'm saying."

Meg: "You are gorgeous. What are your stats?"

Mara: "Well, ain't you a charmer! I'm 5'7". As for measurements, I'm not exactly sure these days. Used to be a 36-28-38 back in my prime, but bodies change, especially with the kinda life I've lived. Either way, I've always been built sturdy, and I like to think I've aged like a fine wine."

Meg: "If you don't mind me saying, you are still very chesty, if that is a word. D cup?"

Mara: "(laughs) Well, I've never been shy about it. Yeah, D cup. Genetics, I guess. But trust me, in this line of 'work', it's both an asset and a liability."

Meg: "I could see the liability for sure. I am sure they have been targets. Explain how they can be assets? I mean in a fight. By the look of your cleavage, I already now they are an asset; to me. Sorry, I must confess."

Mara: "(laughs heartily) Well, you're not the first to mention it, and I'm sure you won't be the last. Yeah, they've been targets, but you learn to use what you got. As for assets, distraction's a big one. You'd be surprised how many opponents get fixated on 'em, thinking it's an easy win. While they're focused there, I've got the advantage, a split second to land a solid hit. It's all about psychology and using what Mother Nature gave ya. And hey, thanks for the compliment. You're not so bad yourself."

Meg: "Well, I am only a C. In a tit fight, I think you beat me."

Mara: "(laughs) Oh, honey, it's not just about size. It's about determination, strategy, and experience. But I appreciate the compliment. Every woman's built differently, and every woman brings something unique to the table. It's all in how you use what you got."

Meg: "Do you remember your first black eye? I assume you have had a black eye?"

Mara: "Oh, absolutely. That first fight I mentioned with Becca? That's when I got my first shiner. Wore it like a badge of honor, though. Felt like it was my initiation into this wild world of catfighting. Over the years, I've had my fair share of black eyes, busted lips, and bruises. But each one's got a story behind it, and I wouldn't trade those experiences for anything."

Meg: "Ever had an eye swollen shut? I know what a pain in the ass that is."

Mara: "Yeah, a couple of times. It's a real pain, both literally and figuratively. Makes everything a challenge, from daily tasks to just getting through the day. One of the worst times was after a particularly brutal fight with this gal, Roxanne. She had a mean right hook, I'll give her that. Woke up the next day barely able to see out of that eye. But hey, it's part of the game. Comes with the territory, you know?"

Meg: "I agree, I try to avoid getting hit right along my eyebrow, if possible."

Mara: "Smart move. That area's particularly sensitive and swells up easy. But sometimes, in the heat of the moment, you can't always control where a punch lands. Best you can do is keep your guard up and hope for the best. Over the years, you learn to roll with the punches, both literally and figuratively."

Meg: "I know you are a smoker; so am I by the way. I have heard that it is more than an addiction for you, it is a sexual turn on. Personally, I understand it, and have my reasons. But I want to hear yours."

Mara: "Well, it's a personal thing, ain't it? I started smoking young, way too young, honestly. But over the years, it became more than just a habit. There's a certain power in it, a sort of control. Holding that cigarette, taking a long drag, feeling the smoke fill your lungs and then exhaling it out... it's almost meditative for me. And yeah, there's a sensual side to it too. The way it makes my lips feel, the warmth, the taste. It can be intimate, in a way. I've had partners who found it incredibly arousing, and I won't lie, there's something about sharing a smoke after... well, you know, that just feels right. But hey, it's not for everyone, and I get that."

Meg: "I think it can intimidate some opponents. A bad girl thing. I have faced off before a fight smoking a cigarette."

Mara: "Oh, absolutely. There's a certain attitude, a confidence that comes with it. Standing there, lighting up, taking a drag, blowing out the smoke while you size up your opponent. It's a statement without words, like saying, 'I'm in control, I'm not scared, and I'm ready for whatever you got.' Plus, there's that whole 'bad girl' vibe, like you said. It's a mind game as much as it is physical. Anything to give you that edge, you know?"

Meg: "Well, you are a sexy smoker, I have seen the videos. Especially when you combine a nose and mouth exhale. Wow, you are giving me goosebumps thinking about it. I think it's time we have a smoke while we continue."

Mara: "(laughs) Well, thank you. I've always believed in doing things with style. And yeah, the combination exhale, it's a bit of an art form. But sure thing, let's light up and continue. Nothing like a good chat with a cigarette in hand."

Meg: "Ok, enough about smoking. Well, not quite. I saw a video a few years back where you put a cigarette out in a woman's naval. That was a little shocking to see. Was that planned, or spontaneous?"

Mara: "Ah, that one. Yeah, I remember it. Wasn't one of my proudest moments, to be honest. It was in the heat of the moment, tensions were high, and things got... out of hand. It wasn't planned at all. Sometimes in the heat of battle, emotions take over and you do things you regret later. I apologized to her afterward. We've had our differences, but that was a step too far, even for me."

Meg: "Well, just between you and me. It was sexy as hell. I must admit."

Mara: "(chuckles) Well, everyone's got their thing, don't they? I appreciate the honesty. Like I said, it was a raw moment, and I guess that raw emotion can be captivating to some. But remember, consent and boundaries are important. What might be thrilling for some can be deeply distressing for others. It's always important to find that balance."

Meg: "I will agree with you there. Speaking of belly button, not cigarette related. You seem to like the area around and just below the belly button. Is that a favorite target?"

Mara: "You've got a sharp eye. Yes, I do tend to focus on that area quite a bit. It's a vulnerable spot, especially if your opponent isn't expecting it. A well-placed punch or strike there can wind someone, make 'em double over. It's all about strategy. If you can control the fight and keep your opponent off-balance, you've got a better shot at winning. Plus, there's something very intimate about that area, almost taboo. Going for it can throw off an opponent mentally as well."

Meg: "I hate getting punched in my solar plexus. I would rather take a punch to my pussy. What do you think about getting hit in the solar plexus?"

Mara: "Getting hit in the solar plexus is one of the worst feelings, no doubt about it. It's a shock to the system. Knocks the wind right out of you, and for a moment, you feel like you can't breathe. I've been on both the giving and receiving end of those punches, and it's definitely a game-changer in a fight. As for comparing it to a cunt punch... well, both are uniquely painful in their own right. But the solar plexus, that's a vulnerability that's hard to defend, especially if you don't see it coming."

Meg: "Where do you not like to get hit?"

Mara: "Well, no one likes getting hit anywhere, really. But if I had to choose, I'd say the kidneys. A solid hit there sends a jolt of pain that's hard to shake off and can have lasting effects. The nose is another one; a good hit can make your eyes water and obscure your vision, not to mention the possibility of a break. And, of course, my kitty. That is if the punches are continuous."

Meg: "The cunt punch, using your words, when part of a sexfight, can be a turn on though. In a sexfight, you focus so much down there, and you can get wet. Is there a different sensation when punching, fingering, stretching and such, in a sexfight, as opposed to a real fight?"

Mara: "(Sighs) You ask some fucking hard questions. That's a complicated one. Sexfights are a whole different ballgame. There's a blending of pain and pleasure that can be confusing, intense, and even erotic. In those situations, the line between aggression and arousal is blurred. When it's in the context of a sexfight, those actions, like fingering or stretching, they're meant to both dominate and stimulate. It's a battle of endurance and sensitivity. Whereas in a traditional fight, a hit to the pussy is purely about inflicting pain and gaining an advantage. The intent is different, and so is the sensation. There's a mental component to it as well – in a sexfight, you're somewhat prepared for that kind of contact, even if it's aggressive. In a regular fight, it can catch you off guard and feel much more violating."

Meg: "Can't argue with you there. When was your

last real fight?"

Mara: "About six months ago. Things got heated between me and a long-time rival. We'd had skirmishes and words exchanged over the years, but this was the first time we actually went all out in a proper, no-holds-barred fight. Both of us walked away with our fair share of bruises, but it was a good release. Sometimes you just need that, you know? To let out all that pent-up aggression and tension."

Meg: "Was she around your age? Younger, older?"

Mara: "She was younger, probably in her mid-30s. We've had a bit of history, and the age difference added an extra layer of rivalry. She always saw herself as the new blood, the one to take over the scene, and saw me as the old guard, someone she needed to surpass. Our dynamic has always been charged with that tension, the push and pull of experience versus youthful vigor."

Meg: "Who won? Or was there a winner?"

Mara: "(Chuckles) I like to think I held my own pretty well. We both gave as good as we got. But if we're talking about who was left standing at the end, well, let's just say she had a hard time looking me in the eye for a while after that."

Meg: "So, you worked her over? Don't get shy on me now."

Mara: "(Sighs and smirks) Alright, if you want the nitty-gritty... Yes, I worked her over. Used all the experience I've gained over the years to my advantage. I knew her weak spots, her tells, and I made sure to exploit them. By the end, she was winded, bruised, and I could tell she wasn't expecting me to still have that much fire left in me. Age might slow you down a bit, but it also teaches you how to be smarter, more strategic. And that night, strategy won."

Meg: "What is the oldest woman you have fought? In a real fistfight. And how old were you?"

Mara: "The oldest? Hm, that would be Sheila. A fiery redhead, even in her early 60s. I was around 40 at the time. Sheila had been a notorious fighter in her younger years and still had a reputation. We crossed paths in a bar, and who knows what ignited the spark. It was quite the scene – two women with a combined age of over a century, throwing down like it was our prime. Sheila had strength; I'll give her that. But like I said earlier, experience teaches you strategy. And that's where I had the upper hand."

Meg: "Did you feel bad punching a woman in her sixties? Or is a fight a fight, regardless of circumstances? Does that make sense?"

Mara: "I get what you're asking. Look, in the heat of the moment, a fight is a fight. Emotions, adrenaline, past beef – they all come into play. But yeah, afterwards, there's always a moment of reflection. Did I go too far? Should I have held back because of her age? But you have to understand, Sheila was no pushover. She came at me with everything she had. Age can be deceiving; just because someone's older doesn't mean they're frail or can't handle themselves. That said, I do always try to be aware of the situation and gauge how far I should go. With Sheila, it was clear she wanted to prove she still had it. And in a way, I respected her for that."

Meg: "It was a Bar fight?"

Mara: "Yes, that's right. A dive bar we both used to frequent. It had its fair share of rough nights, and people knew that if they came there, they might witness a brawl now and then. That night, we just happened to be the main event."

Meg: "Did they break you up? Or let you fight? I find public fights never really end. Some Good Samaritan jumps in."

Mara: "Ah, this bar... it wasn't your average place. It had a reputation, you know? People who frequented it knew what they were getting into. Most folks there just moved their drinks out of the way and watched. Some cheered, some placed bets. A few shouted for us to 'break it up,' but nobody physically intervened. Fights were kind of a rite of passage in that joint. As long as things didn't get too out of hand or destructive, they'd usually let them play out. That night, it was no different."

Meg: "Do you prefer public or private?"

Mara: "Private. In a public setting, there are too many variables. Someone might jump in, there's the risk of collateral damage, and the energy is different. In a private setting, it's just you and your opponent. It's more intimate in a way – it's about settling things between the two of you, without distractions or interference. Plus, there's a certain respect in keeping it between the fighters, without making it a spectacle for everyone else."

Meg: "A friend of mine once told me you haven't been in a fight until a fat woman has beaten you. Not sure where that logic came from. Your thoughts?"

Mara: "Hah! That's a new one for me. Look, every fighter brings their own style, their own strengths, and their own challenges to the table, regardless of size. I've fought women of all shapes and sizes, and each fight was unique. A heavier opponent can use their weight to their advantage, sure, but speed, technique, and experience play a huge role too. It's not about the size; it's about the fight in the woman. But I'll say this – never underestimate anyone based on their appearance alone. Every fighter has something to prove, and you'd be surprised at the fire some people have inside them."

Meg: "Your most memorable fight with a large woman. We need details."

Mara: "Alright, let me take you back about a decade. I was in my late 30s and had been in plenty of fights, so I was no stranger to the game. I got challenged by this woman named Tasha. She was around my age, maybe a bit younger, but had a good 150 pounds on me. She stood around 5'10" and weighed close to 300 pounds. Solid, with a lot of power behind her. Our dispute? A petty argument over a mutual lover. The location? A secluded spot by the docks. The setting sun, the sound of water, it was almost poetic. We met up, no words exchanged, just a knowing look. The fight started, and I immediately felt her weight. Every time she landed a hit, it was like being hit with a sack of bricks. My usual tactics of darting in and out weren't as effective; she was surprisingly quick for her size. At one point, she managed to trap me in a bear hug. I felt the air being squeezed out of me. It was in that moment that I realized I was in for a tough fight. I managed to break free by landing a few well-placed elbows. I kept my distance for a bit, trying to wear her down. But every time I went in, she'd respond with a powerful hit. There was a moment where she landed a solid punch, catching me square on the jaw. I remember tasting blood. But I also remember the fire that ignited within me. We went back and forth for what felt like hours. At one point, both of us were on the ground, grappling and trying to pin the other down. Her size was both an advantage and a disadvantage. I was quicker, but she had the raw strength. Eventually, fatigue began to set in. We were both panting, drenched in sweat, with bruised faces and battered bodies. But neither of us was willing to give up. It was in that final stretch that I managed to land a solid blow to that big stomach. It winded her just long enough for me to gain the upper hand. I pinned her down, both hands holding her wrists to the ground, our faces inches apart. She just stared at me. We both knew it could have gone either way. We left that night, not as enemies, but as warriors who had shared a fierce battle. To this day, I remember that fight with Tasha as one of the most challenging and rewarding experiences of my fighting career."

Meg: "Can I be blunt?"

Mara: "Of course. Speak your mind."

Meg: "You can say it's none of my fucking business, but are you into men or women, or both?"

Mara: "I'm a firm believer in living life authentically. I identify as bisexual. I've had meaningful relationships with both men and women throughout my life. But yes, in the world of catfighting and such, almost all my encounters have been with women. Actually, all have been."

Meg: "Have you ever had sex with a woman after a fight?"

Mara: "It's happened, yes. Some fights have been fueled by underlying tension or attraction. After the adrenaline and emotions, things can get intimate. It's a unique dynamic; the lines between passion, aggression, and attraction can sometimes blur. Not every fight leads there, but it has happened."

Meg: "Those are the good ones. Come on now, admit it."

Mara: "Well, there's no denying the raw intensity of it. When two people are locked in such a primal confrontation, and then find a way to channel that energy into something intimate... it's hard to put into words. It's a mix of relief, connection, vulnerability, and desire. It's not for everyone, but for those who've experienced it, it's unforgettable, and extremely erotic."

Meg: "I need another cigarette." (Lights up a cigarette. Mara reached for one as well) "I had a woman really work me over after she beat me once. She used one of those souvenir baseball bats on me and then finished me with her fist. The pain was worse than the beating. Has anyone ever gone too far on you after a fight like that, or have gotten carried away with the after-fight sex?"

Mara: "I've had my fair share of rough encounters, sure. There was this one time, a woman had me pinned and took it upon herself to 'mark her territory', so to speak. There's a fine line between consensual roughness and crossing boundaries. And yes, there have been instances where the line got blurred. It's a wild world, and things can sometimes go beyond what was initially intended. But I've always been a fighter; I stand up for myself and ensure my boundaries are clear."

Meg: "Let's explore the fights you have been in through the years. Kinda like the greatest hits, pardon the pun. Let's talk about the worsts. The worst beating you have taken?

Mara: "That's a trip down not-so-pleasant memory lane. There was this fight... I was maybe 30 at the time. Took on a younger girl, thought I had the upper hand because of experience. But she was a firecracker. Quick, relentless, and knew just where to hit. Before I knew it, she had me pinned, and it went downhill from there. I was left with cracked ribs, a swollen eye, and more bruises than I could count. It took me a while to recover both physically and mentally from that one. It was a humbling experience, to say the least."

Meg: "Ever see her again?"

Mara: "Funny enough, yes. A couple of years later. I was out at a club, and there she was. We locked eyes for what felt like an eternity. But instead of hostility, there was mutual respect. We ended up sharing a drink, chatting, even laughing about that fight. She had gone through her own challenges after our encounter. It's strange how the universe works; that beating, as brutal as it was, brought about a sort of bond between us."

Meg: "Remember what the fight was about?"

Mara: "Absolutely. It was over a guy, of all things.

Can you believe that? We both had been seeing him at different times, neither of us knowing about the other. He was a smooth talker, playing both sides. When we found out, instead of confronting him, our anger turned towards each other. In hindsight, it was foolish. But emotions run high in those situations, and sometimes logic takes a backseat. After our later meeting, we both agreed he wasn't worth the blood and pain."

Meg: "Ok, turn the tables. The worst beating you have ever given someone?"

Mara: "There was this one time, years ago. A woman named Tessa. She had been spreading some nasty rumors about me. Not just about fighting, but personal stuff, trying to humiliate me. I confronted her, and she had the audacity to laugh in my face and challenge me to do something about it. So, I did. We met up in some woods. No audience, just the two of us. The tension was thick. The moment I saw her, I could feel my blood boiling. We didn't even have much of a preamble; it was on from the word go. I remember every punch I landed on her. She was a decent fighter, but that day, my rage was unstoppable. I could feel her bones crunch under my fists. She tried to fight back, but with every hit she took, I could see her spirit breaking. By the end, her face was a mess. I had blackened both her eyes, busted her lip, and I remember thinking I might've broken her nose. She was on the ground, crying, begging me to stop. When I finally did, I felt a mix of satisfaction and regret. Satisfied because I had defended my honor, but regret because I had let my emotions take such a dark turn. It's one thing to fight for the thrill or challenge, but that day, it was pure anger, and it scared me."

Meg: "Remind me never to cross you."

Mara: "Damn, talking about all this is making me chain-smoke." Got anything to drink around here?"

Meg: "Sure, what are you in the mood for? I have some water, soda, wine, maybe some whiskey?"

Mara: "Whiskey would be great, thanks. Takes the edge off a bit."

Meg gets up and walks to a cabinet, pouring two glasses. She slides one over to Mara and raises hers in a toast. "To battles fought and tales shared." Mara laughs, clinking her glass against Meg's. "Cheers to that."

Meg: "You know, it's rare to get such a candid look into this world. Your stories, the rawness, it's both fascinating and terrifying."

Mara: "It's a crazy life, but it's mine. And as brutal as it can be, it has its moments of sheer adrenaline and excitement that are hard to replicate elsewhere."

Meg: "That was nice to take a little break. Back to my questions. Explain some two on one fights you have had. Let's start where you have been beaten. How did that happen?"

Mara: "Two on one situations are always challenging, even for someone with my experience. I've found myself outnumbered a few times over the years, though not often. There's one situation that stands out. I was at a bar out of town, and I'd gotten into a disagreement with a local woman. We both decided to take it outside, but as we were headed out, her friend decided to join in. Before I knew it, I was dealing with two of them. One would hold me from behind, trapping my arms, while the other took free shots. I tried breaking free multiple times and did manage to land a few solid blows. But the numbers game caught up to me. The one in front would distract, and the one behind would choke or restrain. They worked well together, unfortunately for me. By the end of it, I had a busted lip and a bruised ego. It was a humbling experience."

Meg: "Ever been attacked by more than two? I did in college. Three. Let's just say I missed a couple days of classes."

Mara: "Sorry to hear that happened to you. Yeah, I've been in that situation too. Once, when I was in my late twenties, I had a disagreement with a group of women at a party. I can't even remember what it was about, but alcohol was definitely a factor. Three of them decided they'd teach me a lesson. I managed to hold my ground for a bit, using the close quarters to my advantage. But the weight of numbers and being blindsided by unseen punches took its toll. I pride myself on being tough, but three against one is a tough situation for anyone. I got a black eye and some bruised ribs from that encounter. Like you, I had to lay low for a few days to recover."

Meg: "It's all part of the scene if you are in it long enough."

Mara: "True. Over the years, you learn to pick your battles. Sometimes it's about pride, sometimes it's about respect, and sometimes you're just in the wrong place at the wrong time. But every fight, win or lose, teaches you something. Either about yourself, or about the world around you. I wouldn't recommend it for everyone, but in some twisted way, it's shaped me into the woman I am today."

Meg: "Let's flip this around. You and friend ever corner someone and work her over?"

Mara: [Exhales cigarette smoke slowly] "Yeah, it happened a couple of times. Back in my younger, wilder days. There was this one time with my friend Lexi. We had a score to settle with a girl named Tish. Can't remember it that was her real name. Tish had wronged Lexi in some personal way, and I got roped into it. We cornered her in a parking lot one night. It wasn't something I'm proud of. Lexi went at her first, and I made sure Tish couldn't run away. After Lexi was done, I got a few hits in myself. It was messy, unfair, and I regretted it later. But in the heat of the moment, with adrenaline and loyalty blinding you, you don't always make the best choices."

Meg: "For a person who loves to fight, you seem to have regrets a lot."

Mara: [Sighs] "Fighting is a complicated thing for me. I do love the adrenaline, the competition, and the rawness of it. But that doesn't mean I don't recognize when things go too far or when I've crossed a line. Some fights are about respect, others are personal, and some, in hindsight, just weren't worth it. I've learned a lot over the years, and yes, there are moments I wish I could take back."

Meg: "Your most unusual fight?"

Mara: (Chuckles softly) "Ah, I've had my fair share

of odd ones. But if I had to pick the most unusual... it was in a walk-in freezer at a seafood restaurant. A rival and I had a heated argument, and it ended up there. Fighting on icy floors with cold air biting at your skin, while trying to avoid crates of fish? Definitely not something I'd ever imagined I'd experience. The cold made everything feel more intense, and each punch stung twice as much. I can tell you, neither of us lingered in that freezer after the fight was settled."

Meg: "Well, I didn't see that story coming."

Mara: [Grinning] "Life has a way of throwing curveballs, doesn't it? Never thought I'd be telling that story in an interview, but hey, here we are. Fighting has taken me to some bizarre places, both literally and figuratively."

Meg: "Speaking of places, back in the 70's there was this thing called apartment house wrestling. Basically, bimbos in bikinis wrestling for wealthy men. Any truth to those stories? Or urban legends?

Mara: [Exhales smoke slowly] "Oh, I've heard of those stories. In fact, I might have been involved in a few of those so-called 'apartment matches 20 years or so ago. They weren't just legends. Wealthy men would pay good money to see women fight it out, sometimes in private settings, sometimes in more 'underground' locations. But it wasn't always bimbos in bikinis. Some of us were real fighters, just looking for a way to make a living. It was a different time then, but the essence of the fight remained the same."

Meg: "So you admit you fight for cash?"

Mara: [Pauses, taking a long drag from her cigarette] "In the past? Yes, I've taken money for fights. Sometimes it was for the thrill, other times it was out of necessity. Life throws its punches, and you've got to roll with them. But it wasn't always about the cash. Many times, it was about the pride, the adrenaline, the need to prove myself. But yes, there were times when money was the motivator."

Meg: "The scariest person to face?"

Mara: "The unpredictable ones. Someone who's got nothing to lose, or someone who's too emotional, too angry. They don't think, they just act. It's hard to read their next move, to anticipate. They might not be the most skilled, but their raw energy, their willingness to go to any length... that's scary. Every fighter has a pattern, a rhythm, but the erratic ones, they can catch you off guard."

Meg: "On the other hand, the sexiest to fight? One that you can't wait to get real close to after the fight."

Mara: "Hmm, there's something incredibly alluring about confidence, about someone who carries herself with a certain swagger. A woman who knows her body, who's fit and takes care of herself, but also has that hint of vulnerability. The tension, the buildup of a fight, knowing there's mutual attraction and respect, it's electric. You're fighting, but there's that underlying current of desire. When the fight ends, the proximity, the sweat, the heavy breathing... it all comes together. Those are the fights that sometimes seamlessly transition into something more intimate."

Meg: (Takes a drag) "Just curious, personal, what buttons do I push? While you are sitting across from me."

Mara: (Laughs) "Oh, you're quite forward, aren't you? You've got a certain spark, an energy that's hard to ignore. Your confidence, the way you carry a conversation, and of course, the way you hold that cigarette... there's an undeniable charisma. And I've always had a thing for inquisitive minds. Your eyes give away a lot more than you might think. You're intriguing, to say the least."

Meg: "So you're telling me there's a chance."

Mara: (Chuckles) "Well, never say never. Life is full of surprises, and who knows where an evening like this might lead. But for now, let's keep this interview on track, shall we?"

Meg: "Fair enough. Let's talk about more recent stuff. As you get older, do you pick fights or they seek you?

Mara: "Honestly, as I've aged, I've become more selective about the fights I get into. I don't actively go seeking them out as I did in my younger days. However, because of my reputation and history, there are still women who seek me out, either to challenge me or sometimes just to learn from me. The motivation varies."

Meg: "As we have discussed earlier, we are the about the same age. I enjoy fighting mature women now. Grandmas with attitude if you may. What was your most recent memorable fight?"

Mara: "It was a few months ago. Met this woman, Linda, in a bar. She was around 55, so a few years older than me. She had this air of arrogance around her, clearly had a history in the scene. We started off just exchanging words, but it escalated. Took it to a more private setting. It was a tough fight; she had experience, knew how to throw a punch. But in the end, I managed to get the upper hand."

Meg: "Did Linda seek you out, you her, or did it just happen? Elaborate more on the set up. Our listeners enjoy this shit.

Mara: (Pausing for a moment, taking a drag) "So, I was at this bar with a couple of friends. We were just minding our own business, enjoying some drinks. Linda was there with her own group. At some point, one of my friends made a passing comment about a fight they'd seen a while back, and how I was involved. Linda overheard and laughed, saying something like, 'She's still at it? I thought old birds knew when to retire.'

I turned around, met her gaze, and things just sort of spiraled from there. She had this smirk that just rubbed me the wrong way. We exchanged a few words, sizing each other up. She'd been in the scene too, though she didn't recognize me initially. As the night went on, it became pretty clear that we were on a collision course. It wasn't so much that either of us specifically sought the other out; it was like a challenge that neither of us could back down from. By closing time, we had a location and a few witnesses lined up. Old habits die hard, I guess."

Meg: "This is turning me on. Go on. What happened when you arrived?"

Mara: (Chuckling softly) "I figured as much. I

arrived at the spot, an old warehouse in town that one of the guys add keys for. Go figure. The place was dimly lit with just a couple of lanterns, and I could see shadows of some spectators, probably friends of Linda some of mine. Linda was already there. We locked eyes, and there was this undeniable electric tension. I removed me shirt and was in jeans, while she was in a tight-fitting sports bra and leggings, her hair tied back tightly. We circled each other for a moment, exchanging taunts. I tried to keep my focus, and not let the atmosphere distract me. She was formidable, clearly experienced, and wasn't going to be easy. We both knew it. With a nod, we closed in, and the fight began."

Meg: "And?"

Mara: (Sighing, reminiscing) "Well, the first few minutes were a bit of a blur. Both of us trying to feel each other out, looking for weaknesses. We traded blows, some of which landed, some didn't. Linda was strong, but I had the edge in speed. Every time she tried to corner me, I'd slip out and land a quick jab or hook. About ten minutes in, she managed to catch me with a solid punch to the stomach. It winded me, and she tried to capitalize, pushing me against a pillar. We struggled there, each trying to gain the upper hand. At one point, she almost got me in a chokehold, but I managed to break free. The fight continued, neither of us giving an inch. There were times when it felt more like a dance than a brawl. Sweat dripping, muscles aching, but neither of us willing to back down. Every hit, every shove, was a battle of wills as much as strength.

Finally, after what felt like hours, I managed to land a solid punch on her face. It stunned her, and I followed up with a combination that sent her to the floor. But even then, she tried to pull me down with her. We wrestled on the ground until I managed to pin her. Panting, exhausted, we both knew it was over. But let me tell you, the respect I have for that woman after that fight... it's immense. She's one of the toughest opponents I've faced in a long time."

Meg: "So for the most part, a straight up fight, no hair pulling, clothes ripping slap fest like in the movies.

Mara: (Laughing) "Exactly! It's funny how movies and media portray women's fights. Not every fight is a dramatic, hair-pulling spectacle. Linda and I were both experienced fighters. We respected each other's skills, and neither of us wanted to resort to those tactics. A true fighter knows it's about technique, strength, and strategy, not pulling hair or tearing clothes. But I'll admit, there's always a bit of drama in any fight, just not the Hollywood kind."

Meg: "Speaking of hair. Are you a hair puller? Do you like yours pulled?

Mara: (Tilting her head, fingers brushing through her hair) "In my younger days, I've both pulled hair and had mine pulled. It's an instinctive move, especially when you're close and grappling. And to be honest, in the heat of the moment, it can be effective. As for liking it? I wouldn't say I 'like' it, but I understand its place in a fight. Nowadays, I try to avoid it, focusing on more direct techniques. But if someone grabs my hair, you better believe I'll be returning the favor."

Meg: "But in general, let's say not a fight, you and

I are going at, me behind you, working it, if you know what I mean, I grab a handful of hair and work it with the rhythm of my hips, are you enjoying it?

Mara: (Leaning back, a smirk forming on her face) "In that context, it's a whole different ballgame. A tug of the hair can be... stimulating, to say the least. So yeah, in the right circumstances and with the right person, it can be quite... enjoyable."

Meg: "It's all about the right person."

Mara: "Exactly. It's all about chemistry, understanding, and trust. In a fight, hair pulling can be brutal and painful. But in an intimate setting, it's a different sensation altogether. It's about dominance and submission, giving and taking."

Meg: "What would I have to say or do to put you on alert? You know, hypothetically."

Mara: "It's less about words and more about energy and intent. But if you were to, let's say, directly challenge me, make a derogatory comment, or invade my personal space without invitation... that would definitely put me on alert. Why? Planning something?"

Meg: "Mmm. Has anyone ever interfered? Either for or against you?"

Mara: "Oh, absolutely. Especially in those bar fights or the ones that just spontaneously erupted in public. There've been times when a friend or even just a random person would jump in to help me out. On the flip side, I've had instances where someone's buddy didn't like the way things were going and decided to give their friend an unfair advantage. That's the risk with public brawls. You never truly know if it's going to remain one-on-one."

Meg: "Kicking. I am not talking about kicks used in fight. How do I say this? Being kicked while you are down. Let's say you have just beaten a woman and she is down. Kicking her in the side or belly just because. Has that happened to you? Or even by you? Getting that one last act of dominance in?"

Mara: "Yeah, it's happened. There've been times when, in the heat of the moment, after a particularly brutal or personal fight, I've given a downed opponent an extra kick. On the flip side, I've been on the receiving end too. After being beaten, some opponents want to leave their mark, make sure you remember them. It's a dirty move, but it happens in this world. You have to be ready for anything."

Meg: "Leaving a mark, I like the way you put that."

Mara: "It's a way of staking a claim, a reminder. Sometimes it's about ego, sometimes about sending a message, and other times... it's purely personal. In any case, those marks... they fade, but the memory of them doesn't."

Meg: "Do you have a personal favorite you use? How does Mara mark her opponent?"

Mara: "Depends on the situation and how the fight went. Sometimes it's a hard slap across the face, leaving a handprint. Other times, a bite mark. But one of my favorites... pressing a lit cigarette into their skin. It's a reminder they won't forget."

Meg: "I have snubbed out a cigarette in a woman's belly button. I am not ashamed to admit it, I loved it."

Mara: "Seems we have more in common than I initially thought. But remember, darling, there's a big difference between doing it to someone and having it done to you."

Meg: (Taking a final drag on her current cigarette and twisting it back and forth in the ashtray before a final crush with her finger) "I agree 100%. Absolutely."

Mara: (Watching what Meg just did with her cigarette, knowing exactly what Meg was doing) "I've seen that look before. The mix of curiosity and defiance. It's captivating. But don't get ahead of yourself. It's one thing to reminisce and chat about past experiences... and another to be in the thick of it."

Meg: "Any missed opportunities? A fight you should have had, but for whatever reason it didn't take place? Making you wonder what if?"

Mara: "Oh, there's always been a few of those. Moments where the tension was thick enough to cut with a knife, but for one reason or another, it never escalated. There was this one woman, a few years back...we had this undeniable tension every time we crossed paths. It was electric. But circumstances never allowed for us to settle things. Sometimes, I do wonder 'what if? But life has a way of coming full circle. Maybe one day."

Meg: "It is always when you least expect it. Here is something I am curious. In an arranged fight, have you and your opponent ever chosen to use a safe word? You know, I'm case things get out of hand?"

Mara: "I've been in situations where we've set boundaries, sure. Especially in fights that have... let's call them, 'alternative rules' or added stakes. Safe words can be useful. It's not so much about backing down as it is about ensuring things don't go too far or get too dangerous. There's a difference between wanting to dominate and wanting to genuinely harm someone. But not every fight has those precautions. It depends on the level of trust and the intensity of the animosity."

Meg: "I find safe words, if given the chance to have such a discussion before a fight, very useful. It allows us to go to extremes, or near it, knowing that whatever is happening is still consensual up to point the word is used."

Mara: "Absolutely. It's like a safety net. It allows you to push boundaries and explore limits without crossing into genuinely dangerous territory. It's a form of communication in the heat of the moment, and it ensures that both parties have a level of control over the situation. It's about respecting each other, even when you're in direct conflict. The heat of a fight can be overwhelming, and sometimes it's easy to lose oneself in the intensity. A safe word serves as a reminder, a tether to reality."

Meg: "You mentioned alternative rules and stakes. Here is another very personal question. I must be careful how I word this or it will be edited out. (Mara laughs). Things happen in a stakes fight. The post-fight sex can become, um, rather difficult. This has had to happen to you or by you. The winner is exploring her opponent's womanhood, and one finger becomes two. Two become three, four, and the next thing you know, the loser has a fist inside of her. Has it been done to you, have you done it? And how comfortable are you as either giver, receiver or both. Personally? I love it."

Mara: "Oh, you don't shy away from the tough questions, do you? Look, I've been in some very intense stakes fights. Yes, things can escalate, and they can become... primal. There's an element of dominance and submission, especially in the post-fight activities. As for fisting, It has happened, often, both ways. As a giver, there's an immense sense of control and power. As a receiver, it's an overwhelming sensation, both physically and mentally. It's not something I'd just dive into without some level of understanding with my opponent. It's intimate, even in the context of a fight."

Meg: "I agree and love your answer. It is all about trust. Unfortunately, and not that long ago, I was in a spontaneous situation, where time did not permit any prefight discussions of boundaries. I wasn't strong enough that night. With the help of her friend, she fisted me without regards to anything. And you know what made it worse? I had an orgasm. I had a bloody mouth, a black eye and I fucking soaked the carpet under me."

Mara: "That's heavy. Even in our world, there's supposed to be respect and boundaries. It sounds like they took advantage of the situation. It's also not uncommon for the body to react in ways we don't expect, especially when we're overwhelmed. It doesn't mean you enjoyed or wanted it. It just means your body responded. I'm truly sorry you went through that."

Meg: "That's ok, like you said, the past shapes you.

As a result, fisting is now part of my tool belt. In case you ever need to know that."

Mara: "Life has a funny way of teaching us, doesn't it? It gives us tools and scars in unexpected ways. Whatever comes next, I respect your journey."

Meg: "' Do you need a final break before we conclude the interview? I can use a refill."

Mara: "A refill sounds good. Let's take a short break, and then we can wrap things up."

(Meg stands up and takes hold of Mara's glass at the same time Mara reaches for it. Mara's hand rest on top of Meg. She gives Meg a tight squeeze that isn't accidental)

Mara: "I think we've ventured into territory far beyond a standard interview. Maybe it's the whisky, or maybe it's the conversation, but there's an energy here that's... undeniable."

Meg: "I feel it. Oh, how I feel it."

(Mara, with an air of confidence, gently flips Meg's hand so her palm faces upward. She traces a slow, deliberate circle on Meg's palm with her fingertip, each rotation adding to the electric tension in the room)

Mara: "I've had many interviews, but none quite like this. Maybe it's time we explore this... chemistry."

Meg: "Damn, I am not sure if you are wanting to fight or fuck?"

Mara: "Why choose. Sometimes the line between passion and combat is razor thin. The question is, which do you want first?"

Meg: (taking a drag from her cigarette as she pours more whisky) "Can we table this for a little bit longer? I must finish this interview."

Mara: "Of course. Business before pleasure."

Meg: "So, do have a move you like to go to first in a fight?"

Mara: "I usually like to gauge my opponent first, read their movements. But if I were to choose an initial move, it's often a quick fist to the face. It can throw them off, give me a moment to assess the situation better. But every fight is different, every opponent is different. It's all about adapting on the fly."

Meg: "Are there any quirks you have, subtle, um, something that are giveaways for your opponent?"

Mara: "You're trying to get a fucking edge on me, aren't you? Everyone has tells, I suppose. Maybe I lean slightly to one side before making a move or maybe there's a specific look in my eye. But it's not something I'm going to freely divulge. If you're that curious, you might just have to find out firsthand."

Meg: "Oh, this is going to happen, and you want it as bad as I do. Unless all of a sudden, I have lost the ability to read people."

Mara: (Taking a deliberate drag from her cigarette) "Reading people is one thing, but predicting how a dance between two fighters will play out is quite another. There's a thrill in the unknown."

Meg: "How do you know that a fight is going to lead

to extracurricular activities?"

Mara: "It's hard to pinpoint exactly, but there's a certain chemistry and tension in the air. Beyond the physicality of the fight, there's a dance of eyes, subtle gestures, and unspoken invitations. When two fighters are drawn to each other beyond the physical clash, it becomes palpable. The energy changes from just the drive to dominate to something... more intimate. Sometimes it's in the way they hold each other a tad longer than necessary or the way their breaths synchronize. The lines between aggression, passion, and attraction blur. But it's not always predictable. It's about reading the room and the person in front of you."

Meg: "Are you always prepared for a fight? I mean, the spontaneous stuff? Purely hypothetical, you agree to, let's say, an interview. And the next thing you know, hypothetically, you find yourself on your back getting punched? Just an example.

Mara: "While I don't walk around expecting every situation to turn into a brawl, I've learned to always be alert and aware of my surroundings. It's that instinct, the fighter's sixth sense, that keeps you on your toes. You never truly know when a situation might escalate. But in a situation like this? With the tension we've built up. I'd say I'm more than ready, hypothetically speaking."

Meg: "Before I turn the recorder off, is there anything else you would like to comment on?"

Mara: "Just that life is full of unexpected moments. Embrace them, learn from them, and always be true to yourself. And sometimes, a good fight is just the beginning of something even more thrilling. Thank you for the interview. It's been... enlightening."

Meg: "Are you ready to go off the record?"

Mara: "I am absolutely ready to go off the record."

(With her cigarette between her lips, Mara starts to remove her clothes)

Meg: "I am a little more casual when I am not at work."

(Mara follows suit and starts to remove her own clothes)

Meg: (Looking at Mara's naked body) "I never thought to ask during my interview, but, looking at you now, that's a nice landing strip you have. Enough to entice, but not quite enough to fully grab onto."

Mara: "Well, thank you. It's always nice when someone appreciates the little details. I find it strikes a good balance between practicality and aesthetics. But I must say, the all-natural look suits you quite well."

Meg: "I like to be vulnerable."

Mara: "Vulnerability can be both a strength and a weakness. In the right hands, it can be used to one's advantage. Are you ready to see what my hands can do?"

Meg: "I thought you would never ask."

The tension in the room could be cut with a knife, the air thick with anticipation. With one challenging look from Meg, the fight begins. Mara, drawing on her experience, takes the first move. She feints a left jab, trying to throw Meg off, but follows through with a quick right hook. The punch grazes Meg's cheekbone, the sting sharp and immediate. Quickly, Meg retaliates, sending a straight punch to Mara's midsection, making her grunt in response. Meg's knuckles meet the soft skin of Mara's stomach, pushing the wind out of her. Taking advantage of the momentary distraction, Meg pulls her arm back and aims a fist at Mara's face. Mara tries to dodge but isn't fast enough, Meg's fist colliding with the corner of Mara's mouth, drawing first blood.

Mara tastes the metallic tang, and it only fuels her. She swings a heavy hook at Meg's jaw, and Meg feels a sharp pain. But she doesn't back down, retaliating with a solid right cross that connects with Mara's nose. There's an immediate flare of pain in her eyes, and Meg sees blood begin to trickle down, staining her upper lip. The fight continues with both trading punches, each one more calculated than the last. Both women measure each other's strength, trying to find a weak point. Suddenly, Mara tries to grab at Meg's waist, attempting to take here down. But Meg twists her body, grabbing onto her Mara's arm and turning it into a firm grip around her neck. She chokes slightly but fights against Meg's grip, managing to land a hard punch on Meg's ribcage. The pain is immediate, but Meg uses it to fuel her next move.

Meg pushes Mara off, gaining a bit of distance, and the two circle each other, both breathing hard, sweat and blood mixing. Eyes locked, both look for an opening, knowing that one wrong move could end the fight. Mara lunges at Meg again, aiming for her face, but Meg dodges just in time, sending a quick jab to Mara's ribs. She cries out, but it's cut short as Meg sends another punch to Mara's jaw. Mara retaliates with a punch that connects with Meg's cheek, causing it to immediately start swelling. The two continue this dance, the atmosphere filled with grunts, the sound of skin meeting skin, and the occasional gasp of pain. It's clear neither wants to give up, both determined to prove themselves. The room is heavy with tension, passion, and a fierce competitiveness that neither can deny.

Mara, seeing an opportunity, feints to Meg's right and then quickly moves to the left, her fist connecting with Meg's abdomen. The wind is knocked out of her momentarily, but Meg refuses to let it show. Using her momentum against Mara, Meg grabs Mara's wrist and pulls Mara towards Meg, sending a knee to Mara's midsection. Mara grunts in pain, doubling over. Meg sees her chance and deliver an elbow to the back of Mara's neck, making her stumble forward. But she recovers quickly, spinning around and landing a solid kick to Meg's thigh. Meg feels the muscles tense and spasm, making it hard to put weight on that leg. Despite the pain, Meg digs deep, launching herself at Mara, grabbing her hair and yanking her head back to expose her throat. She gasps, struggling against Meg's grip, but Meg uses her free hand to land a punch to Mara's cheek. Meg can feel the warmth of Mara's blood on Meg's knuckles.

Mara's eyes blaze with anger and determination. She uses her leg to hook Meg's, causing Meg to lose balance and the two tumble to the floor. The impact is jarring, and for a moment, both are disoriented. On the ground, the fight takes on a new intensity. Mara, being on top, tries to pin Meg down, but Meg manages to use her legs to flip Mara over. Now with the upper hand, Meg tries to land a punch to Mara's face, but Mara blocks it, grabbing

Meg's wrist and twisting. Pain shoots up Meg's arm, but she retaliates by headbutting Mara. Mara yells out, blood now streaming from a cut on her forehead. Both women roll around, each trying to gain the dominant position. The floor is now stained with a mix of sweat, blood, and bruised skin. Every move, every grip, every punch is calculated, both knowing that one misstep could cost the fight.

As the minutes drag on, exhaustion begins to set in. Breaths come in ragged gasps, muscles scream in protest, and the pain from the blows becomes more pronounced. Yet, neither woman is willing to yield, the desire to win and the electric tension between the two driving both forward. It's clear this fight, as drawn out and intense as it is, is about more than just physical dominance; it's a battle of wills, a test of determination, and a dance of passion and fury. Meg's eyes lock, both women searching for a weakness, an opening. You take advantage of a brief lapse in Mara's concentration, sweeping her legs out from under her. As she falls, Meg follows her down, straddling her waist. Meg delivers a series of rapid punches to Mara's sides, each one eliciting a groan of pain.

However, Mara is not one to be easily subdued. She manages to wrap her legs around Meg's waist, using her heels to dig into the small of Meg's back, sending jolts of pain through Meg's spine. As Meg's momentarily distracted, Mara delivers a hard punch to Meg's jaw, causing her vision to blur. Rolling to the side, Mara manages to reverse Meg's positions. Pinning Meg's arms above her head with one hand, she uses her free hand to slap Meg hard across the face. The sting is sharp and immediate. But Meg refuses to let her have the last word.

Using all her strength, Meg bucks her hips and manage to throw Mara off, the two separating momentarily to catch their breath. Meg can see the fatigue in Mara's eyes, but it's mirrored in her own eyes. This fight is taking its toll on both women. They circle each other warily, sizing each other up. Meg's movements are slower now, each punch and kick more deliberate. A powerful right hook from Mara connects with Meg's cheek, causing her head to snap back. Meg tastes blood in her mouth. In retaliation, Meg sends a hard knee to Mara's stomach, making her double over.

The two women are on the brink of exhaustion, but neither is willing to admit defeat. Every muscle aches, every breath is a struggle, but the desire to prevail pushes both forward. In a final act of desperation, Meg tackle Mara to the ground, pinning her beneath Meg. Meg can feel her heart racing against her chest, Mara's hot breath on Meg's neck. Meg holds her there, their bodies entwined, waiting for Mara to yield. After what feels like an eternity, Mara whispers, "Enough." Mara and Meg lay there, catching their breath, a mixture of pain, respect, and an undeniable connection between the two. The fight is over, but the journey has only just begun.

Mara, panting heavily, pushes a strand of sweat-soaked hair from her face and looks up at Meg. "Guess we both had something to prove," she says with a slight smirk, pain evident in her eyes. The tension between the two, mixed with the adrenaline, leaves an atmosphere thick with emotion. "Didn't think you had that in you," she adds, her voice softer, more vulnerable. Both women know that the fight was more than just a physical clash; it was a battle of wills, of egos, of unspoken emotions.

It was a way to communicate without words, to let out frustrations and to understand each other on a deeper level. Meg extends a hand to help Mara up, and she takes it gratefully. The two stand, bruised and battered, but with a newfound respect for each other. "You're one hell of a fighter," Mara admits, wiping the blood from her lip. "Didn't see that coming." Meg chuckles lightly, wincing from the pain. "Likewise," Meg replies, eyes locking with Mara's once more. In that moment, all the barriers are down, and both women see each other for who they truly are.

Mara's breath catches as Meg touches her, and she bites her lip, a glint of desire now evident in her eyes. She leans closer, her fingers finding their way to Meg's face, tracing the bruises and cuts gently. The contrasting sensations of pain and pleasure create a heady mix. "You sure know how to make a girl feel... special," Mara murmurs, her voice husky. Meg smirks, taking a step back and reaching for her discarded cigarette pack. "I think we both earned a smoke," Meg says, lighting one up and offering another to Mara. She accepts with a nod, lighting it and inhaling deeply. The two stand in silence for a moment, the only sound being the gentle exhale of smoke. The intensity of the fight, the intimacy that followed, and now the shared cigarette – everything seemed to draw the two closer, building a connection that was unexpected but undeniably powerful. Finally, Mara breaks the silence. "So... what happens now?" she asks, looking at Meg with a mix of curiosity and hope. "I really want to see if that landing strip of yours can safely guide all my fingers into your hanger. It was a cheesy line, but Meg said it before she thought about it. Mara chuckles at her comment, raising an eyebrow in amusement. "Well, that's one way to put it," she says with a playful smirk. "But if you're asking what I think you're asking... I'm game." The atmosphere in the room changes once again, turning from post-fight tension to charged anticipation. Both women move closer, drawn to each other by a mix of attraction and the thrill of what's to come.

The atmosphere between the two is thick with tension and shared bruises. Mara's teasing eyes and that playful smirk from moments ago has since turned into a vulnerable and anticipatory gaze. Taking a step closer to her, the air feels electric. Gently, Meg places a hand on Mara's hip, drawing her closer. Meg's fingers trace the soft skin of her abdomen, dancing their way down to the enticing landing strip that had intrigued Meg earlier. Mara gasps softly, her eyes fluttering as she feels Meg's fingers brush against her most intimate parts. The touch is both gentle and exploring, as if Meg's savoring the sensation of her soft warmth. Gradually, one finger slips inside, exploring her depths. It's followed by another, and then another. Each movement is met with a deeper gasp, a soft moan, a twitch of Mara's hips urging you further. The heat between the two is electric, and both are slick with sweat, each touch creating a sizzle.

Mara looks deep into Meg's eyes, a mixture of anticipation and fear. Meg can feel Mara trembling beneath Meg's touch. Mara has never been this vulnerable, not with an opponent. But there's trust there, a shared intimacy borne from the fight and the raw emotion of the evening. With a gentle push, Meg begins to work your entire hand inside Mara, folding her fingers and easing her way. Mara's breathing is labored, a soft whimper escaping her lips. Every inch Meg explores, she can feel Mara's body responding, muscles contracting, warmth enveloping Meg. The room fills with the sounds of heavy breathing, the occasional soft cry, and the unmistakable sounds of two bodies connecting in the most intimate way. Mara's back arches, her fingers clutching at the floor as she rides the waves of pleasure. And then, just like a tidal wave crashing onto the shore, Mara climaxes, her entire body convulsing in ecstasy. The intensity of the moment is unexplainable, the culmination of a night filled with tension, fighting, and now, this profound connection. As Mara catches her breath, Meg gently pulls away, allowing her a moment of respite. Both lie there, spent and intertwined, a silent understanding passing between them. Whatever this was, whatever it will become, for now, it's just the two of them, in the aftermath of a raw and passionate evening.

After a few moments of heavy breathing, the roles reverse. Mara's eyes glow with a devilish intent, reflecting her hunger for dominance. She sits up, pulling Meg with her. Meg meets Mara's intense gaze, the chemistry between them is strong. "You enjoyed being the victor," Mara purrs. "But let's not forget who the seasoned fighter is." Meg can only nod, caught in Mara's intense gaze. With one swift motion, Mara has Meg on her back, Mara's body hovering over Meg's. Her fingers trace Meg's body, but there's a marked difference in her touch. It's assertive, demanding. Mara doesn't waste any time. She goes directly for Meg's most sensitive parts, punching and prodding, her movements forceful and assertive. Every touch is a reminder of her strength, her dominance. She's not being gentle; Mara is claiming Meg.

With each punch, Meg gasps, her back arching

off the floor. The pain is intense, but it's coupled with pleasure, the two sensations blending into a heady cocktail of arousal. Mara watches Meg's face intently, her fingers working Meg with a practiced ease. She knows exactly how to elicit those moans, those gasps, those cries of pleasure. When she begins to push more forcefully, adding more fingers, Meg can only writhe beneath her, completely at her mercy. The sensations are overwhelming. Meg's body is on fire, every nerve ending alive and tingling. Mara's relentless assault only intensifies, her fingers now fully inside Meg. The rhythm she sets is punishing, but Meg craves it, needing the rough treatment after the evening's events. And just like before, the climax crashes over Meg, wave after wave of intense pleasure that leaves Meg breathless and trembling. Mara keeps her fingers inside her for a moment longer, watching as Meg comes down from the high. Pulling away, Mara collapses next to Meg, both are completely spent. There's an understanding between them, a mutual respect that has formed from this raw and intense exchange. The night's events have brought out a side that neither expected, but neither regret.

The room is filled with the heavy scent of passion and sweat. Both women lie there, side by side, breathing heavily. Every so often, their eyes meet, and there's a shared understanding that words can't capture. The line between rivalry and intimacy is a blurred one, and tonight, both have been explored in their fullest extents. Mara breaks the silence first, her voice soft and husky. "I didn't expect tonight to go this way." Meg chuckles, turning to face Mara. "Neither did I. But I'm not complaining." Mara smirks, propping herself up on an elbow. "We should do interviews more often." Meg laughs at that, the tension of the night finally breaking. "Maybe next time, without the bloody noses." Mara's fingers trace Meg's jawline. "But where's the fun in that?"

The two chat, about the fight, about life, about everything and nothing. It's odd, how easily the conversation flows, considering the night's events. But perhaps it's precisely because of the night's events that there's this newfound bond between them.

As dawn approaches, both decide it's best to part ways for now, to process everything that happened. It's a silent agreement that this won't be the last time they see each other. Whether it's for another fight or another night of passion, only time will tell. But one thing is for sure, neither will forget this night anytime soon.

A RIVALRY SETTLED UNDER THE BLEACHERS

Throughout the football season, Samantha and Jennifer's rivalry had been building. Their sons, teammates on the high school football team, were oblivious to their mothers' increasing animosity. The two moms couldn't be more different, and every parent in the booster club was aware of the tension between them. During a crucial game in the fourth quarter, with the stands packed and the cheers deafening, Samantha approached Jennifer, whispering in her ear. "This ends now. Under the bleachers. Now." Jennifer, never one to decline a challenge, smirked and nodded. "Let's."

While the rest of the spectators were engrossed in the game, the two women snuck away, meeting in the dim, dusty space beneath the roaring stands. With no words, they squared up. Samantha, in her heels, took a quick swipe at Jennifer, who deftly dodged and threw a punch that grazed Samantha's cheek. Both women, dressed in their best game day attire, quickly realized their clothing might be a disadvantage. Jackets were shed, jewelry quickly removed. The blows exchanged were sharp and fast. Samantha managed to grab Jennifer by the hair, yanking her head back, while Jennifer landed a stinging punch on Samantha's face. The noise from the game above shielded the sounds of their scuffle. Jennifer was able to recover from the face punch to deliver several hard punches to Samantha's midsection. While slumped over, Samantha was open for Jennifer to get her in a headlock. With Samantha's neck firmly in Jennifer's right arm, Jennifer delivered a series of punches onto Samantha's head and face. Samantha's only move was to take her right arm and drive her fist into Jennifer's stomach, below her belt. Jennifer released the headlock and both women, bruised and slightly bloody, back away from each other.

For several more minutes, they grappled and wrestled. Their clothes were streaked with dirt, and their hair was wild. Both had scrapes and emerging bruises, testament to the ferocity of their fight. During their struggle, Jennifer managed to pin Samantha down, her forearm pressed against Samantha's throat. They locked eyes, both their faces red with exertion and anger. Finally, gasping for breath, Samantha tapped Jennifer's arm in surrender. Jennifer, also panting heavily, released her and sat back, assessing the damage. They were a mess. "That's done then," Samantha rasped, pulling herself to her feet. Jennifer nodded. "Yeah. It's done."

They helped each other clean up as best they could, both knowing they'd have to make some excuse for their disheveled appearances. But as they emerged from beneath the bleachers, they shared a silent pact: their feud was over, settled in private, away from prying eyes.

THE RETURN OF MARA. ONE YEAR LATER

At 52, Mara Callahan was a legend in the underground catfighting circles. Her journey spanned over two decades, with a history of paid fights, website-arranged catfight videos, spontaneous street battles, and now her newest venture in the over-40 mature amateur porn niche. On this platform, Mara showcased her skills in catfighting, sensuous lesbian encounters, and smoking fetishes. With her earnings concealed, whispers in the circuit estimated she raked in around $200,000 annually just from this site. The industry was abuzz when a tantalizing offer surfaced: a fight against Sylvia Langford, another popular star from the mature amateur scene. Sylvia, a 50-year-old brunette with a statuesque figure and piercing blue eyes, was a force to reckon with. Unlike Mara, Sylvia was a relative newbie in the catfight world, but her gym-toned physique and erotic escapades had garnered her a significant fanbase.

The offer was irresistible. The bout would be streamed live on the dark web, with viewers shelling out $1000 each. A pot of gold awaited the two fighters, as they'd be splitting the viewer fees. The monetary incentive was further sweetened with bonuses which payments would be dished out per viewer: $5 for every 15-minute duration they endured, and additional bonuses paid by viewers for each black eye, bloody lip, bloody nose, strip-down, and blood drawn from scratches to the breasts. Mara, well-versed with the brutalities of her world, felt a swirl of emotions. The payday was substantial, possibly her biggest yet. But this wasn't just any fight. The rules, the audience engagement, and the unprecedented stakes amplified the intensity. She pondered over her strategies as the day neared. Sylvia's reputation preceded her. Mara had seen her videos, witnessed her sultry charm, and her deceptively delicate moves. Sylvia was unpredictable, which made her even more formidable.

Meanwhile, Sylvia was burning with anticipation. She knew of Mara's legendary status in the catfight world. Taking her on was both a challenge and an honor. However, the dark web setup added a tinge of danger and unpredictability. She wasn't just fighting for money or pride but to prove to herself and her fans that she could hold her ground against the best. As news of the bout spread, the underground community went into a frenzy. Forums were overflowing with predictions, stats, and debates. Who would reign supreme: Mara with her vast experience or Sylvia with her raw power and sensuality? The selected venue was a secretive underground club, known only to the insiders. As the night approached, the dimly lit club, equipped with advanced cameras for the live stream, was abuzz with the elite catfight enthusiasts. The atmosphere was electric. Mara, in a shimmering silver bikini, felt the weight of the occasion.

The murmurs, the clinking glasses, the hushed tones - all added to her anxiety. Sylvia, in contrast, seemed the epitome of confidence in her gleaming gold bikini.

Both Mara and Sylvia were aware of the potential windfall that awaited them. The buzz surrounding the event had elevated it to more than just a typical fight; it was a high-stakes game where every move held financial implications. An elaborate yet discreet financial system was in place. As the punches landed and the crowd roared, money would be electronically siphoned into their respective bank accounts. The unnamed organizer had made sure of the transaction's secrecy, masking the massive inflow as a mere "consultant fee." A special announcement was made just moments before the fight began. The winner, apart from the hefty sum collected from the streaming and in-person audience, would be awarded a $10 bonus from each spectator. This announcement amplified the stakes and, in turn, the tension. The loser, despite all the physical and emotional exertions, would leave empty-handed. But the fight itself wasn't the only source of income for the evening. Whispers had spread about a possible post-fight engagement between the two competitors. If the two decided to engage in a sensual rendezvous after their battle, a significant additional payout awaited them. It was a proposition that many in the audience were hoping for, and the potential earnings from this side spectacle alone could touch $30,000 for each fighter. For the victor, the financial rewards would be even more astronomical.

As the two women sized each other up in the ring, it wasn't just about physical prowess or technique. It was also a game of mental endurance and strategic thinking.

Every move had implications, not just in terms of the fight's outcome, but also financially. They both knew that each punch, each dodge, and each tactic could inch them closer to a life-altering sum. The allure of the money added an extra layer of complexity. It wasn't just about pride or proving one's superiority in combat. It was also about securing their futures, about achieving something monumental, and perhaps even about indulging in pleasures beyond the fight. The atmosphere was thick with expectation. The crowd, the fighters, even the silent dark web spectators, all sensed that this was not just any other fight. It was a monumental event, the outcome of which would resonate far beyond the confines of the underground club. With the stakes set so high, both Mara and Sylvia had everything to fight for and a lot to lose. Suddenly, the bell rang.

The atmosphere was electrifying, the weight of expectation, anticipation, and tension, heavy in the air. The hushed silence of the audience was interrupted only by the shuffling of feet and the distant murmur of bets being placed. The opening moments of the fight were a tense standoff, each woman carefully gauging the other's movement, searching for any sign of weakness or hesitation. Mara, known for her precision and technique, made the first move, lunging at Sylvia with a sharp jab. Sylvia, not to be outdone, parried and countered with a swift right hook. The crowd gasped. The first contact had been made. Minutes seemed like hours as each woman gave and took blows. Neither wanted to give an inch, knowing too well the implications of every landed punch, both physically and financially. They danced around each other, their movements almost balletic. The sweat and determination visible on their faces.

It was clear that this fight wasn't going to be won through sheer physicality alone. It was a game of endurance and mental fortitude. Each fighter trying to outthink, outlast, and outmaneuver the other. Punches to the face were met with bloody lips and the occasional black eye, each earning its respective bonus. There were moments when it seemed one had gained the upper hand, only for the tide to turn suddenly. Sylvia managed to pin Mara against the ropes, landing several body blows, but Mara countered with an unexpected uppercut, sending Sylvia staggering back. The crowd cheered and jeered in equal measure. As the fight drug on, fatigue began to set in. Their movements became slightly more sluggish, their defenses a tad more vulnerable. But neither was ready to give up. The potential payout and the promise of the bonuses kept them pushing forward, even as their bodies screamed in protest. The raw brutality of the fight was evident in their battered faces and bodies. Blood smeared on their skin, bruises forming in real-time. Their breaths came out in ragged gasps, but their eyes burned with determination and fire.

The bell signaling for a break was both a relief and a curse. It meant a few moments of respite, a chance to catch one's breath, but it also meant the fight was not yet over. The stakes were too high, the potential payout too tempting. Neither Mara nor Sylvia was willing to back down. As they both returned to their corners, their coaches whispered strategies and words of encouragement. They were patched up, watered, and sent back into the fray, time and time again. The crowd was on the edge of their seats, living and breathing every punch, every dodge. The atmosphere was electric, each round more intense than the last. The question on everyone's mind: Who would emerge as the victor in this epic battle of wills and endurance?

At the one-hour mark, the electronic counter hanging prominently above the ring displayed the earnings for each fighter:

Mara:
- Base Earnings: $5 x 4 (for every 15 minutes) = $20
- Black Eye Given: 2 x $10 = $20
- Bloody Lip Given: 1 x $10 = $10
- Bloody Mouth Given: 1 x $10 = $10
- Blood per Breast Given: 1 x $10 = $10
- Bloody Nose Given: 0x $10 = $0

Total for Mara: $70 x 947 viewers = $66,290

Sylvia:
- Base Earnings: $5 x 4 (for every 15 minutes) = $20
- Black Eye Given: 1 x $10 = $10
- Bloody Lip Given: 2 x $10 = $20
- Bloody Nose Given: 0 x $10 = $0
- Blood per Breast Given: 2 x $10 = $20

Total for Sylvia: $70 x 947 viewers = $66,290

The one-hour mark brought a brief respite, allowing the two battered fighters a moment to breathe and regroup. The electronic counter hung prominently above, serving as a stark reminder of what was at stake. The equal earnings were an unanticipated twist; neither Mara nor Sylvia expected to be neck and neck at this point.

Sylvia, taking a swig from her water bottle, locked

eyes with Mara. Sylvia's lips were swollen, with blood trickling from a cut. Both eyes were turning a shade of deep purple. Mara, though her face was relatively less bruised, was feeling the effects of Sylvia's powerful punches on her torso. Their trainers, working diligently, applied cold packs and dabbed the wounds to stem the bleeding. But the clock was ticking. They had mere minutes to prepare for the next round. The in-person audience murmured amongst themselves, placing side bets on the outcome, while the online chat feed was blowing up with comments, speculations, and cheers for their favored fighters.

The bell sounded once more. Mara and Sylvia stepped forward, with the mutual understanding that this wasn't just about the money. Their professional rivalry had personal undertones, and pride was on the line. Mara initiated with a sharp left jab towards Sylvia's already injured eye, attempting to capitalize on the damage. Sylvia retaliated, swinging hard at Mara's ribs, trying to wind her. The battle resumed in earnest, each blow carrying the weight of their combined determination, pride, and the promise of the hefty purse. The sound of fists on skin echoed under throughout the room, mixing with the cheers from the audience. The two fighters were evenly matched, but as the fight progressed, fatigue began to show its signs. Both women showed incredible resilience, but with each punch and each defensive maneuver, they were being pushed closer and closer to their limits. The big question was, who would reach theirs first?

Both women knew that endurance was crucial. In such a high-stakes battle, one misstep or a momentary lapse in concentration could spell the end. Despite the wear and tear, neither of them was prepared to give up, not with so much on the line. Sylvia attempted a feint, drawing Mara to her left before swinging a strong right hook aimed for Mara's temple. But Mara, with her years of experience, narrowly dodged and countered with an uppercut, catching Sylvia off-guard. The punch connected squarely with Sylvia's chin, snapping her head back. However, Sylvia's resilience and her reputation for being a tough fighter weren't for nothing. Shaking off the dizziness, she responded with a series of body shots, targeting Mara's sides, which were already turning an ugly shade of blue and purple from earlier blows. Each fighter's corner shouted encouragement and strategy, but the cacophony of cheers and gasps, made communication challenging. Both women had to rely on instinct, experience, and sheer will.

Mara, seizing an opportunity, grabbed Sylvia by the hair and pulled her down, attempting to land a knee to Sylvia's face. Sylvia, however, twisted out of Mara's grasp at the last second, causing Mara to lose her balance. Without missing a beat, Sylvia lunged, tackling Mara to the floor. Now on the ground, the fight became even more intense, a blend of punches and kicks. The women writhed and twisted, each attempting to pin the other, to land blows that could give them a definitive advantage. The audience was on the edge of their seats, their cheers and shouts creating a deafening noise. Despite the apparent chaos, there was a method to the madness. Both women, seasoned fighters, were continually strategizing, looking for openings, conserving energy, and waiting for the right moment. After what seemed like an eternity, but was only a few minutes, the bell rang again, indicating the end of another round. Both fighters were panting heavily, their faces and bodies a roadmap of pain and determination.

The electronic counter updated, revealing Mara at $75,760 and Sylvia still at $66,290. Both Women were nearing another 15-minute bonus. If Sylvia could bloody Mara's mouth, they would be equal. The small difference was primarily due to the bonus for Drawing blood on Sylvia's second breast. Both fighters locked eyes, neither was prepared to give an inch. Though bloodied and bruised, both women still had their clothing intact. The clothing bonus was significant, and each woman knew that successfully stripping the other could not only provide a psychological advantage but also a considerable boost to their earnings. The bell rang to signal the start of another round. This time, there was a shift in strategy. Both Mara and Sylvia eyed each other's clothing, calculating the best way to get the upper hand. Sylvia made the first move, lunging at Mara with the intent of grabbing her top. But Mara, always a step ahead, sidestepped the advance and threw a punch. It was a feint, and as Sylvia moved to block, Mara swiftly reached for the hem of Sylvia's shirt, pulling it upwards. Sylvia, in a reactionary move, grabbed Mara's wrists, but the momentum was already in Mara's favor. With a quick yank, the shirt came off, exposing Sylvia's sports bra underneath. The crowd roared in excitement, and the counter above the ring added the bonus to Mara's total.

Not to be outdone, Sylvia retaliated. Using her legs, she tripped Mara, bringing her down. Pinning Mara's arms with her knees, Sylvia began to fumble with the clasps of Mara's sports bra. It was a risky move; leaving her face exposed to Mara's headbutts. Mara, however, was more focused on freeing her arms and avoiding the humiliation of being stripped further. After a brief struggle, Sylvia succeeded in unclasping Mara's bra but was unable to fully remove it before Mara managed to wriggle free. As they both got to their feet, breathing hard, they eyed each other, knowing that the fight had shifted to a new level of intensity. The clothing bonus was now on both their minds, adding another layer of strategy to their moves and countermoves. The stakes were higher than ever.

The sight of the two women, battered and bloodied, made for a powerful image. The dim lighting above the ring cast dramatic shadows on their faces, emphasizing the swollen contours of Mara's double black eyes and Sylvia's split lips. With every punch that landed, a spray of perspiration and occasionally blood misted the air. But beyond the visible injuries, it was the unseen fatigue setting in that threatened to be each woman's undoing. Muscles screamed in protest, lungs burned for air, and the dull throb of accumulated injuries became harder to ignore. Sylvia, sensing her strength waning faster than Mara's, decided to leverage the only advantage she had left: her single undamaged eye. She started focusing her punches on Mara's already injured eyes, trying to further compromise her opponent's vision. Each jab, hook, and uppercut were aimed precisely, and with every successful hit, Mara's vision grew blurrier.

Mara, in turn, tried to close the distance and grapple Sylvia, hoping to use her slightly superior strength to pin Sylvia down. In the clinches, the two women tried desperately to land body shots, their fists thudding against ribs, stomachs, and backs. Mara, sensing an opportunity, managed to trap Sylvia in a headlock. Sylvia struggled, her hands reaching up to scratch and claw at Mara's arms, leaving angry red welts. But Sylvia wasn't done; using her legs, she managed to unbalance Mara and the two tumbled to the floor. It became a ground fight, with both trying to gain the dominant position. Each attempted to pin the other, their limbs tangling in a sweaty knot. Mara, in a desperate move, managed to trap Sylvia's arm and began twisting. The pain was immediate, and Sylvia cried out, but her determination didn't waver. Using her free hand, she reached up and grabbed at Mara's already damaged eyes.

The scream from Mara was visceral. Releasing Sylvia's arm, she tried to pull away, but Sylvia didn't let go. Only when Mara's thrashing became too violent did Sylvia finally release her. Both women, exhausted, pulled apart and lay on the floor for a moment, gasping for breath. The referee began a count, and the tension in the room was tense. The question on everyone's mind: Could they continue?

As the two women lay on the ground, gasping for breath, the counter above continued to tick upwards. The viewers, both online and in-person, were treated to close-ups of the injuries sustained by both fighters, with the dollar amounts corresponding to each damage inflicted flashing on the screen. Sylvia had drawn even in earnings after a punch to Mara's mouth drew blood. The identical amounts were a testament to how evenly matched the two fighters were. However, the all-important winner's bonus still hung in the balance, an extra $10 per viewer, potentially $9,470, was on the line for whoever emerged victorious.

The audience, both online and in person, were at the edge of their seats. The chat rooms were buzzing, some urging the women to continue, others expressing concern for their well-being. Bets were being placed on the eventual winner, with odds shifting with every passing second. As the referee's count neared its end, both women, driven by determination and the tantalizing promise of the payday, began to stir. Mara, using the ropes, pulled herself to her feet, her vision blurry but her spirit unbroken. Sylvia, wiping the blood from her mouth, pushed herself up, her body screaming in pain but her will unbowed. The referee checked in with both fighters, ensuring that they were willing and able to continue. Both women gave a resolute nod, albeit through swollen eyes and blood-stained gritted teeth.

The bell rang, signaling the next round.

Sylvia, seemingly reinvigorated by the short break, lunged towards Mara with renewed vigor. She targeted Mara's midsection with a punch. Mara responded with a quick jab to Sylvia's already bleeding lip, causing her to reel back. Taking advantage of Sylvia's momentary imbalance, Mara attempted to strip Sylvia's clothing, aiming for the bonus. She managed to pull off Sylvia's top before Sylvia retaliated with a sharp elbow to Mara's side. Gasping in pain but undeterred, Mara pressed her attack, focusing on Sylvia's exposed torso. The two fought, each attempting to gain the upper hand and strip the other of her remaining clothing. The crowd's cheers and shouts filled the room as the two combatants continued their fierce battle. Sylvia, using her strength, managed to pin Mara against the ropes and began to work on removing

Mara's clothing. But Mara, always the seasoned fighter, used this position to her advantage. She wrapped her legs around Sylvia's waist and executed a powerful throw, flipping their positions. Now on top, Mara went for the win. She rained down punches on Sylvia, targeting her already injured eye. Sylvia's defenses wavered, and it looked like Mara might emerge as the winner. However, as the minutes ticked by, fatigue set in. The pace of the fight slowed. Every punch, every grab, every move was deliberate and measured. They were both exhausted, but neither was willing to give up. The money counter continued to climb, but at this point, it seemed secondary.

Suddenly, Sylvia saw an opening. With a burst of energy, she delivered a powerful punch to Mara's midsection, winding her. Seizing the moment, she tackled Mara to the ground, aiming to pin her down and claim victory. But Mara wasn't done yet. She used her legs to trap Sylvia, attempting to flip their positions once again. The two women rolled and tumbled, each desperate to gain the upper hand. As the clock ticked down, it became clear that this fight was about more than just the prize money. The outcome was uncertain, but one thing was clear: both women had earned the respect of everyone watching. The counter above the ring reflected the bonuses earned so far, and the audience was well aware of the remaining bonuses up for grabs. Their cheers seemed to take on a new intensity, urging the fighters to push their limits. Mara, eyeing the money counter and realizing that there was still a lot to play for, decided to change her strategy. She began aiming her punches at Sylvia's still unbruised eye, hoping to score the black eye bonus. Sylvia, aware of Mara's intentions, used her forearm to shield her face and tried to target Mara's nose in retaliation.

The two women continued to exchange blows, with Sylvia landing a solid punch to Mara's cheek, making her stagger slightly. Sensing an opportunity, Sylvia made a lunge, aiming for Mara's nose. However, Mara quickly sidestepped, making Sylvia miss and lose her balance. Mara capitalized on this, grabbing Sylvia's hair and delivering a solid knee to her midsection. Sylvia gasped for air but managed to land a punch directly on Mara's nose. Blood started flowing immediately, and the audience erupted in cheers as the bloody nose bonus was finally achieved. The two continued to battle fiercely, sweat and blood mingling as they each tried to secure the win. The energy in the room was electric. Every spectator was on the edge of their seat, wondering who would emerge as the victor. Mara cornered Sylvia and repeatedly pounded her midsection. Sylvia could only hold onto Mara's shoulders to prevent from falling. After what felt like an eternity, the bell finally rang, signaling the end of the fight. Both women, battered and bruised, stood in the middle of the ring, awaiting the decision. The judges convened, and after a few tense moments, they announced Mara as the winner. The crowd erupted in applause, acknowledging both fighters' incredible tenacity and skill. As the cheers died down, the two fighters exchanged a brief, respectful nod. The mutual admiration was evident. But the night was far from over. The post-fight bonus was still on the table, and given the chemistry between the two fighters, the audience was in for a treat.

Mara and Sylvia, beaten and bloodied, stood side by side in the center of the ring, catching their breaths. The raucous underground arena, dimly lit by overhead spotlights, echoed with the murmurs of the 100 spectators present. In addition to the attendees in the shadows, the digital counter displayed 847 – the number of online viewers who had paid to watch the brutal fight.

The LED counter blinked and updated in real time, quickly calculating the earnings of each fighter:

Earnings Breakdown:

- Attendance Earnings: 847 online viewers + 100 in-person = 947 attendees. Each fighter receives $100 per attendee.

Mara: $94,700
Sylvia: $94,700

- Base Earnings x each 15 minutes + Injury Bonuses: Both had achieved an equal bonus.

Mara: $113,640
Sylvia: $113,640

- Clothing Removal: Both had managed to strip each other naked.

Mara: $9,470
Sylvia: $9,470

- Winner's Bonus: Mara had won the fight by decision.

Mara: $47,350
Sylvia: $0

Tallying up the totals, Mara had earned a staggering $170,460 while Sylvia, despite the loss, still walked away with a commendable $123,110.

As they acknowledged their massive paydays, the MC reminded the crowd of the one last potential earning – the post-fight sex bonus, the amount of which was yet to be disclosed. The tension in the air was deafening. Everyone knew this fight was about more than just pride or money; it was about the journey these two fighters had embarked on together, and the choices they'd make next.

As both Mara and Sylvia take long drags from their cigarettes, the atmosphere in the makeshift arena is electric. The crowd is divided: some are here for the violence, some for the eroticism, and many are here for both. Their cheers become a mix of anticipation and excitement as the bonuses are announced.

The counter above the ring flashes the new potential bonuses:

1. Forced Orgasm Bonus:
   - The first to force an orgasm: $10x 947 = $9,470
   - The second to force an orgasm: $5 x 947 = $4,735

2. Face Straddle Bonus:
   - Holding down and straddling the opponent's face: $5 x 947 = $4,735

3. Fisting Bonus:
   - This brutal act has the largest potential payout: $100 x 947 = $94,700

With the stakes clearer than ever, both women consider their options, weighing the potential for further pain against a significantly bigger payday. The audience can't help but lean forward in their seats. The final act of this fierce competition is about to unfold, and with these lucrative bonuses on the line, anything could happen.

Their decision is unanimous. Both women, battered but still fiercely competitive, nod in agreement. The allure of the bonuses and the competitive spirit is too strong to resist. They glance at each other, eyes locked in a mutual understanding. The spark of rivalry, mixed with the potential for a significant payday, ignites their determination. Sylvia, taking another drag from the cigarette, blows out the smoke with a smirk, "Let's do this." Mara, smirking right back, replies, "You're on." The crowd roars in approval, eager to witness the next phase of their intense showdown. The air is thick with anticipation as the two women prepare to face each other once again, this time in a battle that blurs the lines between fierce combat and raw sensuality.

The atmosphere is electric as the two women, already well-acquainted with each other's physicality from the fight, circle each other once again. This time, however, their movements are more deliberate and measured, their eyes not just scanning for an opening to strike, but also searching for vulnerabilities, areas of sensitivity and pleasure. Mara makes the first move, lunging towards Sylvia with a surprising quickness. Their bodies collide, and as they embrace, Mara aims a quick jab towards Sylvia's unprotected face, trying to force her dominance. Sylvia, ever the fighter, retaliates with a low punch. The two women are tangled in a dance that is both aggressive and intimate. Hands roam, not just to strike, but to explore, to tease. Sylvia, seeing an opportunity, suddenly grabs hold of Mara's womanhood. Mara, however, has other plans. With a swift move, she pushes forward and finds herself on top of Sylvia. She grins down at Sylvia, her intentions clear.

In their entanglement, Mara, with a sly smile, starts using her fingers to explore Sylvia's body, aiming to be the first to force an orgasm. Sylvia moans but fights back, trying to distract Mara by digging her fingers into those sensitive breasts. Their battle is a mixture of pleasure and pain, with each woman determined to outdo the other. The crowd watches with bated breath, every movement and moan echoing in the silence. Suddenly, Mara, with a determined look, begins her attempt to claim the biggest bonus of them all: the fisting bonus. Sylvia's eyes widen in surprise and a mix of fear and excitement. She battles back, trying to evade Mara's advances. Their movements are frenzied, passionate, filled with both the desire to win and to experience the raw pleasure of the moment.

Mara, sensing a shift in momentum, uses her strength and positioning to try and maneuver Sylvia beneath her. She aims to capitalize on the straddle bonus, knowing full well the implications it carries both financially and in terms of domination over her opponent. She quickly moves, trying to pin Sylvia's arms and slide her body upwards, aiming to position herself over Sylvia's face. Sylvia resists, but Mara's determination is evident. After a brief struggle, Mara successfully straddles Sylvia's face, forcing Sylvia to taste her. The crowd erupts in both shock and excitement. Sylvia, momentarily stunned, realizes that resistance would only prolong the situation. She begins to use her tongue, granting Mara waves of pleasure. Mara catches herself and realizes that she must reposition as to not accidently reach the point of orgasm, and a bonus for Sylvia. Mara leans back slightly, giving Sylvia a bit of breathing room. But it's not out of kindness; she's gearing up for her next move. Using one hand to steady herself on Sylvia's chest, she uses the other to explore, searching for that untouched bottom lip, and aiming to draw blood.

But Sylvia isn't one to be underestimated. She uses her free hands to grasp at Mara, pulling her closer and trying to gain control of the situation. As Mara tries to land punches to her face, Sylvia uses her mouth as a weapon, biting and sucking, trying to distract Mara and make her lose focus. The raw intensity of their actions is a sight to behold. The mix of pleasure and pain, dominance and submission, is incredible. The crowd, silent at first, begins to cheer and shout, placing side bets on who will claim the next bonus.

Sylvia, using all her strength, manages to reverse their positions, flipping Mara beneath her. The crowd's roar is deafening, as Sylvia takes her chance to dominate. With Mara momentarily disoriented, Sylvia tries to capitalize on the moment and goes for her lips, aiming to draw more blood. The two continue to wrestle, their naked bodies slick with sweat. Sylvia's mouth finds Mara's neck, biting and sucking. Mara, on the other hand, uses her hands to explore Sylvia, searching for any advantage she can find. Both women, though exhausted from the previous fight, find a renewed energy in this contest of sexual dominance. Sylvia, feeling confident, begins her descent, aiming to force an orgasm from Mara. But Mara, always the fighter, doesn't make it easy. She wriggles and resists, trying to throw Sylvia off balance. But Sylvia is determined. She uses her fingers expertly, searching for Mara's most sensitive spots.

Mara gasps and arches her back, a testament to Sylvia's skills. But she's not about to give in so easily. With a sudden burst of strength, Mara manages to throw Sylvia off her, reversing their positions once again. Now on top, Mara decides to take a more direct approach, positioning her fingers and preparing to go for the biggest payout - the fisting bonus. The crowd, sensing the climax of the evening, watches with bated breath. Mara takes her time, ensuring every move is deliberate, every touch meant to tantalize and tease. Sylvia, for her part, tries to resist, but the combination of pleasure and pain is overwhelming.

Mara's hand hovers just outside of Sylvia, teasing and testing. Both women's breathing grows more ragged, a testament to the strain of their ongoing contest. Mara's knuckles press against Sylvia, the first step in an act that promises to be as intense and raw as their earlier battle. Sylvia's body tenses, bracing for the impending intrusion. Every fiber of her being is attuned to Mara's hand, to the pressure and the promise of what's to come. The crowd's cheers grow louder, a cacophonous backdrop to this intimate dance. Mara slowly, deliberately begins to push forward. Her fingers curl, forming the beginning of a fist, and she presses harder, using her other hand to steady Sylvia and keep her in place. Sylvia grits her teeth, her body quivering with a mix of pain and pleasure. Their eyes lock, two fierce competitors sharing an incredibly intimate moment. Mara's hand moves steadily, inch by inch, the depth increasing with every passing second. The intensity is palpable, with both women giving and receiving in equal measure. Mara's hand finally reaches its destination, her wrist the final barrier. Sylvia gasps, a sound of surprise, pain, and pleasure all rolled into one. The two women pause, letting the moment sink in. The crowd's roar is deafening, but in this moment, all that matters is the connection between Mara and Sylvia. Time seems to stand still. The two women, locked in this intimate embrace, ride waves of pleasure and pain. The intensity of the act mirrors their earlier fight, a testament to their strength, determination, and sheer willpower. Eventually, the act comes to its natural conclusion. Mara slowly, carefully withdraws her hand, and the two women collapse, spent and satisfied. The counter above the ring updates, displaying their impressive earnings for the evening. The applause and cheers of the crowd wash over them, but in this moment, all that matters is the bond they've forged in battle and intimacy.

As the crowd's applause reverberates around the dimly lit room, the lights brighten, revealing the full extent of the two warriors' battle scars. Mara, still breathing heavily from the exertion, pulls herself up to a sitting position and extends a hand to help Sylvia up. The two women, though competitors moments ago, now share a newfound respect for each other. Sylvia, her face flush and her body showing the wear of the night's events, accepts Mara's help and pulls herself up. The two women stand facing each other, silently acknowledging the intensity of their shared experience. It's a connection that only they can truly understand. The organizer of the event steps into the makeshift ring, microphone in hand. "Ladies and gentlemen, what a night! Let's give it up for Mara and Sylvia!" The crowd erupts in applause once more.

He continues, "The final bonuses have been

calculated and will be added to their respective accounts. But, before we conclude tonight, let's hear from the two stars of the show."

Mara takes the microphone first. "This... this was unlike anything I've ever experienced. Sylvia, you're a worthy opponent, and I respect you. To everyone who watched, supported, and bet, thank you. This is a night I won't soon forget." Sylvia, wiping away sweat and blood from her face, chimes in, "Neither will I, Mara. We may have been adversaries tonight, but I feel like we've built a bond that's unbreakable. And to the fans, your support means everything. Thank you." As the crowd begins to disperse, the two women, battered but not broken, exit the ring together. The night's events, both the brutal and the intimate, have left an indelible mark on them, and their lives will never be the same.

THE BATTLE FOR A SIGNATURE

The cavernous space of the vacant building echoed with every sound, amplifying the tension in the room. A few old chairs and tables scattered about were the only remnants of its once active past. Shelley and her husband, Frank, sat comfortably, owning the room with their power and affluence. A whiff of smoke floated in the air as Shelley, regal and poised, lit a cigarette, its glow illuminating her face in the dim lighting. Frank cleared his throat, "Ladies, thank you for coming. As you know, Shelley is about to acquire a new business. She needs a partner." His eyes flicked between Fran and Monica, two competent women who had always proven their worth in Shelley's enterprises. Monica, with her lustrous black hair and piercing blue eyes, shifted uneasily. Beside her, Fran, a determined woman with an athletic build and sharp features, clenched her jaw. Shelley exhaled a cloud of smoke and said, "Both of you are exceptional, but I can only choose one. Decide amongst yourselves." Holding up a contract, she added, "The only thing missing here is a signature."

The implication was clear. A physical confrontation, one where the victor would earn her place by Shelley's side. Fran looked Monica dead in the eye, asking, "Are you willing to walk away?" Monica responded in kind, her voice firm, "Are you?" Their response was simultaneous, "No." Monica was the first to move, her disdain for Fran evident. "I've worked too hard, Fran. This is my chance, and I won't let you take it from me." Fran's eyes flashed with anger, "You think you deserve this more than me? Let's find out." With that, the two women lunged at each other, the sound of their struggle echoing in the vastness of the building. Hair was pulled, punches were thrown, and the two grappled intensely, each vying for dominance.

Frank and Shelley remained seated, the latter's smoke rings punctuating the intensity of the scene. Their faces were inscrutable, revealing nothing of their thoughts as they watched the two women they valued battle it out. Each woman was a formidable opponent in her own right. Monica, with her agility, tried to use her height to her advantage, aiming high kicks and punches. Fran, however, had strength on her side, often pinning Monica down, landing powerful blows. Their clothes bore the brunt of their aggression, getting ripped in the process.

The cold concrete floor beneath them only intensified the pain of each fall. Both women were heaving, their chests rising and falling rapidly, with sweat mingling with the smudges of dirt on their faces. The eerie silence of the empty building was punctuated only by their grunts, the scuffle of shoes, and the occasional thud of a body hitting the floor. Fran managed to land a well-placed kick to Monica's midriff, causing her to stagger back. Monica's eyes blazed with fury, using the momentum to charge headfirst, knocking Fran off balance. They tumbled together, rolling across the floor in a desperate struggle for dominance. The atmosphere was thick with tension, and not just from the fight. There was the looming weight of the partnership on the line and the watchful, expectant eyes of Shelley and Frank. Shelley took another drag from her cigarette, her face an unreadable mask, while Frank's hand rested on the arm of his chair, his knuckles white from the grip.

Monica pinned Fran's arms above her head, her knee digging into Fran's stomach. But Fran wasn't one to be subdued easily. Using her legs, she wrapped them around Monica's waist and flipped her over. Now on top, Fran rained down a series of punches, but Monica deftly moved her head, avoiding most of them. She then retaliated by punching Fran in the ribs. Their energy was waning, but their determination was as fierce as when they started. There were no rules in this gritty battle for supremacy; everything was fair game. Suddenly, Fran, spotting an old piece of rope among the discarded furniture, managed to grab it. She tried wrapping it around Monica's wrists to bind her, but Monica fiercely resisted, biting Fran's arm in the process. Fran screamed in pain and anger, pulling the rope tighter. Just when it looked like Fran might have the upper hand, Monica, with a burst of adrenaline, pushed Fran off her. Both women got to their feet, circling each other, sizing up their next moves, their faces streaked with blood, sweat, and determination.

Both women, though battered and bruised, seemed to have a second wind. Their faces, a testament to their willpower, were set in fierce determination, teeth gritted, and eyes narrowed. Fran's bite wound on her arm still throbbed, a stark red against her pale skin. Monica's eyes were slightly swollen from Fran's punches, and her lip was split, giving her a fierce, wild look. They continued to circle each other, the tension palpable, neither wanting to make the first move and leave herself vulnerable. The contract sat tantalizingly close, a reminder of what was at stake. Suddenly, Monica lunged, aiming for Fran's injured arm. Fran winced as Monica's fingers dug into her wound. However, Fran used Monica's momentum against her, throwing her over her shoulder. Monica crashed onto the concrete; the wind knocked out of her. But she wasn't down for long. Rolling to the side, she avoided Fran's attempt to pin her down.

They clashed again, their grunts and the sound of flesh hitting flesh echoing in the vacant room. The fight had moved from a series of calculated moves to a brutal slugfest. But as the minutes dragged on, it became evident that Monica was starting to flag. Her movements were slower, more labored, and Fran, sensing her opponent's waning strength, pressed her advantage. A swift punch to Monica's midsection had her doubling over, gasping for breath. Fran then followed with a right hook that sent Monica sprawling to the floor, dazed. Fran, not wasting any time, quickly straddled Monica, pinning her down. Monica, in a last-ditch effort, tried to unseat Fran, but the exhaustion and the pain had taken its toll. Fran's fists rained down on her, and with a final punch, Monica's resistance faded. Her body went limp, consciousness slipping away.

Fran, panting heavily, rose to her feet, her eyes never leaving the defeated form of Monica. Shelley, having finished her cigarette, stood up and walked over, contract in hand. Her gaze met Fran's, a look of approval in her eyes. "Well done," she murmured, handing over the contract. Fran took a shaky breath, looking at the document that represented her victory and the partnership she had fought so hard for. She then looked down at Monica, a mix of pity and respect in her eyes. The cost had been high, but in the brutal world of business, sometimes the price of success was paid in blood and sweat.

Monica, groggy and disoriented, leaned heavily on Frank as he gently lifted her from the floor. Shelley approached, her face a mask of concern as she looked over the two fighters. The once pristine room now bore the marks of their brutal confrontation: scattered chairs, scuff marks on the floor, and the faint smell of sweat and blood. Frank gently brushed a strand of hair away from Monica's swollen face, his fingers lightly touching a forming bruise on her cheek. "You alright?" he murmured; his voice full of concern. Monica managed a weak nod, her eyes still slightly glazed. "I've had worse," she whispered hoarsely, her pride refusing to let her show just how much pain she was in. Shelley, ever the businesswoman, looked between Fran and Monica. "This was...intense," she began, searching for the right words. "But it's settled now. Fran will be my partner for the new venture." Fran, clutching the contract to her chest, nodded solemnly. "I won't let you down, Shelley."

Monica, with Frank's support, managed to stand straighter, wincing slightly as she did. "Congrats, Fran," she managed to say, her voice strained. "You earned it." Fran looked at Monica, her eyes softening. "Thank you," she replied, her voice thick with emotion. "You're a very tough opponent." The atmosphere in the room had shifted from one of intense rivalry to one of mutual respect. Both women recognized the lengths they had gone to and the sacrifices they had made. Frank and Shelley exchanged a look, both knowing the weight of the decision they had set in motion. But business was business, and sometimes, the path to success was paved with difficult choices.

Shelley lit a couple of cigarettes. As the smoke swirled, she handed one to Fran. Both women inhaled deeply, allowing the nicotine to calm their frayed nerves. With a final glance back at the room, they walked out together, their steps echoing slightly in the large empty space. Meanwhile, Frank gently helped Monica sit down on one of the few chairs that hadn't been knocked over during the intense confrontation. He knelt in front of her, taking a moment to look into her eyes. "Monica," he began, his voice low and sincere, "I've always admired your tenacity, dedication, and drive. That fight was proof of your determination." Monica, still catching her breath and feeling the throbbing pain of her injuries, looked at him, puzzled. "Frank, I appreciate that, but I lost. Fran is getting the partnership."

Frank smiled softly, "Sometimes, one door closing leads to another, even better one, opening." Reaching into his jacket pocket, he produced an envelope, handing it to her. Curious, Monica carefully opened it. Her eyes widened in shock as she scanned the contents. It was a job offer for a senior executive position in one of Frank's other companies, with benefits and a salary that far exceeded anything she had ever expected. "I've been meaning to offer this to you for some time," Frank confessed. "Seeing you today, how you gave everything, just solidified my decision. This isn't a consolation prize, Monica. This is an acknowledgment of your worth." Tears welled up in Monica's eyes, not just from the pain of her injuries but from the overwhelming emotions she felt. "Frank... I don't know what to say." "Just say yes," he replied with a grin. With a nod and a teary smile, Monica agreed, sealing the start of a new chapter in her life.

In the months that followed the intense face-off between Fran and Monica, the dynamics between the four main players in the business world evolved. Monica, under Frank's mentorship, was flourishing in her new role. She had quickly assimilated into her position, taking on her responsibilities with zeal and innovation. Frank couldn't be happier with his choice; Monica proved herself not just with her determination in the fight, but with her strategic mindset, and people skills that made her an asset to his other companies. Her approach was a mix of diligence and creativity, and she had a knack for making those around her feel valued and heard. Fran, on the other hand, was proving to be a double-edged sword. While she excelled in her new partnership role with Shelley, her ambition was leading her down a path of arrogance. She had started to question Shelley's decisions openly, and at times, even belittled her in front of other business leaders. Fran felt her win in the face-off was a validation of her superiority and she began wielding it like a badge of honor, often reminding others of her hard-earned position.

Shelley, ever the professional, tried to manage Fran's ego, often smoothing over ruffled feathers after their meetings. But as days turned into weeks, the strain was becoming evident. She missed the synergy she had with Monica. Their work relationship had been based on mutual respect and understanding, and Shelley now felt she was constantly in a battle of wits with Fran. One evening, after a particularly tense board meeting where Fran had openly criticized Shelley's strategy, Shelley and Frank found themselves in his office, sipping on aged whiskey.

"Monica is really shining, Frank," Shelley remarked, trying to shift the conversation from the recent meeting. Frank nodded, "I couldn't be happier. She's become indispensable." Shelley took a deep breath, "I wish I could say the same about Fran. Her attitude is becoming a liability. She's great at what she does, no doubt, but her arrogance... It's pushing boundaries." Frank swirled his drink, "I've noticed. But remember, we chose them for their fire, their determination. It's a double-edged sword." Shelley sighed, "I know. But sometimes, I can't help but feel you got the better end of the deal with Monica." Frank smiled, "It's not a competition, Shell. We'll manage. We always do." Shelley nodded, appreciating Frank's calm demeanor, "You're right. I'll figure it out." And with that, they clinked their glasses, to challenges and the hope of better days.

Shelley's patience had reached its limit. Having clawed her way up from the very bottom, she wasn't about to let Fran, with her newfound authority, undermine her position, especially not in front of important business associates. It was time for a confrontation. Late one evening, after an exhausting day of meetings, Shelley, cigarette in hand, found Fran alone in her office. She walked in, the soft ember glow of her cigarette illuminating the dimly lit room. Without a word, she closed the door, signaling that this was a private matter. "You've been running your mouth quite a lot recently," Shelley began, taking a long drag and exhaling the smoke slowly.

Fran, never one to back down, shot back, "Just calling it as I see it, Shell." The tension between the two was thick. Shelley took another drag, holding Fran's gaze. "You think because you've had a few good months here that you can speak down to me? I built this place. Before Monica, before you, I was here. I've faced down bigger threats than you, darling." Fran smirked, "You mean like Frank's ex-secretary?" Shelley's eyes flashed with anger, "Exactly. She underestimated me and paid the price. I hope, for your sake, you don't make the same mistake." Fran stood up, getting face-to-face with Shelley, "What are you going to do, challenge me to a duel?" Shelley exhaled smoke directly into Fran's face, never breaking eye contact. "If that's what it takes to put you in your place, don't think I won't." Fran coughed but remained defiant, "You may have your history, Barbara, but this is my time now. Don't make the mistake of thinking I'm scared of you." Shelley smirked, crushing out her cigarette. "Then perhaps we need to settle this the old-fashioned way. To show you exactly who you're dealing with." The stage was set. The tension between Barbara and Fran had reached its boiling point.

Shelley informed Frank of her confrontation with Fran. Frank leaned back in his chair, the weight of years and countless deals evident in the lines on his face. He looked at Shelley, his partner in both business and life, and could see the familiar fire in her eyes. It was a fire he'd seen many times before, one that had carried them through countless challenges and obstacles. "You really going through with this, Shell?" he asked, though he already knew the answer. Shelley took a moment. "She needs to understand, Frank. Understand her place, and the respect she owes. Not just to me, but to us, and everything we've built." Frank nodded slowly. "Just... be careful, okay? This company, our legacy, it's bigger than just one rivalry." She smiled wryly, her crimson lips curving in a way that was both affectionate and dangerous. "Don't worry about me. I've been through worse and come out on top. I've no intention of letting Fran change that track record." Frank sighed, rubbing his temples. "I trust you, Shell. Always have, always will. Just remember what's at stake." Shelley leaned forward, placing a gentle hand on Frank's. "I know what's at stake. And I also know Fran's ego is her biggest weakness. She's not prepared for what's coming."

Shelley's luxurious office bore witness to the tension brewing between the two women. An expensive mahogany desk separated them, and behind it, large windows provided a panoramic view of the city. In the soft light, Shelley, the powerful business magnate, lit a cigarette. Offering the pack to Fran, she prompted, "Remember the last time we shared a smoke privately?" Fran, always defiant, shot back immediately, the corners of her mouth twitching in a smirk. "The night I defeated Monica, you mean?" Fran took a cigarette, lighting it, her gaze not leaving Shelley's. The room was filled with the slow, rhythmic sound of their breathing, punctuated by the occasional exhale of smoke.

"Monica isn't cozying up with Frank yet, is she?"

Fran said with a teasing edge. Shelley's eyes flashed dangerously. She took a long drag from her cigarette before letting the smoke escape slowly, the acrid smell cutting through the room. "You're treading on thin ice, Fran. Bringing Frank into this is a low blow, even for you." Fran tilted her head, her rebellious streak evident. "Just stating the facts, Shell. You married into power." Shelley leaned forward, her icy demeanor never faltering. "And you, dear Fran, think you can just talk your way to the top. But let's get one thing straight. Monica was soft; I'm not. And I've had enough of your insubordination." A tense pause ensued before Shelley continued, "You might not be aware, but there's some fine print in your contract. To put it plainly, I own you. You dance to my tunes, remember?"

Fran's defiant facade wavered for a moment, processing the gravity of Shelley's words. But she wasn't going to back down so easily. "What do you want, Shelley?" Shelley scribbled an address on a piece of paper, sliding it across the table towards Fran. "Be there in two hours. And bring someone to drive you home. Frank will be with me." Fran's eyes widened, but she said nothing. She knew exactly what Shelley was implying. Shelley took a final drag of her cigarette, her gaze never leaving Fran's. "You can choose not to show up. But either way, remember this isn't about your job. This is about respect. It's time for an attitude adjustment." The gauntlet had been thrown; the challenge issued. The next two hours would determine the outcome of this power play.

Fran's mind raced as she left Shelley's office. She was confident in her own abilities, but she knew Shelley wasn't someone to be taken lightly. As she walked, she remembered hearing whispers in the company about Shelley's rise to the top. They talked about a brutal confrontation years ago in a warehouse between Shelley and Frank's former secretary, which ended with the secretary's abrupt departure from the company. Shelley had then smoothly transitioned from Frank's secretary to business associate, then partner, and finally, his wife.

Pulling out her phone, Fran called her friend Carla, a tall, robust woman with a past in amateur boxing. Fran briefly explained the situation, leaving out certain details, but emphasizing that she needed someone in her corner. Carla agreed, intrigued and slightly amused by the high-stakes drama. Two hours later, at the address Shelley had given, Fran arrived in her sleek black sedan. Carla, sitting beside her, looked out to see an old warehouse, the windows dusty and walls showing signs of age. Fran's heart raced as she remembered the whispers about Shelley 's rise to power. Stepping out of the car, they were greeted by the low hum of a car engine. A black SUV pulled up, and out stepped Frank and Shelley. Frank gave a nod to Carla, acknowledging her, but his gaze was fixed on his wife.

Shelley looked every bit the confident, powerful businesswoman that she was, even in this grimy environment. Her eyes fixed on Fran, assessing her opponent. "Glad to see you took my advice and brought someone to drive you home," she remarked, taking a drag from another cigarette. Fran smirked, "Thought I'd give you a proper audience." Both women circled each other, sizing each other up, the stillness only interrupted by the occasional crackling of a cigarette being smoked. The battle for power, respect, and dominance was about to begin.

Inside the warehouse, both women stood a few feet apart. Shelley wore loose-fitting trousers and a comfortable shirt, her hair tied back in a no-nonsense ponytail. Fran had chosen a similar ensemble, her auburn hair pulled into a tight bun, highlighting her defiant eyes. Shelley took a deep drag from her cigarette, the smoke obscuring her face for a moment before she exhaled slowly. "You know, Fran," she began, her voice calm, "you're incredibly valuable to the company. What you don't seem to understand is that respect isn't given, it's earned. And right now, you're lacking in that department. This," she gestured around, "is going to be a little lesson for you." Fran chuckled, the fire in her eyes blazing. "You think I'm afraid of you? Just because you've slept your way up doesn't mean I won't put you in your place. Frank needs to see who the real powerhouse is."

Frank, watching intently, shifted uncomfortably. He knew both women were capable, but this was not how he had envisioned things going. It was, however, too late to intervene. Shelley dropped her cigarette, crushing it under her heel. "This isn't about Frank, dear," she smirked. "This is about teaching you a lesson in humility." Fran's eyes narrowed. "Let's see if you can, old lady." The two women lunged at each other, fueled by a mix of professional rivalry, personal vendettas, and the desire to assert dominance. Their movements were calculated, each trying to gain the upper hand, both determined to prove their point and emerge victorious. As Fran lunged at Shelley, she aimed a right hook towards her face, anticipating a swift victory. But Barbara, with her years of experience, easily sidestepped the blow, grabbing

Fran's wrist and pulling her off balance. Fran stumbled but quickly regained her footing, swinging her leg in a sweeping motion to knock Barbara off her feet. But Shelley was ready. She hopped over Fran's leg and, with a swift motion, attempted a takedown. Fran, however, was quicker than she appeared. She avoided Shelley 's hands and sent a sharp punch towards her midsection. The blow connected, and Shelley grunted in pain, momentarily winded.

Using the brief window of opportunity, Fran grabbed Shelley by the shoulders and pushed her hard against a nearby stack of crates. Shelley's back slammed against the wood, and she hissed in pain, her eyes watering. But she wasn't out yet. She responded with a headbutt, catching Fran off guard. The impact dazed Fran, giving Shelley the chance to push her away and regain some distance. Both women, panting heavily now, circled each other, eyes locked. Frank, as a spectator, felt a mix of anxiety and anticipation. He had seen Shelley in action before, but Fran was a surprising force to be reckoned with. Suddenly, Fran lunged again, her fingers aiming for Barbara's eyes. Shelley swatted her hands away, but the diversion allowed Fran to land a punch square on Shelley's jaw. Shelley staggered back, tasting blood. Fran, seeing her advantage, pressed on, throwing a flurry of punches and kicks.

Shelley, however, wasn't ready to give up. She ducked and dodged, blocking most of Fran's blows, waiting for an opening. And when she saw it, she didn't hesitate. With a fierce cry, she landed a solid punch on Fran's stomach, followed by a swift uppercut to her chin. The blow sent Fran reeling backward, crashing into a pile of discarded pallets. Seizing the moment, Shelley lunged, pinning Fran down. The two struggled for dominance, each trying to gain the upper hand. But with a combination of determination and sheer willpower, Shelley managed to pin Fran's arms to the ground. Face to face, both women were panting, sweat and blood mixing on their skin. Shelley's voice was low and fierce. "This isn't about power, Fran. This is about respect. You may not like me, but you will respect me." Fran, her defiance still apparent but physically outmatched, swallowed hard. The realization that Shelley wasn't just a figurehead but a force to be reckoned with was evident in her eyes. The warehouse fell silent, save for their heavy breathing, as the two women locked eyes, an unspoken understanding passing between them.

Fran's defiant glare slowly softened into begrudging respect. It was clear that Shelley had made her point. "Alright," Fran panted, "I get it."

Shelley, maintaining her position of dominance but with a slight smirk, replied, "I knew you would." She followed up with one last punch to Fran's mouth. "That's for talking shit about me." Shelley then released Fran, allowing her to sit up. Both women took a moment, catching their breaths, feeling the weight of bruises forming and the sting of their injuries. Frank, with a hint of admiration in his eyes, approached the two women, offering a hand to help Shelley up. "Impressive," he commented, nodding toward both women. "Fran, you've got fire, but Shelley's got experience. Remember, it's not just about strength; it's about strategy." Fran, wiping the sweat from her brow, looked at Shelley. "You didn't have to go this far to make your point," she said, her voice a mixture of pain and exasperation. Shelley, lighting another cigarette and taking a long drag, replied, "Sometimes, words aren't enough. You needed to understand the hierarchy, and this was the only way." Fran, rubbing her aching limbs, conceded, "Fine. But just know, I still think I'm better suited for the job." She paused, adding with a smirk, "Just not better at fighting, apparently." Shelley laughed, "Glad you see the difference." She extended a hand to Fran, helping her to her feet. "Now, let's get back to work. There's a company to run." The tension in the room began to dissipate as mutual respect formed between the two powerful women. They may not have seen eye to eye on everything, but they now understood each other's strengths and weaknesses. And in the cutthroat world of business, such understanding was invaluable.

RETRIBUTION RENT

Samantha and Julia, both in their early thirties, shared a modest apartment in the heart of the city. They had lived together for five years and had seen their fair share of ups and downs. However, the most constant pain in their lives was their landlord, Mrs. Carver. With platinum blonde hair, porcelain skin, and striking features, Mrs. Carver could easily have been mistaken for a former model. But behind that veneer of beauty was a soul tainted with malice. Today, Mrs. Carver had arrived for a surprise inspection. The women knew what this meant - it was her infamous tactic before evicting someone. As Mrs. Carver went from room to room, her eyes meticulously scanned every inch of the apartment, finding fault wherever she looked.

"The cracks on this wall, the stain on the carpet, the slightly chipped countertop - all of these will cost you," Mrs. Carver said, jotting down notes on her pad, her tone dripping with satisfaction. Julia clenched her fists, trying to control her rising anger. "This is outrageous! We've kept this place in impeccable condition." Mrs. Carver turned her icy gaze to Julia, "Oh, dear, if you thought the rent was high, wait till you see these charges." Suddenly, the atmosphere in the room grew thick with tension. Samantha had reached her breaking point. In a swift move, she lunged at Mrs. Carver, gripping her from behind and restraining her arms. Samantha's sudden move took Mrs. Carver by surprise. The grip was ironclad. Mrs. Carver, with her fiery spirit, thrashed and tried to break free, her sharp heels clicking against the wooden floor in a futile effort. But Samantha's hold was unyielding. "You're not going anywhere," Samantha whispered menacingly into Mrs. Carver's ear.

Julia, her face flushed with a mix of anger and determination, took a deep breath and then started delivering focused punches to Mrs. Carver's soft midsection. Each hit landed with precision, causing the older woman to gasp and grunt in pain. The air was thick with the sound of flesh meeting flesh. With each punch, Mrs. Carver's once arrogant demeanor began to crumble. Her eyes, once cold and calculating, now reflected shock, fear, and disbelief. Every blow pushed the air out of her, leaving her gasping. Her face turned a shade paler, her lips quivering, beads of sweat forming on her forehead. Julia's movements were rhythmic, each punch methodical and purposeful. As she continued, Mrs. Carver's resistance weakened, her body sagging more and more into Samantha's grasp. Her moans of pain grew louder, echoing eerily in the confines of the room. After several moments that felt like an eternity, Julia finally paused, her breath ragged from the effort. She leaned in close to Mrs. Carver's face, ensuring the defeated landlord could see the fire in her eyes. "We're even now. No additional charges," she declared.

After what felt like an eternity, Samantha finally released her grip, and Mrs. Carver crumpled to the floor, gasping for breath. Julia, panting from the exertion, leaned down, her face inches from Mrs. Carver's. "We're even now. No additional charges." Mrs. Carver, clutching her bruised abdomen, managed to nod weakly, the realization hitting her that she had pushed these women too far. The roommates didn't stick around for much longer after the incident, quickly finding a new place to call home. But for Mrs. Carver, the lesson was clear: never underestimate the power of those you oppress.

SMOKE AND MIRRORS

Amelia, a woman in her early thirties, had an addiction that was unlike any other. It wasn't just the nicotine; it was the act itself. Smoking for her was a ritual, a gateway into her deepest, darkest desires. The cigarette was more than just an object; it was a symbol of her power, her seduction, and her rebellion against norms. Growing up, Amelia was always the shy one. Timid and overlooked, she often found solace in the novels she read, where fierce female protagonists took charge of their lives, often with a cigarette dangling from their lips. They were strong, defiant, and unapologetically themselves. And that's what she yearned to be.

It started innocently enough. In college, at a party, she took her first drag. The rush wasn't just from the nicotine but also from the awareness of the eyes on her. She felt seen, powerful, and in control. From that moment on, the cigarette became an extension of her. As Amelia's confidence grew, so did her desire to explore more of herself. She found that the act of smoking heightened her senses, especially during intimate moments. The slow drag, the release of the smoke, and the slight burn became intertwined with pleasure. The men and women she brought into her bedroom would often comment on the intoxicating blend of her natural scent mixed with the lingering aroma of tobacco. But her true passion, the deepest depth of her fetish, was when she combined smoking with confrontation.

In her professional life, Amelia was known to be fierce and direct. There were countless times when she'd light up a cigarette during tense negotiations, using the act as both a distraction and assertion of dominance. Opponents would be caught off guard, allowing her the upper hand. Her personal life, however, was where the real thrill lay. Amelia sought out challenges with other strong-willed women. These confrontations, often culminating in physical fights, became her most exhilarating escapes. The set-up was almost ritualistic: a shared cigarette, an escalating argument, and then the physical release. For Amelia, the combination of the sensory stimulation from smoking and the adrenaline rush from fighting was intoxicating. It was a way to reclaim the power she never felt she had growing up. Every drag of her cigarette and every confrontation was a reminder of how far she had come from that shy girl in the corner. The question always lingered in the back of her mind: Why this specific blend of fetishes? Maybe it was a rebellion against her upbringing, a way to assert control, or perhaps a way to feel alive in moments of numbness. Whatever the reason, it was intrinsically Amelia. She wore her scars, both from fights and from the occasional cigarette burn, with pride. They were reminders of her journey, her growth, and her unabashed embrace of her desires.

Amelia had always prided herself on being the center of attention wherever she went. But the day

Isabelle walked into the local bar, all eyes, including Amelia's, were on her. Isabelle was undeniably magnetic. With raven-black hair that cascaded down her back in loose waves, she had a chiseled jawline, piercing blue eyes, and an air of confidence that was palpable. But it wasn't just her beauty that made heads turn. It was her demeanor, an exquisite blend of raw strength and sensuality. Her leather jacket, combined with a flowy skirt, defied traditional fashion norms. The way she smoked her cigarette, not with fragility, but with a power that commanded respect, was hypnotic. Amelia watched from across the room as men tried to approach Isabelle, each trying to woo her with their best pickup lines. But Isabelle dismissed them effortlessly, her sharp wit cutting through their advances. As the evening progressed, Amelia felt an irresistible pull. It wasn't just physical attraction; she felt a kinship, an unspoken understanding, like they were both wolves among sheep. Summoning her courage, Amelia approached the bar counter where Isabelle was seated. Lighting her own cigarette, she opened with, "You handle attention well." Isabelle took a drag from her cigarette, her blue eyes locking onto Amelia's, and replied with a smirk, "It's not the attention I seek, it's the thrill of the challenge."

Amelia felt a rush, a mix of excitement and apprehension. She realized that in Isabelle, she might have met her match. Their conversation flowed effortlessly, touching upon their shared love for adrenaline, their experiences with confrontations, and the primal satisfaction they felt in asserting dominance. Amelia found herself not just attracted to Isabelle, but also deeply intrigued by her. She sensed a story behind Isabelle's mysterious aura, and she was eager to unravel it. Isabelle, leaning against the bar, took another drag from her cigarette and exhaled slowly, her eyes never leaving Amelia's. "You ever wonder why some of us are so drawn to the thrill? The rush of facing off with someone? And then mixing it with the slow, sensuous pull of a cigarette?"

Amelia leaned in closer, her own cigarette forgotten between her fingers. "I've always felt it. It's like two sides of the same coin for me - the aggression, the desire to dominate, and then the calm, the control from smoking. But most don't get it." Isabelle nodded, a playful smile curving her lips. "Most people seek peace and avoid confrontation. But for some of us, it's in the confrontation where we truly feel alive. The physicality, the adrenaline... it's intoxicating. Then, lighting up a cigarette afterward? It's the perfect way to revel in that post-confrontation calm."

Amelia, feeling an unusual vulnerability, shared a memory. "I once got into a confrontation with a woman at a club. She was being obnoxious, and things escalated quickly. After I'd... let's say, established my dominance, I stepped outside and lit a cigarette. The juxtaposition of the aggression inside and the calm outside, with the smoke curling around me, it felt poetic." Isabelle laughed softly. "I get that. There's something profoundly satisfying about asserting yourself and then retreating into the quiet embrace of a smoke. It's almost ritualistic." Their conversation deepened as the night wore on. They shared stories of past encounters, of the times they felt powerful and the times they were humbled. They talked about past relationships and how their unique inclinations often made things complicated. But with each shared tale and every puff of smoke, a bond formed between them.

By the time the bar announced the last call, Amelia and Isabelle had delved deep into each other's psyche, finding a mirrored reflection of their desires and inclinations. They stepped outside, the cool night air enveloping them. Amelia lit a cigarette, offering one to Isabelle. "Same time next week?" Isabelle asked, taking the offered cigarette. Amelia smiled. "Definitely. There's a lot more to unpack, and I think we're just scratching the surface." Isabelle grinned, "Here's to new beginnings and shared... passions." They both laughed, sealing the start of a mysterious, thrilling journey ahead.

The bar's ambiance was electric with the hum of chatter and clinking glasses, but Amelia felt like she was in her own world, replaying their last conversation in her mind and the anticipation of the next. Every time the door opened, she'd glance hopefully, searching for Isabelle's distinct silhouette. After what felt like hours but was probably only thirty minutes, the door opened, revealing Isabelle. The dim lighting of the bar illuminated her strong features, making her look even more enigmatic than Amelia remembered. Isabelle, spotting Amelia, gave a playful smirk and sauntered over. She took a seat next to Amelia, leaning in to look closely at her eye. "Rough week?" she inquired, her voice dripping with curiosity. Amelia smirked, taking a sip from her drink. "You could say that. Let's just say a woman at the laundry mat didn't take too kindly to some friendly advice. We had a little disagreement." She paused, looking into Isabelle's eyes. "The cigarette after was the most satisfying I've ever had." Isabelle chuckled. "I can imagine. There's something about combining pain and pleasure that's incredibly... invigorating." She signaled the bartender, ordering a drink for herself.

Amelia, feeling emboldened by the alcohol and the company, confessed, "You know, ever since our conversation, I've found myself more enticed by physical encounters. It's like you've opened up a door inside me, one I didn't even know existed." Isabelle looked deeply into Amelia's eyes. "And how do you feel about that door being open?" Amelia exhaled, her breath slightly shaky. "Excited. Overwhelmed. But mostly... curious." Isabelle leaned in closer, their faces mere inches apart. " Good. Curiosity can lead to profound self-discovery. But always remember to be true to yourself, no matter where it takes you."

Their shared experiences and conversations had created a bond deeper than had anticipated. The allure of their mutual interests was a heady mixture, both thrilling and terrifying. Amelia took a deep breath, steadying herself. "You know, Isabelle, every confrontation, every fight I've had, it's like a dance. A push and pull of power dynamics, and when it's over, the calm that washes over is... euphoric." Isabelle nodded in agreement, her gaze intense. "Exactly. It's like two energies colliding, fighting for dominance, and when it settles, there's this serene aftermath. The dance of aggression and the solace of a smoke." They sat in contemplative silence for a moment, lost in their thoughts. The atmosphere around them seemed to quieten, making the world feel like it had shrunk to just the two of them at the bar. Breaking the silence, Amelia said, "I think I'm beginning to understand my desires better, thanks to you. But there's so much more I want to explore, to experience." Isabelle smiled, her eyes gleaming with mischief. "Well, life's an adventure, isn't it? And it seems like we're on a similar journey. Maybe we can explore it together."

The nights that followed were filled with the same tantalizing dance. Each time Amelia and Isabelle met up, the conversations would take on more flirtatious and daring undertones. They would sit across from each other, sharing stories of past confrontations, teasing each other about how they'd fare in a fight against one another. The air was thick with the tension of unspoken desires. One evening, as they shared drinks at Amelia's apartment, the conversation took a particularly intense turn. Amelia, after taking a drag from her cigarette, blew out a cloud of smoke and said, "You know, Isabelle, every time I see you, there's this urge inside me, like I want to test my strength against yours. Just to see who would come out on top." Isabelle, ever the dominant one, leaned in closer, her face inches from Amelia's. "Is that a challenge?" she whispered. Amelia, not one to back down, met Isabelle's gaze squarely. "Maybe. What if it is?" Isabelle smirked, circling Amelia slowly, taking in every detail. "You're brave, Amelia. But remember, challenging me might not end the way you think it will." Amelia stood up, closing the distance between them. "Who says I'm thinking about the end? Maybe I'm more focused on the journey." She emphasized the last word, making her intentions clear.

The atmosphere between them was electric. The desire to fight, to wrestle with each other, to test their strengths and resolve, was undeniable. It wasn't about hatred or anger. It was about understanding, pushing boundaries, and exploring the depths of their connection. Both women knew that their relationship had reached a tipping point. The dance around the subject could only go on for so long before one of them made the first move. The question remained: who would it be? And what would be the consequences of their actions? Isabelle's dark eyes glittered with mischief as she looked at Amelia, a half-smile playing on her lips as she exhaled a stream of smoke. "This journey we're on," she mused, "I hope it's one of those long, thrilling novels with unexpected twists and turns." Amelia raised an eyebrow, intrigued by where Isabelle was taking the conversation. "Oh? And how do you see our story unfolding?"

Instead of answering verbally, Isabelle reached for the hem of her top and began to slowly pull it over her head. The soft lighting of the room cast a soft glow on her skin, accentuating the curves of her toned physique. As the fabric slid off, revealing more and more, her intent was clear. Amelia's heartbeat quickened. She was caught off guard but also entranced. Here was Isabelle, a woman she had been dancing around with for weeks, making a bold move in their tantalizing game of push and pull. "The first chapter," Isabelle whispered, her voice husky, "is always about setting the stage, introducing the characters, and giving a hint of what's to come." She stepped closer to Amelia, her fingers lightly tracing the faint bruise around Amelia's eye. "It seems you've already had a taste of the action." Amelia smirked, leaning into Isabelle's touch. "That was just the prologue. The real story starts now." The two women stood close, their breaths mingling.

Isabelle's gaze was locked onto Amelia's as she took a drag from the cigarette tucked between her teeth. The room was filled with the sharp, seductive aroma of the smoke. Each exhalation framed their faces in a delicate mist. "I think it's only fair," Amelia murmured, the cigarette still held in place as her fingers began to work on the buttons of her blouse. Slowly, one by one, she revealed more of herself. The ambient lighting reflected off the sweat on her skin, amplifying the intensity of the moment. Isabelle watched with rapt attention, each successive button heightening the anticipation. By the time Amelia was done, her blouse hung open, revealing a simple black lace bra that contrasted strikingly with her skin. The room's temperature seemed to have risen several degrees.

She took a final drag from her cigarette and flicked it into an ashtray. "Your move," she said, the challenge evident in her voice. Isabelle smirked, pausing for a moment to appraise Amelia. With a swift motion, she unzipped the side of her skirt, letting it drop to the floor and revealing matching black lingerie. The two women stood there, equally exposed yet defiant, neither willing to be the first to truly surrender. The combination of their shared fetishes and the undeniable attraction between them was creating an electric atmosphere. "Seems we're on equal footing now," Isabelle whispered, stepping closer. The distance between them was rapidly closing, but the question remained: who would make the next move? Isabelle smirked, her gaze unwavering as she met Amelia's. "I've never been one to shy away from a challenge," she purred, taking a step closer, their bodies almost touching. "How about this: we see who can remove the other's first." Amelia's eyes sparkled with mischief. She had never met anyone quite like Isabelle, who exuded confidence and sensuality in equal measure. "Deal," she whispered.

The room was thick with tension as the two women circled each other, each trying to gauge the other's next move. The game had begun, and the stakes were high. This wasn't just about clothing; it was a test of dominance, desire, and determination. Suddenly, Isabelle lunged, her fingers grasping for the delicate strap of Amelia's bra. But Amelia was quick, sidestepping and attempting to catch Isabelle's panties' waistband. They tumbled together onto the soft rug, a tangle of limbs and laughter, each trying to best the other in their playful duel. Through the roughhousing and teasing, it was clear there was chemistry between them. Isabelle paused, her fingers hovering just above the clasp of Amelia's bra. Looking directly into Amelia's eyes, she said, "Remember, whatever happens here, this is just chapter one. I don't want us to hurt each other and part ways forever. This is just the beginning for us." Amelia, her breath slightly ragged from the excitement, nodded in agreement. "I don't want this to end either," she admitted. "No matter who wins this little game, I want to see where this journey takes us."

The moment was charged with anticipation, but also a newfound understanding. Both women knew that the intensity of their connection was undeniable, and that they were on the precipice of something much bigger than just a playful skirmish. Amelia, a freshly lit cigarette dangling from her lips, drew back her arm and threw a punch directly into Isabelle's stomach. The unexpected impact forced the air out of Isabelle, and her eyes widened in surprise. She doubled over slightly, trying to catch her breath. Isabelle looked up, locking eyes with Amelia. The initial shock of the blow faded into a smirk, and there was a wicked glint in her eye. "So that's how it's going to be?" she whispered, regaining her breath. Amelia, not breaking eye contact, smirked right back. "I thought I'd take the initiative." The atmosphere in the room thickened even more. Both women now knew the game had truly begun, and neither would back down easily.

Isabelle took the cigarette from Amelia, inhaling deeply and savoring the taste. The sight was almost hypnotic - the ember glowing brightly, the wisps of smoke curling around Isabelle's face, and the defiant look in her eyes as she exhaled, sending a cloud of smoke towards Amelia. She dropped the spent cigarette in an ashtray. "You're full of surprises," she murmured, circling Amelia slowly, like a predator sizing up its prey. Amelia braced herself, her stance wide and ready. The initial strike had set the tone, but she understood the real test was about to begin. Both women moved cautiously, respecting each other's strength and skill. They were equally matched, and this wouldn't be a quick skirmish. It would be a battle of wills, determination, and raw physicality.

The first few seconds were a blur of motion and raw aggression. Amelia lunged at Isabelle, aiming a punch at her face. Isabelle turned, avoiding most of the blow, but Amelia was quick on her feet, immediately following with a side hook to Isabelle's ribs. The sound of the impact echoed in the room. Isabelle winced but retaliated with a swift uppercut that made Amelia stagger back, gasping for breath. It was evident that neither woman was holding back; every punch, every move was made with the intention to overpower the other. The two were locked in a fierce exchange, blows landing on faces, chests, and stomachs. The echo of their impacts and their labored breathing were the only sounds in the room. There were moments when it seemed one had the upper hand, only for the other to surprise with a counterattack.

Isabelle, using her slightly larger frame, managed to pin Amelia against the wall, throwing a series of punches at her midsection. Amelia grunted with each hit but managed to twist out of Isabelle's grip, delivering a powerful punch that sent Isabelle sprawling backward. Both were sweating, strands of hair sticking to their faces. Their breaths came in short, ragged bursts, but their determination was unyielding. They exchanged fierce looks, trying to find a momentary weakness or hesitation in the other. As minutes turned into what felt like hours, fatigue began to set in. Every punch thrown had slightly less force behind it, and their movements became a bit more sluggish. Yet, neither was willing to yield. Their pride, their competitive spirits, wouldn't allow it. Amelia, trying to end the exhausting brawl, threw a flurry of punches at Isabelle, but Isabelle, summoning her last reserves of strength, ducked and dodged. She then delivered a fist to Amelia's jaw, causing her to stumble back, dazed.

Isabelle didn't waste the opportunity. She lunged, tackling Amelia to the floor. They wrestled, rolling and struggling for dominance, but Isabelle managed to pin Amelia's arms above her head. Both women panted heavily, their chests heaving. "I... I yield," Amelia whispered, the fight finally drained from her. She looked up into Isabelle's triumphant yet equally exhausted eyes. Isabelle nodded, releasing Amelia and sitting up. She extended a hand to help Amelia to her feet. They stood, swaying slightly, their bodies covered in sweat, bruises forming on their skin. "That was... intense," Amelia managed to say, a hint of a smile on her lips. Isabelle grinned, her teeth slightly stained with blood from a split lip. "Just the first chapter, remember?"

Amelia, a lit cigarette clutched between her teeth, narrowed her eyes playfully at Isabelle. The wisps of smoke curled around them as the tension in the room thickened. With a smirk, Amelia reached out suddenly, her fingers latching onto the front of Isabelle's bra, yanking it hard enough to snap it free. Isabelle looked down at the tattered remnants of her favorite bra before raising an eyebrow at Amelia, a smirk playing on her lips. She took a drag from her own cigarette, which was confidently held between her lips, and blew out the smoke teasingly in Amelia's direction. "That was my favorite one," she remarked with faux disappointment. Without missing a beat, Isabelle retaliated by lunging forward and managing to grasp the straps of Amelia's bra, ripping it off in one swift motion. The room was filled with the scent of their perfume, and the smoky aroma from their cigarettes. Amelia took a deep drag, and laughed, "Guess we're even now."

The silence between them grew, filled only by the soft crackling of their cigarettes and their synchronized breathing, which seemed to rise and fall in tandem. Isabelle took a long drag, the ember glowing brightly, illuminating her face momentarily, before exhaling a plume of smoke towards the ceiling. "You're full of surprises, Amelia," she finally said, breaking the silence. Her voice carried a hint of admiration. Amelia chuckled softly, her eyes never leaving Isabelle's. "Life's too short for predictability," she responded, taking another drag from her own cigarette. Isabelle slowly approached Amelia, their bodies almost touching, the heat between them undeniable. "What now?" Isabelle whispered, her voice husky. Amelia met Isabelle's gaze intently. "Now? We decide if this was a one-time thing or if we're just getting started." She blew out a stream of smoke, watching as it danced between them. Isabelle responded by placing her hand on Amelia's cheek, her thumb gently grazing the bruise that had started to form from their earlier scuffle. "Something tells me we're just scratching the surface," she murmured.

With the smoke from their cigarettes lingering between them, Isabelle's fingers trailed from Amelia's cheek to her chin, lifting it slightly. The distance between them closed in an instant. Isabelle pressed her lips against Amelia's, a soft, tentative gesture that quickly deepened into something more passionate and hungrier. The taste of tobacco intertwined with the taste of their own unique flavors. It was a heady mix, amplified by the adrenaline that still pulsed through their veins from their earlier confrontation. Amelia's hands found their way to Isabelle's waist, pulling her even closer. When they finally broke apart, both were gasping for breath, their eyes locked in a gaze filled with a mix of surprise and desire. Amelia's voice was raspy, "That... was unexpected." Isabelle smirked, taking another drag from her cigarette. "Like you said, life's too short for predictability."

Isabelle's grip tightened on Amelia's hand as they moved towards the bedroom. The intensity of their earlier physical confrontation seemed to have only heightened the tangible tension between them. As they crossed the threshold, Amelia paused, glancing sideways at Isabelle. "You know," she said, her tone half-serious, half-teasing, "I'm not known for being gentle in situations like this, especially after the adrenaline rush of a fight." Isabelle's eyes glittered with mischief and challenge. "Neither am I. But that's part of the allure, isn't it?" She leaned in, her voice dropping to a husky whisper, "If you're having second thoughts, this is your chance to turn away. From here on out, things might get... bumpy." Amelia's gaze held Isabelle's, her lips curling into a small smile. "Bumpy sounds interesting. Let's see where this takes us."

Isabelle rummaged through a drawer and produced a sizable strap-on, her eyes never leaving Amelia's. "Given our earlier little exchange," she said, smirking, "I think it's only fair I get to wear this first. But if you want a turn, sweetheart, you'll have to earn it." Amelia, catching her breath and taking a moment to size up the situation, replied with a playful defiance, "You seem pretty confident for someone who's barely caught her breath from our brawl. If you think that punch to your belly hurt, wait till you see what I can do here." Isabelle leaned in, her face inches from Amelia's, her breath hot and heavy with anticipation. The flicker of a lighter briefly illuminated the room, and soon both women were puffing on their cigarettes, the faint glow casting an ethereal light onto their already flushed faces.

With a predatory smirk, Isabelle moved into

position, showcasing her prowess with the silicone cock she had introduced. Each movement was calculated, a delicate balance between granting pleasure and asserting dominance. With every thrust, Amelia gasped, a cocktail of sensations coursing through her — pleasure, pain, and a dizzying rush from the nicotine. The wisps of smoke that spiraled from their lips seemed to join in their dance, mingling and intertwining in the dim light. The room was filled with their soft moans and the faint crackle of burning tobacco. Isabelle, while in control, was attentive to Amelia's reactions, adjusting her rhythm and angle based on the arch of Amelia's back or the catch in her breath. Amelia, though pinned beneath Isabelle, was far from passive, meeting her advances with equal fervor.

As Isabelle continued her expert motions, the ember of her cigarette glowed brighter with each inhalation, reflecting the rising tension between the two. The subtle combination of smoke, passion, and the lingering pain from their earlier fight created an intoxicating mix for Amelia. Amelia could feel herself nearing the edge, and Isabelle, sensing this, slowed her pace slightly, wanting to draw out the moment. Every touch and movement became more deliberate, intensifying the sensations coursing through Amelia. With the cigarette smoke slightly stinging her eyes and the blend of pain and pleasure mounting, Amelia felt a tidal wave of sensation building within her. The culmination was fierce and vocal, a release of all the tension, frustration, and passion that had been building between the two women. Amelia's orgasmic cries filled the room, echoing off the walls and mingling with the smoky haze. The deep satisfaction of the moment was evident in both of their expressions, a perfect blend of exhaustion and contentment.

Isabelle gently pulled out of Amelia; her own face flushed from the intensity of their shared experience. She carefully set the silicone accessory aside and turned her attention back to Amelia, who was still trying to steady her erratic breathing. Amelia's eyes, glazed and slightly out of focus, darted towards Isabelle. The dampness on the sheets beneath her was a testament to the potency of her orgasm. She felt a slight embarrassment, but the reassuring smile on Isabelle's face quelled any lingering insecurities. The two women lay beside each other, their bodies still tingling from their passionate encounter. The room was filled with the mixed aroma of their lovemaking and the faint trace of their shared cigarettes. They both took a moment, allowing the afterglow to settle over them. Isabelle broke the silence first, "Well, that was... intense." Amelia let out a soft, exhausted chuckle, "Understatement of the year. I told you I wasn't gentle." Isabelle smirked, "And neither am I. I believe we're a match made in... well, wherever wild things like us come from." They both laughed softly, a comfortable silence returning as they intertwined their fingers, letting the night's events bond them even closer.

Isabelle propped herself up on one elbow, using her free hand to light a fresh cigarette. As the flame illuminated her face, the play of shadows gave her an almost feral look. The first inhale was deep and deliberate, with her exhale a wispy dance in the dim room. Her gaze was locked onto Amelia's, a mix of challenge and desire evident in her eyes. Amelia, not one to back down from any challenge, leaned closer to Isabelle. Her fingers traced a path down Isabelle's body, taking her time to explore every curve and contour. When Amelia's fingers brushed against Isabelle's intimate areas, Isabelle's reaction was instantaneous. Her back arched, and she let out a soft moan, a clear indication of the pleasure she was feeling.

Despite the gentle start, Amelia began to intensify her movements. Just as they had been in their earlier physical confrontation, Amelia's touches became more forceful and demanding. Isabelle's body responded with jerks and spasms, each one more intense than the last. Her moans gradually morphed into screams of pleasure, each one echoing the raw passion of the moment. Isabelle took another deep drag from her cigarette, the smoke mingling with her ragged breaths. The intense sensation Amelia was causing was pushing her to the edge. The combination of the nicotine and the skilled touch of Amelia made everything feel amplified. As the climax approached, Isabelle's grip on the sheets tightened, her knuckles white. The culmination of sensations, from the aftereffects of their fight to the intense pleasure now coursing through her, was almost too much to bear. Finally, Isabelle let out a scream, signaling her release. Her body relaxed, and she took a few moments to catch her breath. Amelia, satisfied with her handiwork, moved up to lay beside Isabelle. The two shared a deep, passionate kiss, a mutual acknowledgment of the intense bond they had just deepened.

Isabelle looked Amelia deep in the eyes, a sense of primal intimacy hanging thick in the air between them. Amelia, with a confident smirk, brought her moist hand up to Isabelle's face, tracing a wet path over her cheek, down to her lips. Isabelle, her breathing still uneven from the recent orgasm, opened her mouth slightly, letting Amelia's fingers slip between her lips. With a sultry gaze, she sucked on Amelia's fingers, tasting herself, the rawness of the moment making their connection even more profound. The act was not just erotic, but also a form of acknowledgment of their shared experience and the intensity of their feelings.

Amelia, with Isabelle's taste still on her lips, leaned in, capturing Isabelle in another deep and passionate kiss. Their bodies pressed close, the heat from their previous activities still lingering on their skin. As they kissed, they found a rhythm, hands exploring and caressing each other's bodies with a newfound familiarity. Isabelle broke the kiss to catch her breath, her forehead resting against Amelia's. "I've never felt anything like this," she whispered, her voice hoarse. The intensity of their connection was something neither had anticipated. Amelia softly chuckled, "Neither have I. And to think this all started with a fight." Isabelle grinned, "A fight that I won." Amelia rolled her eyes playfully. "For now. We still have many more rounds to go." Isabelle's eyes darkened with mischief. "And I look forward to every single one of them."

They cuddled, their naked bodies intertwined, drawing comfort from the warmth and softness of the other. The room was filled with the scent of their activities, the lingering traces of cigarette smoke, and the deep connection that had formed between them. Outside, the early morning light began to creep through the curtains, signaling the start of a new day. But for Amelia and Isabelle, it was more than just a new day. It was the start of a new chapter, one that promised countless adventures, both in and out of the bedroom.

5 CARD STUD (M/M)

The Friday night poker game was not going as well as I would have liked. I was down to my last $5 as the final round was being dealt. Frank was the big winner so far, with Dean a close second. Mark was doing better than I was and had a few dollars to play with in this final round. The four of us get together one Friday night a month for poker and had been doing this for about 4 years now. Frank and I were the elders of the foursome, both in our late 40's. Dean was a couple of years younger, and Mark was the baby of the group at 28. We typically played dealer's choice and Dean, having won the previous round of 7 Card Draw was given the honors of choosing the final round, Five Card Stud was his choice. The first card facedown and the remaining four to be displayed for all to see. I didn't care for Dean's choice of game for this, the final round. Stud poker showed too many cards and players were quick to fold.

I needed a decent size pot if I were to have any chance of leaving with a little cash in my pocket. After putting in my $2 ante, I was left with three $1 bills to play the round with. Dean dealt the first facedown card to each of us. I lifted the corner to find a fucking seven of Hearts. Since I sat to the left of Dean, I was first to bet. With a hidden seven and only $3, I decided to check. Mark, who was sitting to my left, peaked down at his cards, looked over at me, then the other two at the table and put down a $20 bet. With my $3, I was fucked. Frank took a drag from his cigarette, saw Mark's bet and raised it $10. Frank took another drag. "That's $30 to you Cock Sucker," Frank joked at Dean. Dean studied his card for a few seconds and proceeded to call; tossing a 20 and a 10 on the pile. Dean looked over at me. "Looks like the end of a shitty night for you, my friend." I grabbed a cigarette from the pack next to me and lit one. I took a deep inhale and as I slowly exhaled, I laid it out on the table for the three. "I need a little help. Who can offer up a little credit?" I really wanted to stay in the game and would deal with whatever payback was required after the game. Frank lit up another cigarette. "Well, Stud, you know what my bank terms are, and this bank is always open." Frank tried to drag out the "always."

Each of us was always eager to float a table loan to another. The terms were simple; you pay back a dollar for dollar. If you run out of dollars and are still in the hole, you receive a punishment to be immediately served until all debts were settled. Each of us had a different method of debt settlement if one of us still owed money. Frank's method was painful, especially if there was a large sum of money still owed. If you were unable to pay back Frank, he would have the other two at the table hold your arms and he would deliver a single punch to your gut for each dollar owed him until the ledger was balanced. I am not talking about love tabs from Frank. The Fucker punches hard; hard enough to make you really consider the option of getting a "loan." Mark's preferred choice of payback was a good old-fashioned blowjob.

Mark loves to have his cock deep throated all the

way to his balls. That typically wouldn't be too bad if it weren't for the fact that Mark was hung at a solid 8 inches uncut. I am very careful of the amount I borrow from Mark, as I am not too keen to be having the back of my throat fucked. Dean was a motherfucker in all the literal sense. Whether you owed him $5 or $50, Dean was going to fuck your ass until he was ready to cum. Dean had a sinister skill of ejaculating at will. He could blow his load in 60 seconds or 20 minutes. It was an art. Dean once fucked Frank for 15 minutes before shooting his load into Frank's sore ass. As for me, I am a mixture of the three. As for tonight, I was the guy in need of cash and was willing to pay the price. Frank and Dean agreed to equally cover me through this last round. I agreed, although being in debt with two meant possible double trouble at the end of the night. It didn't matter now; I was all in and could now only hope for some hot cards and win this round. I called and was now $15 in debt each to both Frank and Dean.

The remaining four cards would be face up. Dean began to toss out the next cards. I was given a 7 of Clubs, Mark got a 2 of Diamonds, Frank received a 4 of Hearts and Dean dealt himself an Ace of Clubs. I didn't feel confident at this time, but at least I had a pair of sevens. With his Ace high showing, Dean began the next round of betting with a call. I quickly called as well, as did Mark and Frank. The pot stood at $128, and I was in the hole for $30. Dean quickly distributed our third card. I was given a 3 of Clubs. Mark got a 9 of Hearts, Frank, a 5 of Spades and lastly, Dean dealt himself a 2 of Spades. Dean was still showing the high card and made a $10 bet. I called his $10, which now had me at $40 in debt to the Bank of Frank and Dean. Mark decided to end the bleeding and fold. "It sucks to have this shit hand showing." Mark complained while reaching for one of Frank's cigarettes. "I will watch you guys end this." Mark said. Frank took his lighter and lit Mark's cigarette before producing one from his pack and lighting one for himself as well. "I call boys." Frank tossed in $10 onto the small pile of cash in the middle of the table. "Looks good," Dean followed, and we were ready for the fourth card. The pot was at $158.

I was in the hole for $40 and we had two cards left. I was showing a seven high. Mark was out, Frank was showing a five high and Dean had the Ace. The 4th deal revealed an Ace of Diamonds for me, an Ace of Hearts for Frank and a 6 of Diamonds for Dean. Dean was still high and called on this fourth bet. I quickly called as well. "Fuck boys, it's only money. I bet $5." Frank said. Dean and I matched the bet and that was the end of the fourth deal. I was feeling confident with my sleeper pair of sevens and was happy to see my last card was a 7 of Diamonds. "Three God Damn sevens," I thought to myself. Frank was dealt a 2 of Hearts and Dean got a Jack of Hearts. For the last round of bets, my two 7's showing were high. I bet $10. Frank saw my bet and raised it another $10. Dean could see that he was beat on the table and folded. I felt good about my three 7's. With that, I saw Frank's raise of $10 and raised it another $10. Frank took a long drag on his cigarette and thought for a few long seconds. Frank finally matched my extra $10 and then raised it another $10.

"What the Fuck Frank?" I said loudly. "It will cost you another ten of my dollars for you to see what I have, Cock Sucker." Frank seemed very confident with his Ace high showing. I was already in it too deep with both Frank's fist and Dean's cock if I were to somehow lose;

but then again, I could see that Frank was not showing shit on the table and I had Three of a Kind nicely hidden. I had no choice but to call Frank's raise and end the betting. "Alright, I called motherfucker, show me what you have hidden." I demanded of Frank. "With pleasure," Frank laughed as he turned over a three of Hearts. "God Damnit," I cried out. With my full attention on my Three of a Kind, I had completely forgot about the possibility that Frank was holding a Straight. I flipped over my third 7 and crushed out the cigarette in the ash tray. Dean stood up to stretch his legs. He grabbed a cigarette and lit it. While exhaling, he took his hand and grabbed the hair from the back of my head, tilting my head backwards.

"Time to see the banker Cock Sucker," Dean smiled down at me. With his cigarette clinched between his teeth, Frank leaned forward and slid the money towards him. "That was a good hand." Frank said gleefully. Mark stood up, collected what little money he had saved from the nights play and declared that it was time to head out. Frank asked if he was sure he wanted to leave so soon. "We still have some business to settle here before we all leave." Mark responded that he had to get up early in the morning and needed to head out. "You boys will have to have fun without me this time." Mark mused as he made his way to the door. As Mark was leaving, Dean got up to get himself a beer from the kitchen. Frank and I sat across from each other as Dean made his way back to the table with three cold beers. Frank asked to bum a cigarette from me, and I obliged. We both lit up as Frank began to speak.

"Looks like you have some settling to do. "Frank seemed to be enjoying himself. I replied "Yep, just wasn't my night." "I guess Frank will get his rocks off working me over." I said to Dean. "$55 worth is a little more than a work over if you ask me," Dean commented, as he took the cigarette from my hand and took a drag. "Don't forget, I get about $30 worth myself" Dean said. Frank stood up and walked next to Dean. Dean crushed out my cigarette and pulled me up by my hair. He then grabbed both of my arms and secured them behind me, facing Frank. "Don't hurt him too bad Frank, I need him alert for me." Dean pleaded with his friend.

"Fuck you Frank" was all I could say as Dean's hold on my arms was tight. Frank smiled, crushed out his cigarette in the ashtray on the table and then turned toward me. He unbuttoned my shirt and exposed my chest and belly.

Dean temporarily released his grip on my arms as Frank removed my shirt. Once my shirt was off, Dean resumed his grip. Frank ran his right hand down my chest, past my belly until he had a firm grip on my cock over my jeans. While his right hand massaged my cock, his left fingers began to play with my right nipple. Frank would twist and squeeze, then switch to my other nipple. If it weren't for the fact that he was about to beat me up, I would be enjoying this stimulation. In fact, my cock was beginning to get hard as Frank played with it. "Well, this fucker is enjoying this." Frank spoke to Dean. In response, Dean tightened his grip on my arms and arched his back, further exposing my chest and gut. Frank loosened my belt and unzipped my jeans. He reached through my briefs and got a good handful of my cock and balls. "Yeah, this Cock Sucker is enjoying this." Frank confirmed. With his left hand firmly around my cock and balls, Frank delivered the first of what would be many punches into my gut. I grunted and doubled over slightly. "Fuck," I cried out. Dean lifted me back up.

Frank continued. "Now, I will continue to beat you until you beg Dean for his blowjob." "Say the words and I will stop." I gave him another "FUCK YOU!!!!" This time, I said slow and deliberate, as to if he was hard of hearing. With that, Frank began to land hard right fists into my gut. With each punch Dean would straighten me up, ready for another punch. "You can stop this Cock Sucker," Frank said, as he landed more punches into my stomach. "I am owed about 50 of these fists, but all you have to do is beg me for Dean's cock and I will stop." The punches were beginning to hurt, and Frank seemed to have no intention of stopping. Dean made sure that I could feel his fully erect 7-inch cock straining inside his jeans as he pressed against my ass. One, two, three punches. Frank paused. "You stubborn motherfucker." Frank fired a fourth, fifth, then sixth punch. My belly was on fire and I felt the urge to hurl. Grabbing hold of both my nipples, Frank Twisted in a clockwise, then counterclockwise direction. "Say it Stud. Beg me to let you suck Dean's cock." I didn't speak.

"God Damnit," Frank called out as he turned toward the table. He grabbed a cigarette from one of the packs on the table and lit it. Pointing, Frank spoke to me. "you do realize, we aren't even halfway through what you owe me." With that, Frank motioned to Dean, who released his grip on me. I leaned forward, panting, as I placed my hands on my knees. My stomach was red and on fire. I had no idea how many punches Frank had given me, but I knew there were many more left before my debt was paid. It also occurred to me, that if he continues, or I do as he says and beg him to stop, Dean is going to throat fuck me anyway. That was his re-payment requirement and there was no way in hell he was not getting his. As I was contemplating the decision to swallow my pride and beg for a blowjob, Frank walked back over to me and straightened me up by my hair. With his right hand clamped to my hair, he placed his cigarette in his mouth and fired two punches with his left fist below my belly button. My knees hit the ground. "Well, what will it be?" "Do you want me to continue?" "Please Frank," I spoke. "Please Frank what?" He followed. "Please Frank, stop." I muttered. "Just say the word," answered Frank. "Suck yourself Frank."

With my comeback, Dean violently grabbed my arms again and tucked then tightly behind me. "You just earned yourself an ass fucking Stud." Frank landed another punch into my gut. "OK Frank, you win." I said softly. "Please stop and let me suck off Dean." With that, Frank stepped back, took a drag off his cigarette and proclaimed to Dean that I was all his. Dean did not release his grip, but rather pushed me over to the table. "Grab the ashtray and smokes," Dean ordered Frank. Frank quickly moved them off the table and onto a chair. Still with a firm grip on my arms Dean order Frank to pull down my pants and briefs. Afterwards, Dean slammed my belly and chest onto the table. He released his grip and dropped his pants. My back was to Dean, but I did not have to see what he was doing to know what was about to happen. As he mentioned a minute earlier before Frank's last punch, Dean was about to ram his rock-hard cock into my awaiting asshole.

Frank took a quick drag off his cigarette and dropped it into the ashtray. He placed his hand over the back of my neck to hold me in place. Once the tip of his cock made contact with my hole, he started to push it in. I held on tightly to the edges of the table as Frank continued to press down onto my neck. I nearly passed out as Dean's thick dong sank into my chute. Once he was balls-deep, he pulled out. Then he shoved his cock back in. Hard. Over and over he did this, until I couldn't stop my own orgasm any longer. Streams of my jism spilled onto the table under and to the sides of me. "You're fucking milking me, Bitch." Dean slapped my ass and slammed his cock in my hole harder. He pulled his cock out again, only to ram it back home. He continued to roughly fuck me will Frank held the side of my face onto the table. I groaned when I realized he was emptying his balls up my ass. His cum was hot and thick, squirting deep inside me.

After Dean fucked me, he slapped my ass several times before taking is cock in his hand and smearing what was left of his cum all over my reddened ass. Frank grabbed me by the hair and dropped me to my knees. "It isn't fucking fair." Frank spoke out to Dean as Dean was pulling up his briefs and pants. "You shot your load up this fucker's fuck chute, He shot is load all over your table and I am standing here hard as a motherfucking rock and dry." Dean agreed. "You're right, it doesn't seem fair." I was exhausted. My abs were on fire with pain, my asshole had been ploughed open and now Frank is complaining. Despite the fact I was in no condition to protest, I could still be a cocky prick. "It isn't our fault you stood there like a dumb fuck while Dean and I were blasting cum everywhere. Instead of holding my head down, you should have used that hand of yours and jerked yourself off." Dean leaned over the chair to grab a cigarette. "Well, the Cocksucker does have a point," Dean laughed while lighting up. Unzipping his fly and pulling out his throbbing cock, Frank positioned himself in front of me. Grabbing a handful of my hair, Frank took his other hand and in one jerking motion removed his belt from his jeans. "This should settle your debt." With that said, Frank whipped the belt around my neck, took the other end in his other hand and pulled my mouth over his cock until my lips were touching his balls. I immediately gagged.

Dean moved around and stood close behind, leaning forward to fondle Frank's nipples. Frank tightened the grip on the belt and held my head in place while he began to throat fuck me. Frank looks forward at Dean, then down at me, as I look back at him. His full cock is in my mouth, slick with my spit. I must have hit a good spot because Frank threw back his head in ecstasy. As Frank's pleasure increased, so did Dean's working over his nipples. With my head held tightly in place by the belt around my neck, I was swallowing his manhood whole; my muscles contracting around it, gagging on it. If it were even possible, Frank began to get a little rougher, thrusting his hips with my head tethered to him. Frank's legs stiffened as he released a wave of semen into my mouth and down my throat. The last dribbles of cum run down my face as he pulls his cock out of my mouth. Dean released his grip on Frank's nipples and stepped over to drop a lengthy ash into the ashtray on the chair. I could now add my throat to the list of body parts that burned like hell. All three of us were a hot fucking mess.

The room reeked from the smell of cigarette smoke, sweat, body odor and a gallon of cum from the three of us. We each took a seat in our respective chairs at the table, which now was home to scattered cards, semen and cigarette butts. "These cards will have to be replaced before next Friday's game," Dean joked, finally breaking the silence. "What the fuck got into you Frank?" I asked, knowing full well that Friday nights typically ended with a post-game fight, or fuck or, whatever the hell tonight was. "Is anyone complaining?" Frank asked. "I will let you both know tomorrow." I joked. "And what the fuck was up with Mark leaving right after the game?" Dean asked puzzled. I took a drag from my cigarette. "He needs to be punished for walking out on us like he did." I answered. "Fuck yeah we do." Dean replied. "Well, let's discuss that later. I need to leave myself." Frank said as he got up, adjusting his clothes and replacing the belt around his waist. "You two fuckers wore me out." Frank began to walk toward the door. He gave me a kiss as he was leaving. "No hard feelings, Stud?" Frank asked of me. "Not at all. Be ready next Friday night. I plan to run the table on you and have a little fun afterwards; At YOUR expense." Frank smiled and left. I turned to Dean, who was still seated. "Do you mind if I stay over tonight? I don't feel like the drive home." "Not at all, after being such a good fuck, you can sleep in the Master Bedroom." I picked up my smokes and lighter and started to make my way upstairs. "I desperately need a shower," I said. "Do you mind company?" Dean asked, as he stood next to me at the foot of the stairs. I grabbed a handful of Dean's hair and tilted his head back. "Not at all." I whispered. "Not at all."

BIKER BITCH BATTLE

The sun was quickly setting behind the mountain range as Connie made her way towards Grady's Cabin. Connie slowed her Harley to a stop along the winding gravel drive, about a hundred yards from the structure. She could see Helen's Dyna Low Rider parked under the tin overhang next to the old hand-hewn oak cabin. She noticed the flickering light of an oil lamp burning in the one room shack. By the looks of only one bike, Helen had showed up alone. Connie was concerned that Helen may pull some shit and bring backup. Their meeting tonight was not going to be pleasant, and Connie had not been completely convinced that Helen would be completely honest in her agreement to privately meet alone. Connie figured the rumble of her Fat Boy had already announced her arrival even though she was still a good distance from the cabin. There was no need to make a stealthy entrance; this "get together" had been planned for many days. With the engine still running, Connie took a few moments to take in the beauty.

The cabin sat in the middle of a small valley in the heart of North Carolina's Smoky Mountains. This location was familiar to members of The Iron Dolls. 30 acres, several cabins, along with a gorgeous mountain stream has been in Helen's family for over 100 years. The Dolls frequently used the property for gatherings. Connie, in her mid-forties, had been a founding member of the Iron Dolls which was formed over twenty years ago. Her first taste into the world of biker gangs was shortly after high school, when she was a Mama in a gang in Arizona. As a Mama, Connie was the plaything for the male members of the gang. Connie was tough and sexy. She knew how to use her fists to establish respect among the women and her pussy to gain the admiration of the men. Her "talents" quickly graduated Connie from a Mama to Ol' Lady; the "property" of the Gang's number two leader. To this day Connie carries a scar under her left ear; the result of a fist fight she had with Number Two's original Ol' Lady. After several years of hard living and the abuse of being in a motorcycle gang, Connie took to the road one day, headed east and never looked back.

At 5' 9" and 150 pounds, the 44-year-old dirty blonde Connie could still turn heads, despite the years on the road and way too much sun beginning to show its signs on her face. Connie's biggest assets were a pair of firm D cup boobs that still hung high on her chest. A couple of tattoos adorned the outer edge of her breasts and both nipples were pierced with barbell nipple rings. Connie switched from circled hoop rings to the straight barbells after a woman, during a catfight, tried to use her hoops as hitches and almost ripped open her nipples. Connie was as tough as they came and never walked away from a would-be challenger. Shortly after settling in North Carolina, Connie began to hang out among the gay and lesbian community of Asheville. She became friends with several women, who shared a common interest in bikes, rough housing and sex. One of the women that

Connie became good friends with was a young, recent divorcee, Helen. Together, they formed the Iron Dolls. That was 20 years ago. Tonight, her focus was solely on Helen and the fate of that 20-year bond, as it would surely be put to the test. As Connie began the final 100-yard ride to the cabin, she was unsure on how the night would unfold, but she knew it was too late to turn back.

Helen patiently sat in an old ladderback chair. The only light in the one room cabin was from an oil lamp sitting on a small end table next to Helen. Helen had just lit her 5th Marlboro Red since she arrived less than an hour ago. The ray of sunlight through the dirty window was fading fast, as nighttime would arrive shortly. Helen arrived earlier than expected and had spent most of her time pacing, smoking and thinking. The 5'8", 145-pound brunette agreed to meet Connie, in private, at the cabin, as she didn't want to settle the dispute she had with her longtime friend and occasional lover in the middle of an audience of Iron Dolls. She knew that each would take sides as to who they favored. Besides, with just the two, in private, the chances of an all-out brawl would be avoided. Helen was very comparable to Connie in height and weight. What she lacked where the legendary boobs of her longtime partner.

Helen's breasts were what could be considered average; more of a full B than a C. She was in a white tank top and was in a firm fitting, well-worn pair of blue jeans. She preferred wearing cowboy boots as opposed to the heavy buckled work boots of Connie's. Her Dolls leather vest was resting on the back of the chair she was sitting in. Helen heard Connie's Harley in the distance. She pulled out another cig and lit it with the one she had just finished. Helen dropped the cigarette butt on the dirty wood floor beneath her and crushed it out with the tip of her boot. She had started a small collection of crushed butts on the floor. Helen took a drag and paced around in the darkening room. "What the fuck is she waiting for?" Helen spoke softly to herself. Helen looked out the window and could see the lone headlight of Connie's Fat Boy at beginning of the drive in the distance. She was relieved to only see one headlight. Helen turned, took another drag, and went back to her seated position in the uncomfortable chair. Helen knew that very soon Connie would open the door and all Hell would break loose.

Connie made her way down the drive, revving the engine of her Harley as if Helen didn't already know she was coming. Parking her bike next to Helen's, Connie pulled a cigarette from the pack she had tucked in the inner pocket of her leather Iron Dolls vest. Uncharacteristic of her rough and tough demeaner, Connie's preferred smokes of choice were Virginia Slims. It had been that way since she started the habit in high school. Connie made her way through the overgrown grass and brush onto the porch of the old, dilapidated cabin. Slowly opening the creaky door, the dirty blonde-haired biker slowly entered. The only light coming from the oil lamp on the table, below a yellowed window. Adjusting her eyes to the lack of light she saw that the floor was covered in a layer of dust. It had been a long time since any of the Dolls had come to the cabin. Cobwebs hung from the corners of the wall. The only sign of any recent occupant was a nest that some small animal had made. The air was thick, smelling of mildew and cigarette smoke. The silence was broken by Helen's soft, but raspy voice. "I was wondering if your ass was going to show up." Closing the door, Connie saw the reason she had traveled to the cabin.

Helen rose from the chair, cigarette dangling from her lips. She was clad only in the white tank top, blue jeans and boots. Her hands resting on her waist, fists clenched, eyes full of hate. "Fuck you" Connie said to Helen as she slowly removed her vest, hanging it on the doorknob. Connie was equally wearing a white tank top, jeans and boots. Connie took a long drag from her cigarette, exhaling a large plume of smoke from her lips and nostrils. Each woman stared at each other from opposite corners of the single room cabin. The two were compatible in size. The only measurable difference was the larger boobs that hung from Connie's chest. Both had known each other for 20 years. They were the founding members of the Iron Dolls. Both had fought each other over the years; settling disputes and general horse play. Tonight, would be different. Each knew their friendship could survive the night, but each also knew that this evening could not be avoided. There was a violation of trust and a debt had to be paid. "Why did you do it?" Connie asked Helen. "If you needed cash, you could have asked. I would have given it to you." "You know that if I had..." Helen tried to speak but was immediately interrupted. "Shut your fucking mouth, Helen." Connie was in no mood for understanding. "Just tell me you stole my money. You owe me that much." Connie knew that a confession was not going to make things right, but she sought it anyway. "Why? It won't change anything. Whether I took it or not, a confession won't matter nor will the fact that I can't pay you back." Helen continued as Connie listened. Helen took a last drag from her cigarette before tossing it on the floor at her feet. "There are other ways to pay back a debt instead of cash." Connie assured. "So, you didn't suggest we meet to get me to pay you back?" Helen asked; almost sarcastically. "Oh, I am here to collect; every last dollar's worth." Connie spoke, then took a drag off her cigarette and dropped it to the floor.

As she crushed it beneath her boot, she continued. "So, you tell me. How bad must I beat you to get my $400 worth?" "Wait a goddamn minute; it was only $300." Helen was quick to correct Connie, only afterwards realizing what she had said. "You fuckin' cunt. I knew you stole it." Connie walked closer to Helen. It was completely dark outside by now and the oil lamp provided little light. As if on cue, both women untucked their tank tops from under their belts. Connie proceeded to completely pull her shirt off and toss it onto the chair next to where her rival was standing. "So, you want to come after me tits a blazing." Helen commented. "Better to remove it now, then have it ripped off later." With Connie's comment Helen removed her tank top and put it down on the chair as well. "I am finished talking Helen." Connie said. She proceeded to pull a pair of brass knuckles from her back pocket and toss them across the room onto the floor in a darkened corner. "Looks like you are serious." Helen commented; while at the same time, removing the motorcycle chain belt that she always wore around her waist.

The heavy belt made a loud thump onto the floor in the corner opposite the brass knuckles. "And I thought our 20-year friendship meant something to you. I thought we were like sisters" Helen concluded. "Oh, we are still sisters. I will still love you. But that's tomorrow.

Tonight, you are nothing but a piece of meat to me and I am getting my monies worth out of your ass." Connie coldly laid it down for Helen. Helen followed. "Well then, since this shit hole belongs to my family, I get to set the rules. There are none. We fight until one of us can't or won't continue." "In other words," Helen continued; "easy enough for a cunt like you to understand." "Fuck you," was Connie's only reply.

Connie started walking towards Helen who put her fists into a fighting stance. The two circled slowly, their eyes focused. Suddenly Connie threw a solid left which connected to Helen's cheek. Helen retaliated with an uppercut that stung Connie's chin. The women threw their topless bodies together in a clinch, a real test of strength that saw them rolling against the walls, still standing, struggling for dominance. Helen placed a kick to Connie's pussy. Helen followed up with a hard fist just below Connie's belly button. Helen's knuckles grazed Connie's belt buckle, producing a good size cut across two of the knuckles. The first blood of the fight was not a nose or lip, but rather a fist. "Fuck," Helen screamed out as she saw her fist begin to turn red. The punch was still effective, doubling Connie over. A right fist to the cheek sent Connie to the floor. Helen picked her rival up by the hair, forearmed her and then threw her against the wall. Connie came off the wall with her fists up. She charged Helen and caught her in the belly with a hard punch, a kick to the pussy and Helen was on the floor clutching her now sore cunt. Connie threw back her work boot and kicked Helen in the back and dropped a knee on her. Connie swiftly moved to the corner of the room to retrieve the brass knuckles.

Once she found it on the floor Connie picked it up and slid the fingers of her right hand through it. While making a fist with the knuckles, Connie turned toward Helen. Helen had crawled on her hands and knees to collect her motorcycle chain belt. As Helen was standing, both women made eye contact with each other. In the dimly lit and now dust filled room, both took a second to access the damage they had received. Other than Helen's bloody fist from the knuckle cut, both women showed little signs of damage. Each sported a few red splotches, but their topless torsos and arms only showed dirt and dust mixed with sweat. Both knew things would soon escalate with the introduction of weapons.

Helen grasped the buckle of her belt tightly in her bloody fist and moved toward Connie. A wild swing of the chained belt made direct contact with Connie's left side. The effects of the blow were immediate and painful. Rushing forward, Connie got Helen in a front bearhug and drove her to the floor. Dust flew in all directions as Helen's back came crashing to the floor. Swinging her belt, Helen was able to connect with repeated blows across Connie's bare back, ass and legs. Connie was finally able to use the brass knuckles and started to repeatedly pound Helen's left side. Each punch was answered with a grunt from Helen. Swinging the belt across Connie's back, Helen was able to take hold of the other end and run the belt up Connie's back. Connie let out a scream as the belt drug across the blonde's back. Rolling herself under Helen, Connie was able to stop the back torture. With her free right arm, Connie took her brass fist and landed a couple of soft but still painful blows to Helen's mouth, cutting her upper lip.

The blood from Helen's cut lip poured onto Connie's face. As Helen rose, she planted a hard knee to Connie's pubic bone and fell back onto her belly and breast. Helen straddled Connie and started a vicious punching attack aimed with her chained fist at Connie's face, opening up a cut on her cheek. A few more punches and Connie's mouth was pouring blood. Tiring of hitting her foe, Helen rolled over and sat next to her bleeding opponent. The two women slowly rose to their feet and without speaking a word assumed boxers' stances and started circling. Helen's right hand made a fist with the chain belt while Connie still held onto the brass knuckles in her right fist. As if on cue both women let out screams and lunged at each other. With fists flying the two pummeled each other across the room, blood flowing as a cut opened over Helen's left eye and the gash on Connie's mouth deepened. Helen managed to get Connie in a headlock and dragged her to the floor. Helen applied very little pressure and Connie barely struggled as the two took a few minutes to rest. Suddenly Connie's brass knuckles hit Helen in her belly and then she clamped onto her boobs, digging her nails into the fleshy meat.

Helen retaliated by dropping the belt and digging her own nails into Connie's large D cups. The two started rolling around in the dust, nails in breasts, switching to flailing fists; first one, then the other on top, rolling and struggling for dominance. Connie ended on top, pounding on Helen's cut eye with the brass knuckles until the blood flowed freely. Rolling off and getting to her feet Connie asked Helen if she had had enough. FUCK YOU was her answer as Helen kicked at Connie from the floor placing the heel of her boot into Connie's pussy. Connie fell to her knees clutching her cunt, Helen threw a forearm which sent her to the floor. Helen straddled her enemy and threw punch after punch at her face and boobs, until her arms were too tired to throw anymore. Helen rolled off her opponent as she lay next to her; both women bleeding and breathing hard. The air now smelled of mildew, smoke and sweat. The dust and dirt on the floor were now mingled with blood and sweat. After a few minutes of rest Helen got to her knees. "This isn't over, is it cunt? She asked. She got her response as Connie removed the brass knuckles from her hand and tossed it across the room, spitting blood at Helen. "Then let's finish this," Helen said as she got to her feet. The two women put up their fists. Their eyes glared into each other's. Even though no words were spoken, the hatred in their eyes spoke volumes.

Slowly they started circling, throwing wild jabs as they inched closer and closer together. Suddenly they grabbed each other's boobs, their fingers digging into each other's flesh. Pushing Helen up against the wall Connie kneed her just below her belt line, Helen lost her grip and Connie threw three solid punches to her belly. Grabbing a handful of Helen's hair Connie pulled her head up and threw three more solid punches into Helen's face. Connie slammed the back of Helen's head into the wall. Releasing her hold, she backed away as Helen slowly slid down the wall onto the floor. Connie picked up Helen's tank top and used it to wipe the blood from her face. She then stood over Helen's prone body, unbuckled her belt and dropped her jeans and panties down to her ankles. Connie squatted down and placed her sweaty pussy onto Helen's bloody face. Clenching Helen's hair with both hands, Connie began to grind her pussy across Helen's mouth, forcing her to reward the victor. Connie watched as her juices mixed with the free-flowing blood from Helen's cuts. It only took minutes before Connie erupted with an incredible orgasm. Once again, using Helen's tank top, Connie wiped the juices from her pussy and then threw it on top of Helen.

Connie walked over to the front door to retrieve her Virginia Slims from her vest pocket. Connie grabbed Helen's smokes from the table next to the chair and walked over to her victim who was still prone on the floor. Connie slid her back down the wall and sat on the floor, tossing Helen's cigarette pack onto her. Helen took the cigs and tank top and crawled over to the wall and sat herself up next to Connie. Both girls lit up their cigarettes; neither saying a word to each other. Helen wiped the blood from her face before tossing the tank over to Connie for her to do the same. As both women took drags from their cigarettes, Helen asked Connie if the debt was settled. "Paid in full," Connie answered. "By the way, the next time you need cash, just ask. The interest isn't nearly as bad." Helen attempted to laugh at Connie's comment, but her mouth hurt too bad. Both women sat shoulder to shoulder against the wall, smoking their cigarettes and wiping blood from their face and breasts. "Are we still sisters?" Connie softly asked, exhaling a plume of smoke into the mildew air. Helen took a drag from her cigarette, leaning toward Connie. "Always" was her reply as both began to kiss.

BRONZED RIVALRY

In the heart of the city, "Glow and Go" was the go-to tanning salon for the beauty-conscious. Its clientele included the local elite, college students, and those just wanting to look their sun-kissed best. This particular day saw the arrival of two individuals that the entire town loved to gossip about: Scarlett and Vanessa. Both were equally known for their beauty, ambition, and an unspoken rivalry that everyone seemed to be aware of. Scarlett, with her long, sleek raven hair, walked in, her heels clicking with each confident stride. Vanessa, not too far behind, sported a high ponytail of platinum blonde hair that accentuated her striking features. They caught sight of each other almost instantly. The tension in the room was palpable, with both women exchanging cold glares, their past confrontations flashing before their eyes.

They each intended to have a routine tanning session, but upon seeing the other, an idea, devious and tempting, sparked in their minds. Vanessa approached the counter first. "I need a room for two," she said, her voice dripping with honey, her eyes never leaving Scarlett's. Scarlett, raising an eyebrow, decided to play along, "It's more environmentally friendly to share a room, isn't it?" The attendant, Katie, a young college student working part-time, blinked in confusion. She'd heard of the fierce rivalry between these two, and now they wanted a room together. "Uh, sure," she stammered, handing them the key to the couples' suite. "It's the last door on the right. Remember, there's a fifteen-minute maximum on those beds." The two rivals exchanged a smirk. Fifteen minutes was all they needed.

As they entered the room, the humming sound of the tanning beds was coupled with ambient music playing softly in the background. Scarlett slipped off her shoes, her eyes locked onto Vanessa's, silently challenging her. Vanessa mirrored her actions, her fingers flexing in anticipation. "You sure about this?" she whispered; a hint of excitement evident in her voice. Scarlett grinned, "More than ever." Without another word, they lunged at each other. The initial struggle was fierce, each trying to gain the upper hand. Scarlett managed to pin Vanessa against one of the tanning beds, but Vanessa used her legs to throw Scarlett off, causing her to stumble back. Their grunts and groans echoed off the walls, their every movement filled with a desire to dominate the other. They rolled around on the floor, their limbs tangled, their hair a wild mess. Punches were thrown, some landing, some missing, but each one fueled by their deep-seated animosity.

The sounds from the tanning beds and the music did its job, masking the violence occurring within the room. The minutes ticked by quickly. Every passing second increased the urgency and ferocity of their brawl, knowing their time was limited. The intensity of their fight left them breathless, their clothes disheveled, and marks beginning to form on their skin. With each passing moment, it was becoming more and more difficult to determine who had the upper hand. As the timer on the tanning beds began to wind down, signaling the nearing end of their allotted time, both women paused, panting heavily, their faces inches apart. The pause between them was brief, just a fleeting moment in the grand scheme of things, but it was enough for both Scarlett and Vanessa to regain some composure and come to a stark realization. They had mere minutes left to assert dominance, to prove once and for all who was the superior. They could feel the heat from the tanning beds, and in some ways, it seemed to stoke the fires of their determination.

Scarlett, using her height advantage, aimed a sharp jab towards Vanessa's forehead. Vanessa dodged it by mere inches, but Scarlett's follow-up, a left hook, found its mark on Vanessa's cheek, causing her head to snap to the side. Blood oozed from a small cut on her cheekbone. The metallic taste of her own blood seemed to ignite a fire within Vanessa, and with a roar of defiance, she retaliated. Using Scarlett's momentary self-satisfaction against her, Vanessa delivered a punishing uppercut, catching Scarlett right under the chin. Scarlett stumbled back, tasting blood as her lip split from the force of the blow. But Scarlett wasn't done yet. She charged at Vanessa, catching her off guard, and with all her might, sent a powerhouse of a punch into Vanessa's midsection. Vanessa gasped, the wind knocked out of her, her vision blurred for a moment. But her resilience and determination kept her on her feet. She feinted a move to the right, deceiving Scarlett, and then landed a brutal punch to Scarlett's eye. Almost instantly, a swelling began, promising a dark bruise in its wake.

The sounds of their heavy breathing, grunts of

pain, and smacking of fists on flesh blended into the hum of the tanning beds and the muffled beats of the music outside. Their strength was waning, but neither would give in. The timer on the wall showed that barely a minute remained. Both women, with sweat mingling with blood on their faces, stared each other down, trying to find an opening, a weakness, anything that would give them the edge in these final moments. The struggle between Scarlett and Vanessa intensified as Vanessa deftly dodged a lunge from Scarlett. Seizing the moment, Vanessa tripped Scarlett, sending her crashing to the floor. Before Scarlett could react, Vanessa was on top of her, straddling her waist in a schoolboy pin.

Scarlett squirmed beneath her rival, trying desperately to unseat Vanessa and reverse their positions. But Vanessa's weight and determination kept Scarlett firmly pinned. Vanessa managed to trap Scarlett's arms, pinning them to the ground under Venessa's knees. Locked in this vulnerable position, Scarlett's face became a prime target. Vanessa unleashed a barrage of punches, each blow precise and relentless. Scarlett's face jerked with every hit, her cheeks reddening and swelling, blood oozing from her nose and split lip. Despite being pinned and pummeled, Scarlett's spirit was far from broken. Her eyes blazed with defiance, and she continued to buck and twist beneath Vanessa, attempting to unseat her. But with each passing moment, Vanessa's advantage grew more pronounced, and Scarlett's strength waned. The timer's final beep sounded in the distance, a reminder of the fleeting nature of their brawl. But for Vanessa and Scarlett, trapped in their power struggle, it felt as if the world had fallen away.

Vanessa, breathing heavily, stood over a battered Scarlett, taking a moment to savor her dominance. Her shadow cast a long silhouette over Scarlett, who lay on the floor, dazed and gasping for breath. Scarlett's eyes, though blurred from the pain, still flickered with defiance and challenge. The fluorescent lights of the tanning room illuminated the scene, making the sweat on both women's bodies glisten. Vanessa, feeling the intensity of the moment, taunted Scarlett. "Thought you could handle me?" she sneered. Scarlett, summoning what little strength she had left, spat back, "This isn't over." Their tension-filled stare-down held for a moment longer, a silent battle of wills playing out in the room. Even in her momentary defeat, Scarlett's resolve was evident, and Vanessa knew this fight was just one chapter in their ongoing feud.

As the buzzing of the tanning beds ceased, Vanessa and Scarlett began to gather themselves. They slowly slipped on their shoes, the pain of the recent fight evident in every wince and careful movement. With the towels in the room, they dabbed away the blood on their faces, trying to make themselves presentable for the world outside the room. Despite the intensity of the brawl, there was a silent agreement between them not to make a scene as they left. They wanted to keep their battle private, away from prying eyes. Walking out of the room, they moved in separate directions without uttering a word to one another. Both knew that their rivalry was far from over, but for now, they had other priorities to attend to, like recovering and planning their next encounter. As they exited the tanning salon, the employees and other customers remained oblivious to the intense showdown that had just transpired behind closed doors.

STEEL CHAINS AND DETERMINATION

The scent of gasoline and old oil wafted through the air, mingling with the stale aroma of cigarette smoke. The garage echoed with the anticipation of the fight about to commence. Clarissa, a tall, robust woman with flowing raven hair and fierce green eyes, stood at one corner. Her muscular arms betrayed years of dedication to her craft - fighting. The steel chain attached to the wrist restraint dangled, reflecting the minimal light and adding to the tension. Her lips parted slightly, exhaling a plume of smoke from her last drag. Across from her, stood Giselle, equally formidable, her silver-blonde mane contrasting starkly against her bronzed skin. Her ice-blue eyes watched Clarissa intently, looking for any sign of weakness, any hint of hesitation. The chains attached to her wrists clinked softly, waiting for the moment they'd clash against Clarissa's.

Both women, devoid of any distractions and tops, felt the cool air on their skin. The stillness was punctuated only by the soft hum of a nearby refrigerator. With a final exhale, Clarissa dropped the cigarette and stamped it out, her eyes never leaving Giselle's. It was the cue they'd been waiting for. Almost simultaneously, both lunged forward, chains swinging. Their arms clashed with a deafening rattle, but neither backed down. The fight was on. Blow after blow, their fists found their marks. But the chains made the battle more challenging. Every move required calculated precision to avoid entanglement, every strike risked leaving them vulnerable.

At one point, Giselle used her chain to catch Clarissa's wrist, yanking her forward into a devastating punch. Clarissa retaliated by wrapping her chain around Giselle's arm, using her strength to pull her opponent off-balance, taking the battle to the ground, the sounds of the chain clinking echoing throughout the garage. Each woman's resilience was remarkable. Sweat and determination glistened on their faces, neither willing to yield. The fierce contest was a testament to their strength, skill, and sheer willpower. It became evident that this was not just a physical fight but a battle of wits. The chains, initially seeming like a simple weapon, became an intricate part of their strategies. They were not only used for striking but also for binding, trapping, and ensnaring. Instead of swinging the chain traditionally, Clarissa wrapped it around her fist, creating a brutal makeshift weapon. Giselle, quick to catch on, followed suit.

The once cold steel now felt warm, almost burning against their skin. With each strike, the chains added weight, force, and, most notably, damage. Their tightened fists wrapped in chains made a sickening thud upon impact. Giselle's swing landed on Clarissa's ribs, the chain digging into her flesh, leaving behind an immediate mark of purple and red. Clarissa grunted in pain but retaliated with a rapid succession of blows, aiming for Giselle's midsection. The silver-blonde's skin soon displayed a canvas of bruises, scratches, and the first hints of blood. As the fight progressed, the initial strategy began to wane, replaced by raw emotion and adrenaline. Each punch thrown was not just about landing a hit; it was about proving dominance, about showcasing resilience.

Clarissa's knuckles, even protected in part by the chain, began to bleed. Each punch she threw left a smear of her own blood on Giselle. Conversely, Giselle's face had scratches from where the chain had grazed her, each new mark stinging more than the last. The sound of their heavy breathing, the clinking of the chains, and the muffled grunts of pain filled the air. The garage, initially a silent observer, now bore witness to a battle that was as much about physical prowess as it was about mental stamina. Every hit taken was a challenge, a dare to strike back harder. The chains, which had seemed like an advantage, were now both a weapon and a liability. They inflicted pain, but they also took their toll on the hands that wielded them. Both women, covered in sweat, blood, and bruises, continued their dance of dominance, neither showing any sign of backing down.

The exhaustion was evident in their breaths, but neither Clarissa nor Giselle was willing to yield. As the battle wore on, the strategy evolved, and so did their methods of attack. Giselle was the first to unwrap the chain from her bleeding fist, gripping it by the end and sizing up Clarissa with a predatory gleam in her eye. With a swift motion, she lashed out, using the chain as a whip. It sliced through the air, landing with a vicious snap on Clarissa's thigh. The imprint it left was immediate

– a welt accompanied by a stinging sensation that shot up Clarissa's leg. Taken by surprise but quick to adapt, Clarissa mimicked Giselle's actions. Holding the end of her chain, she aimed for Giselle's upper arm. The chain hit with such force that Giselle staggered back, clutching her arm where a deep red mark was rapidly forming.

The change in tactics added a new dimension to their fight. The whipping motion of the chains required more space and more strategy. There was the challenge of timing and aim, as well as the ever-present danger of backlash. Several times, in their eagerness to land a hit, one of them would misjudge the distance, and the chain would come back, landing on them instead. The garage echoed with the sound of chains slashing through the air, sometimes finding their mark, sometimes hitting the cold concrete floor, leaving small scratches in its wake. Clarissa aimed a particularly forceful whip towards Giselle's midsection, but Giselle, using her chain, managed to block it, causing both chains to get entangled. The two women pulled at their respective ends, trying to free their weapon, but in doing so, they were drawn closer to each other. The proximity gave way to a more direct and brutal form of combat, with knees, elbows, and headbutts being employed as they struggled for dominance. Giselle managed to free her chain first and, using it, ensnared Clarissa's ankle, pulling hard and causing her to fall backward. Clarissa, however, was not down for long. With a furious scream, she lunged at Giselle, and the two once again were locked in a fierce battle of wills and strength. The chains, once the primary weapons, now lay discarded on the floor as the fight became more primal, personal, and intense.

Giselle, having been momentarily taken off guard by Clarissa's sudden lunge, struggled to regain control. Clarissa, using her momentary advantage, attempted to pin Giselle to the ground. However, Giselle's raw strength wasn't to be underestimated. She forcefully bucked, managing to dislodge Clarissa and flip their positions. Now Giselle was on top, her face inches from Clarissa's. Both women panted heavily, their chests heaving as they locked eyes. The intensity of their gaze was palpable, each trying to mentally overpower the other. Their tangled legs wrestled for position while hands sought weak points. Hair was pulled, flesh was scratched, and groans of pain filled the garage. Suddenly, Clarissa managed to shift her weight, throwing Giselle off balance. With a surprising burst of strength, she used the opportunity to wrap her chain around Giselle's neck, pulling tight. Giselle's eyes widened in panic, hands clawing desperately at the chain. But Clarissa's grip was unyielding, her knuckles white from the strain. However, in her bid to choke Giselle, Clarissa left herself open. Giselle, with fading strength, managed to grab her chain and lash out at Clarissa's face. The metal hit its mark, causing Clarissa to release her grip on Giselle's neck. Giselle gasped for air, her hands instinctively going to her neck, feeling the burning imprint of the chain. But there was no time for recovery. Clarissa was back on her, the two of them rolling on the ground, each trying to pin the other.

Minutes felt like hours as they fought. Sweat mixed with blood, staining the concrete floor. Their once forceful grunts and yells had now reduced to weary gasps and moans. Finally, with one last surge of strength,

Giselle managed to pin Clarissa's wrists to the floor, their faces once again inches apart. Both women were drained, their eyes reflecting a mixture of respect, pain, and exhaustion. The fight had reached its natural conclusion, and the two lay there, neither willing to move, caught in a moment of stillness amidst the chaos they'd created.

Clarissa, her breath ragged and uneven, met Giselle's eyes. There was a raw vulnerability there, an acknowledgment of the intensity they'd just shared. She tilted her head slightly, breaking the silence. "Is it over?" Giselle smirked, despite the aches in her body. "For now," she replied, slowly releasing Clarissa's wrists from her grasp. Both women struggled to their feet, using the other for support. They observed their surroundings, taking in the mess of tangled chains and evidence of their scuffle everywhere. "You're one tough bitch," Clarissa commented, her voice hoarse from the strain. Giselle chuckled, wincing as she touched a particularly painful bruise forming on her cheek. "You're not too bad yourself." "You know, there's no point in us continuing this feud," Clarissa said quietly, her eyes darting to meet Giselle's. Giselle nodded in agreement, "There isn't. We've proven what we needed to, to each other at least."

They both leaned against a garage wall, the weight of the night's events settling heavily upon them. It was Giselle who broke the silence, "How about a drink? My treat." Clarissa laughed, a genuine, heartfelt laugh that made her eyes sparkle. "Sounds perfect. But maybe a shower first?" The two women, former enemies now sharing a unique bond forged in battle, left the garage side by side, a testament to the unpredictable paths life often takes.

MIDNIGHT RIVALRY

The fluorescent lights buzzed overhead as the unmistakable aroma of grease, coffee, and pancake syrup enveloped the 24-hour Comet Diner. Mandy, a 5'7" blonde with striking green eyes, had been working the overnight shift for a year and had developed quite a regular clientele. She knew their orders by heart and greeted each with a warm smile, despite the weariness from working long hours. However, her chipper demeanor hid a simmering rage. Sarah, a petite brunette with a fiery spirit and piercing blue eyes, was the newest addition to the Comet team. She had an air of confidence that Mandy found both irritating and threatening. Adding to the tension, Sarah was now dating Tom, Mandy's ex-boyfriend. Though Tom was in the past for Mandy, the sting of betrayal was fresh each time she saw Sarah flash the necklace he'd once given her. Overseeing the night's operations was Lorna, the overnight manager. Lorna, with her overly teased hair and thick makeup, was known for her scandalous tales of her youth and her love for drama. She'd often assign Sarah and Mandy to work in close quarters, sharing sly glances as she watched them exchange passive-aggressive comments. Lorna would chuckle to herself, hoping for a confrontation that would break the monotony of her shift.

On this particular Saturday, tension was brewing

between Mandy and Sarah. With the diner closing from 1 am to 5 am for maintenance, there were fewer distractions to prevent a boiling over of emotions. Sarah, in a bold move, had been using Tom's pet name for her loudly and deliberately, knowing full well it would get under Mandy's skin. "Tom always calls me his 'little firecracker,'" she cooed, while refilling a coffee pot, ensuring Mandy heard every word. "That's only because you're quick to burn out," Mandy retorted, her patience wearing thin. Lorna, sensing the impending explosion, slid into a booth with a clear view of the two women. She lit a cigarette, took a drag, and smirked. "You two gonna dance, or what?" she taunted.

As the diner's lights dimmed for maintenance, the neon "Closed" sign was the only illumination, casting a surreal glow on the scene. Sarah, tired of the constant jabs and resentment, threw her apron on the counter. "Let's settle this," she challenged. Mandy, her hands shaking with a mix of anger and anticipation, responded in kind. The two women squared off, eyes locked, knowing that only one would walk away unscathed. Lorna, her interest piqued, leaned forward in her booth, ready to take in every second of the spectacle she had instigated. The tension between Sarah and Mandy was electric, but Lorna, ever the cunning manipulator, wasn't about to let this escalating feud draw attention from the outside world. "Alright, you two," she interjected, "if you're so keen on settling this, follow me." She led the pair toward the back of the diner, away from the windows and any potential prying eyes.

They passed the kitchen, with its lingering smell of sizzling bacon and hash browns, and approached a nondescript door labeled "Storage." Lorna pushed the door open with her shoulder, revealing a dimly lit, empty room, the walls lined with metal shelves and a single overhead light. It was secluded, out of view, and perfect for what Lorna had in mind. "I don't want any interruptions. No one sees, no one knows. Got it?" Lorna ordered, her voice dripping with authority. Both Sarah and Mandy, despite their anger towards each other, couldn't help but feel a chill at Lorna's cold demeanor. However, their mutual disdain was enough to keep them from backing down. Lorna lit another cigarette. As she inhaled deeply, she eyed the two women up and down. "Those uniforms aren't cheap, you know. Off with the shirts. If you're going to ruin something, it won't be company property." Mandy and Sarah exchanged a glance, their expressions a mix of embarrassment and determination. But neither wanted to give Lorna the satisfaction of seeing them back down. They simultaneously unbuttoned and removed their white waitress shirts, revealing the tank tops they wore beneath.

Lorna settled against a wall, taking another drag from her cigarette, her eyes gleaming with excitement. "Alright then," she purred, "show me what you've got. And remember, I'm here to make sure it stays even." Both women knew what Lorna meant by that. If one of them seemed to be dominating the other too much, Lorna would step in, making sure that neither woman had a clear advantage for long. The stakes had been raised, and the fight that was about to unfold would be one for the books. Lorna took a deep inhale from her cigarette, and then handed it over to Mandy without a word. Mandy accepted it gratefully, her eyes locked on Sarah's the entire time. As she inhaled, the smoke seemed to calm her nerves, and when she exhaled, she felt a rush of determination. Mandy handed the cigarette back to Lorna and took her position.

Sarah and Mandy began to circle one another in the tight space, each trying to gauge the other's intent. Lorna watched intently from her position against the wall, her cigarette hanging lazily from her lips. The quiet was punctuated only by their steady breathing and Lorna's occasional exhale of smoke. Suddenly, Lorna broke the silence. "Begin," she commanded coolly. Sarah lunged first, trying to catch Mandy off-guard with a quick jab. Mandy partially blocked the punch and countered with a swipe aimed at Sarah's face. Sarah quickly ducked, avoiding contact, and the two continued their dance. As the minutes wore on, the confined space of the storage room became increasingly oppressive. The lack of air conditioning made the room hot and stuffy, and sweat began to glisten on both fighters. The physical exertion combined with the close quarters created a palpable intensity.

At one point, Sarah managed to pin Mandy against one of the metal shelves, delivering a few hard blows to her midsection. Mandy grunted with each hit but managed to knee Sarah in the stomach, breaking her grip. The two separated, taking a moment to catch their breath. Lorna, sensing Mandy's momentary disadvantage, stepped in. Lorna gave Sarah a shove, knocking her off balance. Mandy took advantage of the situation, charging at Sarah and tackling her to the floor. For a while, the two women wrestled on the floor, each trying to gain the upper hand. The scuffling of their shoes on the floor, combined with their grunts of exertion, echoed in the small room. They exchanged blows, each fighter landing a few good hits. Finally, Sarah managed to get Mandy in a headlock. Mandy struggled, trying to free herself, but Sarah's grip was strong. Just as it seemed Mandy might be in real trouble, Lorna stepped in, grabbing Sarah by the collar and pulling her off.

Lorna smirked, exhaling a plume of smoke. "I said a fair fight," she drawled, looking at Sarah. Sarah tried to retort, but Lorna swiftly approached her, landing a sharp punch to Sarah's jaw, which made her stagger back. As Sarah tried to regain her footing, Lorna grabbed her by the hair and delivered another punch, this time to her stomach. Sarah let out a gasp, doubling over in pain. Lorna took a step back, smirking as she took another drag from her cigarette. "Keep it even," she warned. Mandy, sensing her opportunity, lunged at the dazed Sarah. They both tumbled to the floor, trading blows. Every time one of them seemed to be getting the upper hand, the other would summon a burst of strength to turn the tide. Their grunts and the thuds of their punches against flesh reverberated in the confined space. Sarah managed to get on top of Mandy, pinning her down. Just as she was about to deliver a crushing blow, Lorna intervened again, grabbing Sarah's wrist and twisting it. Sarah yelped in pain, releasing her grip on Mandy. Mandy seized the moment to roll Sarah off her, scrambling to her feet. Both women were bruised, battered, and breathing heavily. Their eyes locked in a mutual understanding: this fight was far from over, but they also realized that Lorna's intervention could come at any moment, turning the tide in either direction. The unpredictability of the battle made it even more intense.

Lorna watched with glee, her cigarette now a mere stub. She flicked it to the floor, her eyes never leaving the two fighters. "Continue," she urged, her voice dripping with anticipation. Mandy, her face flushed from the intense battle and eyes locked with Sarah's, momentarily forgot about Lorna's unpredictable nature. As Mandy readied herself to take on Sarah again, she felt a sudden grip on her hair. Before she could react, Lorna yanked her back, landing a swift punch to her ribs. "Thought you were getting the upper hand, did you?" Lorna hissed, holding Mandy by the hair, forcing her to look up. Mandy grunted, trying to free herself, but Lorna's grip was firm. Using her other hand, Lorna slapped Mandy across the face, leaving a stinging red mark. Mandy's eyes welled up with tears from the sudden assault, but her fury was evident.

Sarah, seeing her adversary in a vulnerable position, moved to attack. However, Lorna quickly turned her attention, shooting her a warning look, indicating that this was her moment with Mandy. With Mandy still trapped, Lorna landed another punch, this time to Mandy's belly, making her wheeze for breath. The dominance was short-lived, though, as Mandy gathered her strength, landing a punch to Lorna's midsection. The unexpected move caught Lorna off guard, making her release Mandy. Stumbling back, Lorna chuckled, "Impressive." She rubbed the spot where Mandy's elbow had made contact. "Seems you both have some fire left."

Sarah and Mandy exchanged glances, the unspoken realization dawning upon them that their real adversary might not be each other, but the devious Lorna. Still, with heavy breaths, both women readied themselves, not knowing who'd strike next or where Lorna's whims would take the fight. Sarah, using her agility, managed to dodge a fierce punch from Mandy and responded with a swift jab of her own. The momentum shifted, and Sarah began landing a series of blows to Mandy's face and torso. Just when it seemed Mandy was about to buckle under Sarah's aggressive assault, Lorna quickly assessed the situation and intervened.

Grabbing Sarah's arms from behind, Lorna immobilized her, rendering her defenseless. "Thought you could take over, huh?" Lorna whispered into Sarah's ear, her voice dripping with malice. Mandy, still panting and reeling from Sarah's punches, looked up to find her rival defenseless, held tight by Lorna. Seeing the opportunity, she hesitated for a split second before landing a series of punches to Sarah's midsection. Each blow was accentuated by a grunt from Sarah, who tried in vain to break free from Lorna's grip. After several forceful punches, Lorna released Sarah, who stumbled back, gasping for air. The dynamic in the room had changed once again, with Lorna asserting her dominance and ensuring neither woman gained a significant advantage. "You both still think you can beat each other?" Lorna taunted, taking another drag from her cigarette. She blew out a cloud of smoke, her eyes dancing with mischief.

Both Sarah and Mandy looked at each other, battered and bruised, but there was a new understanding between them. Lorna's manipulations were becoming clear, and the realization that they were being played started to sink in. The question now was, how would they respond? Would they continue their feud, or would they find a way to turn the tables on Lorna? "Why the hell did you even step in, Lorna? It was between us," Sarah's voice held a steely edge. Lorna, leaning against a shelf, smirked, taking another drag from her cigarette. "You girls just can't seem to finish anything without a little push. Thought I'd offer a hand." Mandy, smoke swirling around her, narrowed her eyes. "You love feeling superior, don't you? Think you could take us on?" Lorna's laughter echoed in the confined space, creating an eerie atmosphere. "Oh, honey, I've fought bigger and badder than the likes of you two. But if you want a demonstration..."

Sarah, her frustration evident, moved a step closer to Lorna, "You might've seen us fight, but have you ever seen us team up? How about we show you? "The dynamics shifted drastically. The two waitresses, previously at each other's throats, were now united against a common foe. Their earlier conflict overshadowed by Lorna's interference. Mandy took a step towards Lorna. "Sarah's right. Maybe we should give you a front row seat." Eyes darting between the two younger women, Lorna exhaled a cloud of smoke, her confident smirk never faltering. "Try me."

It was clear that the storage room, originally meant to be a pit for Sarah and Mandy's conflict, was about to witness a completely unexpected showdown. The atmosphere in the room had turned into a pressure cooker, the dense cigarette smoke hanging around them acting like a visual representation of the simmering tension. Mandy took a step towards Lorna, but Sarah, eager to have the first move, moved faster. Sarah lunged at Lorna, grabbing her by the collar and pushing her against the wall. Lorna, with experience on her side, quickly retaliated by swinging a fist into Sarah's side. Mandy saw this as her opportunity, lunging herself at Lorna from behind, wrapping an arm around her neck.

Lorna gasped, her face turning red as Mandy's grip tightened. The older woman, however, wouldn't be subdued so easily. With a burst of strength, she sent a sharp elbow into Mandy's ribs, causing her to momentarily loosen her hold. Sarah, recovering from the earlier hit, took this as her opportunity to send a powerful right hook into Lorna's jaw. But as Lorna staggered back, her hand caught Sarah's wrist and twisted it, pulling her forward and off-balance. This move was all Mandy needed to remember her original resentment towards Sarah, and she lunged, taking advantage of Sarah's vulnerable position. The two younger women briefly locked in a struggle, allowing Lorna to catch her breath and watch with an amused grin.

For Lorna, the joy wasn't just about fighting, it was the chaotic dance of dominance, and she relished in the momentary distraction between the two rivals. The three-way melee was a swirl of motion and fury. Just when it looked like two of them had teamed up against the third, the dynamics would switch, and alliances were fluid. Sarah managed to knock Mandy to the floor and turned her attention back to Lorna. They both exchanged heavy blows, each one causing the other to stagger. But Sarah, with younger stamina, managed to push Lorna back against a shelf. Mandy, recovering, decided to return the favor from earlier, pulling Sarah off Lorna and landing a knee into Sarah's stomach. Amid the chaos, with all three taking and dealing blows in equal measure, it was hard to determine where the battle would end. The only guarantee was that none of them would leave the room unscathed.

As the conflict intensified, it became apparent to both Sarah and Mandy that Lorna, with her years of experience and cunning tactics, was the most significant threat in the room. While the younger waitresses might have harbored deep resentment for each other, their mutual disdain for Lorna began to overshadow their personal grudges. Spotting an opportunity, Sarah caught Mandy's eye and subtly nodded towards Lorna. Mandy, always quick on the uptake, understood immediately. They would need to join forces, however temporarily, to take down their cunning manager.

Both women moved in sync, like predators cornering their prey. Sarah feinted a punch, drawing Lorna's attention, while Mandy swooped in from behind, locking her arm around Lorna's neck in a chokehold. Lorna struggled, her nails scratching at Mandy's arm in a desperate attempt to free herself, but Sarah was right there, landing blow after blow to Lorna's midsection. After what felt like hours but was only a few minutes, Lorna's struggles began to wane, her energy sapped from the combined onslaught. Finally, with one last effort, she went limp, the fight drained from her. Mandy and Sarah, panting and bruised, dropped her to the floor. The two women locked eyes, the brief truce between them shattered as quickly as it had formed. Both knew that, with Lorna out of the picture, their unfinished business would come to a head. But for now, they had succeeded in their mutual goal: to stand tall while ensuring Lorna was the one who wouldn't.

With Lorna incapacitated, the confined space of the storage closet felt even smaller, the tension palpable. Mandy, still catching her breath, stared hard at Sarah. "You think just because we teamed up for a moment, we're square? Think again." Sarah, wiping the sweat from her brow, smirked, "Never thought that. But I will thank you for the help. Made that part easier." Mandy scowled, "Your thanks means nothing. Remember why we're in this mess to begin with." Sarah's smile faded. "Oh, I remember. And once we're done here, everyone will know I'm the better woman – both in the fight and for him." The mention of the stolen boyfriend reignited the fiery hatred between them. Without warning, Mandy lunged at Sarah, swinging her fist. Sarah, anticipating the move, ducked and countered with an elbow to Mandy's ribs. The sharp pain momentarily winded Mandy, but she quickly recovered, grabbing Sarah by the hair and slamming her into the wall.

The two grappled, exchanging blows, each trying to get the upper hand. The close confines made it a messy fight, with both women utilizing every available advantage. Elbows, knees, hair pulls – nothing was off-limits. As the minutes ticked by, their energy began to wane, but neither was willing to concede. Every time one seemed to get the upper hand, the other would muster the strength for a counterattack. It was clear that neither would stop until one was declared the undeniable victor. Lorna's resilience was remarkable. Slowly, her senses started to return, and her eyes focused on the vicious battle unfolding before her. The initial shock and pain had subsided, replaced by a fury she had never felt before. Mandy, in a momentarily dominant position, had Sarah pinned against the wall, her forearm pressed against Sarah's throat. But Sarah, summoning the last of her strength, managed to knee Mandy in the stomach, forcing her to stumble back. This created a slight pause, each woman gasping for air, bodies drenched in sweat, faces marked by the evidence of the fierce brawl.

Lorna seized her opportunity. She quietly rose to her feet, and as Mandy tried to mount another attack on Sarah, Lorna forcefully grabbed Mandy from behind, wrapping her arm around Mandy's neck in a chokehold. Sarah, seizing the unexpected assistance, lunged at Mandy, delivering a series of rapid punches to her abdomen. Together, Sarah and Lorna overpowered Mandy, who struggled fiercely but was no match for the combined strength of the two. Eventually, Mandy's struggles weakened, and she slumped to the floor, defeated. Sarah, panting heavily, glared down at Mandy, then turned to face Lorna. The two exchanged a long, calculating look, but this time, no blows were thrown. Instead, a silent understanding passed between them. For now, at least, their battle was over.

In the storage closet, both Lorna and Sarah, visibly winded, stood opposite each other, the tension palpable between them. Mandy's soft groans from the floor acted as a grim background score to this uneasy standoff. Sarah's eyes flashed with defiance and anger, while Lorna seemed to revel in the controlled chaos of the moment. Reaching into her pocket, Lorna pulled out a cigarette and lit it. The initial flare of the lighter momentarily lit up her cunning eyes, and with a smirk, she took a long drag, allowing the smoke to slowly escape her lips. "You want a hit?" Lorna offered, extending the cigarette towards

Sarah. In any other situation, Sarah would have spat in her face, but the adrenaline, pain, and sheer exhaustion made her reconsider. She took a moment, looking at Lorna with suspicion, then grabbed the cigarette. She inhaled deeply, letting the nicotine calm her frazzled nerves momentarily.

The two shared a silent moment, passing the cigarette back and forth, an almost surreal calm amidst the storm. But this momentary truce was just that – momentary. Breaking the silence, Lorna murmured, "Ready for round two?" Sarah, exhaling a cloud of smoke, shot back, "Always." Meanwhile, Mandy began to gather herself, realizing that she might have an opportunity here. She knew the moment of calm wouldn't last, and she needed to be prepared for when the storm began anew. As Sarah and Lorna locked eyes, preparing for the next round, Mandy slowly began pushing herself to her knees. She was battered but not beaten, and the brief interlude provided her with just enough time to recover.

However, as she attempted to rise, Lorna's keen eye caught the movement. "Not so fast," she whispered, sending a sharp kick towards Mandy's midsection. Mandy winced but managed to grab Lorna's foot, pulling her off balance. Sarah, seeing an opportunity, lunged at Lorna, but in her haste, she collided with Mandy instead, causing all three women to tumble into a chaotic heap. It was every woman for herself, a whirlwind of flailing limbs and muffled cries. The lines had blurred; alliances shifted rapidly, and every woman was just trying to gain an advantage. Mandy, having been at the receiving end for most of the fight, found her second wind. She threw punches at both Sarah and Lorna, keeping them at bay.

Sarah, ever the opportunist, saw this as her chance to strike. With Mandy distracted, she lunged, catching her off guard. But Lorna wasn't one to be left out, and she joined the fray, making it a free-for-all once again. The unpredictability of the situation made it clear: any of them could emerge as the victor. The only question was who wanted it more. The intensity in the room reached a fever pitch. The three women, fueled by anger and adrenaline, moved with a vicious determination that left no room for truces.

Mandy, having been the underdog for most of the fight, was now in the spotlight. She managed to catch Sarah with a surprise right hook, sending her into the wall. Sarah crumpled to the ground, dazed. Seizing her opportunity, Mandy turned her attention to Lorna, who was already charging at her with a vengeance. The two exchanged rapid blows, neither giving an inch. Their exhaustion was evident, but neither was willing to back down. Lorna managed to land a solid punch to Mandy's gut, causing her to double over. But Mandy retaliated with a low sweep, knocking Lorna's legs out from under her. Both scrambled to their feet, and in a final, desperate move, Mandy lunged at Lorna, tackling her to the ground. They grappled, each trying to pin the other, but Mandy managed to overpower Lorna, pinning her down with a firm grip on her throat.
Gasping for air, Lorna's eyes filled with a mix of rage and realization. She tried to break free, but her energy was quickly depleting. Mandy's eyes blazed with triumph, not loosening her grip until Lorna's movements grew sluggish and she finally stopped struggling.

Breathing heavily, Mandy slowly rose, standing

amidst the aftermath of their fierce battle. Sarah and Lorna lay defeated, the cost of their vendettas evident in every bruise and cut. Mandy, against all odds, had emerged as the sole victor of the brutal confrontation. Mandy, panting and sweat-drenched, took a moment to survey the destruction around her. The dim light of the storage closet illuminated the bruised and battered figures of Sarah and Lorna, both breathing but unconscious. The stale scent of cigarette smoke lingered in the air, blending with the metallic odor of blood. Pushing back her disheveled hair, she staggered to her feet. With shaky hands, she pulled her shirt back on, her movements slow and deliberate. The weight of what had transpired sunk in, and she felt a cocktail of emotions; from relief to the chilling realization of the intensity of the violence that had just taken place. As she exited the storage closet, the silence of the empty diner enveloped her. The neon lights outside cast a dim glow over the tables and chairs, eerily vacant in the middle of the night.

She glanced at the clock. Only a few minutes had passed since the battle began, but it felt like hours. The diner would open again in a couple of hours, and patrons would be none the wiser of the chaos that had occurred in the back room. Determined not to let this night define her, Mandy decided to leave. She hastily scribbled a resignation letter and left it on the counter. The sun was beginning to rise, casting the first light of day onto the world outside. The horizon promised a new beginning, and Mandy, with a mix of determination and trepidation, walked away from the diner and into the dawn, ready to put this dark chapter behind her.

Three months after the tumultuous night in the

diner, life had shifted for all three women involved. Mandy had moved to another city, taking up a job at a cozy bookshop. She'd found solace in the quietude of the place, with the scent of old pages and fresh coffee surrounding her. Each day, she'd pen a little of her own story, contemplating turning it into a novel. The incident at the diner, though traumatic, became a catalyst for her to seek change and find her true calling. Sarah, having woken up to the aftermath of that night with a renewed perspective, had gone into therapy. Her turbulent emotions needed addressing, and she was determined to get her life on track. She still worked at the diner but had mended fences with the owner and worked mostly during the day shifts, avoiding the memories that the night brought.

Lorna, on the other hand, faced consequences for her actions. The owner, upon hearing of the events, promptly fired her. The rumor mill quickly caught wind of the story, and Lorna found herself struggling to find another job in town. She moved to a smaller neighboring town, taking up a job at a gas station. The nights were long and lonely, often making her ruminate over her choices. The diner, surprisingly, flourished. The tale of the late-night brawl, though initially a scandal, transformed into an urban legend. Patrons would come in, hoping to hear tidbits of the story, and it became a curious draw for the establishment. Life moved on, scars healed, and lessons were learned. But that one night at the diner remained etched in the memory of the town, a reminder of how quickly things could change and the lasting impact of choices made in the heat of the moment.

HAIR SALON SHOWDOWN

Tensions in the plush downtown beauty salon had always been high, given the competitive nature of the industry. But lately, the atmosphere had been particularly electric. Claire, a 57-year-old hairdresser with decades of experience, had been clashing with Emma, a 25-year-old upstart who had recently joined the team. Emma, with her fresh ideas and cutting-edge techniques, had begun drawing in a younger clientele, much to Claire's chagrin. Rumors of Emma undermining Claire's skills and stealing her longtime clients had further strained their relationship. On a breezy Wednesday afternoon, as the clock ticked towards closing time, the salon emptied, save for Claire, Emma, and Zoe, another young hairdresser who had always been close to Claire. The pristine white tiles echoed the silence, a stark contrast to the cacophony that had filled the space just hours before.

Emma, needing a break from the tension, retreated to the back room for a smoke. The aroma of her cigarette wafted into the main salon area. Claire, sensing an opportunity to confront Emma once and for all, exchanged a knowing glance with Zoe. Upon entering the back room, without uttering a word, Claire swiftly snatched the cigarette from Emma's fingers. Inhaling deeply, she let the smoke curl out from between her lips, her eyes fixed on the younger woman with a chilling intensity. Emma, taken aback, tried to recover her composure but was rendered immobile when Zoe gripped her firmly by the arms from behind. The surprise, and the betrayal she felt seeing Zoe turn against her, was evident in Emma's eyes.

Claire, still holding the cigarette in her lips, approached Emma. Each puff she took was like a timer, counting down to the inevitable confrontation. And then, with a suddenness that took Emma off guard, Claire unleashed a flurry of punches. Each hit was fueled by years of frustration, jealousy, and anger. Emma tried to struggle, to scream, but Zoe's grip was too tight. Tears streamed down her face as Claire continued her assault, teaching her a lesson she'd not soon forget. After what felt like an eternity, Claire stepped back, her breathing heavy. Dropping the cigarette on the floor, she crushed it with her heel. "Let that be a lesson to you, young lady," she hissed, "respect is earned, not given." Zoe released Emma, who crumpled to the floor, sobbing.

The atmosphere in the room was heavy, thick with tension and the lingering haze of cigarette smoke. Claire, unfazed by the scene before her, picked up another one of Emma's cigarettes. With practiced ease, she lit it and took a long, luxurious drag. Every movement was deliberate, a display of power. She sat down, crossing her legs, her posture perfect as always, an elegant predator in her domain. Zoe watched from a few feet away, her gaze darting between the defeated Emma on the floor and Claire. The juxtaposition was stark - the older woman exuding confidence and authority, and the young upstart broken and humiliated. It was overwhelming, the raw power Claire emanated, and Zoe felt a strange, irresistible pull toward her.

Emma whimpered, pulling Zoe out of her trance momentarily. The young girl's eyes were filled with pain, confusion, and a touch of fear. But Zoe felt no sympathy, no remorse. The lesson had been necessary. Emma had been a thorn in their side for too long, and the younger hairdresser had needed to be put in her place. As the silence stretched, Zoe felt her resistance waning. She looked at Claire, her lips slightly parted from the pull of the cigarette, and a wild thought ran through Zoe's mind. She wanted nothing more than to close the distance between them and kiss Claire with all the passion she felt in that moment. But she held back, letting the silence and the weight of the evening's events hang heavily in the room. Zoe hesitated for a fraction of a second before taking a step toward Claire. The air seemed to grow even thicker. Claire's eyes never left Zoe's as she took another slow drag from the cigarette, the burning ember glowing brighter, illuminating her face. Zoe stood just a breath away from Claire, looking down into her eyes, searching for a sign. Claire, always one for dramatics, exhaled slowly, the smoke curling around them both, creating a hazy barrier from the world outside. With a slight tilt of her head, Claire brought the cigarette to her lips once more, taking a deep drag. Then, ever so gently, she reached out with her free hand, cupping Zoe's face. Her thumb brushed Zoe's bottom lip, a silent invitation. Zoe's heart raced, the moment feeling like an eternity. Claire's intense gaze held her captive, and Zoe leaned in, their lips meeting in a passionate embrace. The taste of tobacco lingered between them, a testament to the raw intensity of the moment. The world outside ceased to exist, and in that room, with the faint scent of hair products and cigarette smoke, the two women shared an unexpected connection.

As Zoe stood before Claire, the older woman extended the cigarette towards her, silently offering her a drag. Zoe leaned in, lips wrapping around the filter, and took a deep inhale. The familiar sensation of the smoke filling her lungs was intensified by the proximity to Claire. Holding the smoke in, Zoe's eyes locked onto Claire's. The two women were drawn together once more, this time with Zoe initiating the contact. Their lips met again, but this kiss was different, charged with the smoke they both held inside. As they pulled apart, they simultaneously exhaled, the mingling smoke forming a transient veil around them.

Emma, still on the floor and disoriented from her beating, tried to comprehend the scene before her. The last thing she expected was to see Zoe and Claire share such a moment. She coughed weakly from the smoke that wafted towards her, but her attention remained fixed on the two women. Claire, her confidence still apparent, reached out to gently cup Zoe's face. "Looks like we have more in common than I thought," she murmured with a teasing edge. Zoe's face reddened, a mix of embarrassment and attraction. "Claire, I've always respected you. But I never thought..." her voice trailed off. Claire's smirk grew wider, "That we'd share a moment like this after giving our dear Emma a lesson?" She gestured with her cigarette towards the younger girl who was still on the floor. Zoe nodded slowly. "Exactly."

Emma, pushing herself up slightly, interrupted the

moment. "Are you two just going to leave me here?" she mumbled, a mix of pain and frustration evident in her voice. Claire took another drag from the cigarette and blew the smoke in Emma's direction. "You should thank us," she said coolly. "We just taught you a very important lesson about respect." Emma hesitated for a moment, looking between Zoe and Claire. The air was still thick with the tension of recent events. Swallowing her pride and her pain, she carefully made her way over and sat on Claire's lap, facing her. Claire took a drag from the cigarette and blew the smoke to the side. With one arm wrapped securely around Emma's waist to keep her in place, Claire used her free hand to tilt Emma's chin up, forcing their eyes to meet. "I hope this has been a lesson for you," Claire said sternly, her gaze piercing into Emma. Emma blinked back tears, a mix of pain, humiliation, and a begrudging respect for the older woman. "It has," she whispered.

Zoe watched the interaction, her eyes darting between the two. The dynamic was shifting, and she could sense the power Claire was exerting over Emma. Claire took another drag from the cigarette, this time letting the smoke waft in front of Emma's face. "You're going to respect the hierarchy in this salon, do you understand?" Emma nodded quickly. "Yes, Claire." Claire's gaze softened slightly, "Good. Now, apologize to Zoe and make sure this never happens again." Emma looked over to Zoe, "I'm sorry, Zoe." Zoe gave a nod, her expression unreadable, "Just make sure it doesn't happen again."

Claire takes Emma by the hair and kisses her hard. Claire's unexpected move caught Emma off guard. Their lips pressed together forcefully, with Claire's hand firmly gripping Emma's hair, ensuring she couldn't pull away. Their kiss was one of dominance, Claire's way of ensuring Emma understood the new pecking order. Zoe took a long drag from the cigarette. She moved silently behind Claire, letting her fingers sift through Claire's hair, pulling it slightly to expose the nape of her neck. Zoe's breath, mixed with the scent of cigarette smoke, brushed against Claire's skin, causing a shiver to run down Claire's spine. The atmosphere was thick with tension and unsaid emotions. A dance of power, dominance, and submission played out in that small backroom. The dynamic between the three of them had irrevocably shifted in those few intense moments. Each woman's position in the hierarchy was now clearly defined, their roles set. And as the cigarette's smoke swirled around them, the new boundaries were silently established.

After the initial display of dominance and power play, an unspoken understanding passed between the three women. The charged atmosphere in the room, a byproduct of intense emotions and confrontations, now took on a more intimate hue. Claire, always the one to initiate, gently tilted Emma's chin upwards, gazing deeply into her eyes. Their earlier animosity melted away, replaced by curiosity and a touch of desire. Claire's lips met Emma's once more, but this time the kiss was softer, more exploratory. Zoe, still behind Claire, began to trace delicate patterns along Claire's collarbone, her touch light but filled with intent. She leaned in, her lips brushing against the nape of Claire's neck, sending shivers down Claire's spine. Emma, finding her voice, whispered, "We don't have to do this." Claire replied, her voice husky, "We don't. But sometimes, intimacy is the way to heal wounds and find understanding." Zoe chimed in, her voice a seductive purr, "And sometimes, it's just fun."

The three women exchanged amused glances, laughter bubbling up, lightening the atmosphere. The raw intensity of their earlier confrontation slowly morphed into a playful, teasing camaraderie. They began exploring each other, a tangle of limbs and emotions, each touch and kiss blurring the lines between rivalry and intimacy. In this secluded space, away from the world outside, the trio discovered unexpected connections, finding solace, pleasure, and a strange sort of unity in each other's arms.

The sounds of the salon faded into the background, the hum of fluorescent lights and the distant traffic muffled by the closed door. In that secluded space, time seemed to stretch and bend. The strict professional boundaries they'd maintained during working hours gave way to a newfound intimacy. Claire, always confident and in control, allowed herself to be vulnerable for once. With Emma seated on her lap, she caressed her face, trailing her fingers down to Emma's collarbone, enjoying the softness of her skin. Their previous altercation was forgotten, replaced by a mutual desire to explore and understand each other. Emma, despite her initial resistance, melted into Claire's touch. She wrapped her arms around Claire's neck, losing herself in the sensation. The events of the evening had been unexpected and tumultuous, but now, she felt a warmth and connection she hadn't anticipated. Zoe, ever the passionate one, pressed herself against Claire's back, her lips finding the older woman's neck. She reveled in the sensation of Claire's heartbeat beneath her fingers, synchronizing with her own racing pulse. The three of them, once divided by jealousy and professional rivalry, now found themselves united in a shared moment of intimacy. Their differences seemed inconsequential, overshadowed by the magnetic pull drawing them closer. Whispers, laughter, and soft sighs filled the room as they continued to explore the boundaries of their newfound relationship. The dynamics shifted, ebbed, and flowed, but throughout it all, the undercurrent of genuine connection remained. Hours passed, feeling like mere minutes. They lay entangled, their energies spent, basking in the afterglow of shared intimacy. The events of the night would forever change the dynamics between them, making the salon not just a place of work, but a sanctuary of shared secrets and unspoken bonds.

STORMED-IN STRANGERS (M/M)

The snowstorm outside whirled furiously, the kind where white blankets the ground and the skies darken with a promise of more to come. Michael and Richard, two complete strangers, found themselves taking refuge in the last room available at a roadside motel. The clerk at the reception had been apologetic, explaining that due to the storm, many were stranded, hence the lack of vacancy. With their respective histories buried under layers of clothing and years of life, both men agreed to split the room, each appreciating the warmth of shelter over the chill of pride. The room was nothing extraordinary - a king-size bed, a small television, a table, and a pair of chairs.

As they settled in, Michael pulled out a deck of cards from his bag, suggesting a game of poker to pass the time. Richard agreed, adding a hint of stakes to the game by placing a bottle of bourbon he had on the table. Both men chatted as they played, sharing snippets of their life stories; Michael was a salesman from the Midwest, and Richard, a retired journalist who was traveling the country to rediscover himself after a divorce. As hours turned into minutes and minutes turned into moments, they found themselves immersed in conversations about life, loss, love, and all the little things in between. The bottle was soon half empty, and the room was filled with a smoky haze from the cigarettes Richard had been lighting, one after the other.

The intoxication of the alcohol mixed with the confinement of the storm and the proximity of another person led to an unexpected tension. It started with a heated argument over a poker move. Words escalated, and before they knew it, both men were on their feet, posturing, gauging the other, fists clenched. Several punches were thrown. Both men finding themselves fighting on the kind size bed. It was about more than just a game; it was a tussle for dominance in this confined space they were forced to share. The physical altercation was brief but intense. Michael, with a slight height advantage, managed to pin Richard down. Their heavy breaths echoed in the dim room, eyes locked in a mixture of anger, confusion, and an undeniable spark of something more. As Michael loosened his grip, Richard pulled him closer. The line between anger and passion blurred as they shared a rough, desperate kiss, a mix of aggression and need. They fumbled with each other's clothing, exploring each other's bodies, every touch an act of discovery and assertion.

The room was thick with the scent of sweat, smoke, and the remnants of the bourbon. The storm outside raged on, but inside, there was a newfound calm, a quiet understanding between two strangers who had found an unexpected connection amidst the chaos of nature. They lay beside each other, reflecting on the whirlwind of emotions and actions, understanding that the storm outside had not only forced them together but also ignited a storm within, one that they had chosen to explore, challenging societal norms and their own boundaries. The stillness of the room was punctuated by the faint hum of the heater and the soft crackling of the storm outside. Michael held the cigarette delicately between his fingers, the ember glowing a deep orange. Between drags, he would pass the cigarette over to Richard. The sight of Richard's lips around the filter made Michael's heart race just a little faster. Michael took another deep drag, the smoke curling around his fingers before he handed it back to Richard. Both men lay on the bed, bodies still warm from their unexpected passion, heads propped up by their arms, eyes scanning each other for signs of what the night might bring next. "Never thought today would turn out like this," Richard mused, the cigarette smoke wafting lazily from his lips. Michael chuckled, "Neither did I." The two continued to share the cigarette, the silence between them comfortably charged. Their previous clash had awakened a hunger in both; the taste of rough play mixed with intimacy was heady and intoxicating. "You know," Richard began, his voice laced with mischief, "there's something thrilling about fighting it out. No harm meant, just the raw intensity." Michael's eyebrow arched in interest, "You thinking of round two?" Richard smirked, "With stakes. Winner gets to call the shots for the night." The proposal hung in the air; its implications clear. Both men knew that the line between aggression and desire was a thrilling one to tread.

"You're on," Michael replied, his voice low and determined. They sat up, facing each other, the soft light from the lamp casting a glow on their faces. There was a playful yet challenging gleam in their eyes, an understanding that this was about more than just dominance. It was about exploring limits, pushing boundaries, and discovering parts of themselves they hadn't known existed. As they prepared for their next bout, the night stretched out ahead of them, filled with possibilities. Whatever the outcome, both men knew that this was a night neither would forget. The storm outside seemed to mirror the whirlwind of emotions inside the small motel room, two men lost in a dance of desire, competition, and discovery.

The room became a whirl of taut muscles, grunts, and strained breaths. Each man was determined to assert himself over the other. They locked eyes, the atmosphere was electric. Michael threw the first punch, aimed squarely at Richard's midsection. It was met with a grunt, but Richard countered with a swift jab to Michael's jaw. They tumbled onto the bed, their movements more about asserting dominance than causing harm. Hands gripped shoulders and heads, pulling and tugging as they tried to pin each other down. Elbows dug into sides, and knees pressed into thighs. Each hit, each thrust and counterthrust, only added to the growing arousal between them. Every touch, no matter how aggressive, was a testament to their burning desire. The pain was real, the marks and bruises would be testament to that, but so was the pleasure that accompanied it. Richard managed to pin Michael's wrists above his head at one point, staring down into his eyes with a feral intensity. But Michael, using his legs for leverage, managed to turn the tables, flipping Richard onto his back.

Their breathing was labored, faces flushed with both exertion and excitement. Clothes, previously discarded, became weapons of their own, used to tie or restrain, to add another layer to their game of control. It was a dance of strength and wills. Each punch met with a matching force. The fight seemed to go on forever, neither man willing to concede, neither willing to give up the intoxicating mix of pain and pleasure. During the tussle, the room became a blur. The sounds of the storm outside faded into the background, overshadowed by the sounds of their struggle. The line between fight and foreplay became increasingly blurred until it was almost impossible to tell where one ended and the other began. The intensity of their clash, the merging of pain and pleasure, the give and take of power, all culminated in a crescendo of raw emotion. They were two men, both strong and proud, finding solace and connection in the most unexpected of circumstances. The storm outside might have forced them together, but it was their own storm of emotions that kept them entwined.

As the two men wrestled with one another, their fists played a central role in their display of dominance. Richard, with a more pronounced upper body strength, aimed calculated punches at Michael's ribs. Each blow was meant to assert dominance rather than injure, but the force behind them left reddening imprints on Michael's pale skin. Michael, not to be outdone, managed to land a solid punch to Richard's stomach, causing him to momentarily lose his breath. The sound of the impact echoed in the room, momentarily overshadowing the raging storm outside. The sensation of knuckles meeting flesh was as arousing as it was painful, a testament to the thin line they were treading between pain and pleasure. Every punch thrown was met with a grunt or a sharp intake of breath. But it wasn't just about the punches. It was about the anticipation of each blow, the game of predicting where the next hit would land.

Richard, trying to gain an upper hand, swung a right hook towards Michael's jaw. Michael, quick on his feet, dodged and landed a sharp jab to Richard's cheek. The sting of the blow was immediate, and a red mark quickly formed. Their punches became more frantic, more desperate. Richard managed to land a blow to Michael's chest, right above his heart. Michael countered by throwing a punch to Richard's side, making him wince in pain. But as the minutes wore on, their energy began to wane. The punches, though still forceful, were thrown less frequently. Their breathing became more labored, their movements slower. Every blow landed was met with a mix of pain and pleasure, each sensation feeding off the other. In this raw and primal display of dominance and desire, the two men found a connection that went beyond physicality. Through their punches, through their shared pain and pleasure, they found a bond that was as unexpected as it was intense.

Their eyes locked, both panting heavily. The intensity of the fight had left them drained but in its wake was a palpable tension, electric and charged. The room, now filled with the sounds of their heavy breathing and the distant murmur of the storm outside, seemed smaller. Michael slowly approached Richard, his fingers brushing over the reddened skin on Richard's torso, tracing the aftermath of their brawl. Richard responded with a shiver, his own fingers reaching out to touch the marks he'd left on Michael. With their faces inches apart, the scent of sweat, arousal, and the faint remnant of cigarette smoke intertwined. Michael took the initiative, crashing his lips onto Richard's. The kiss was fierce, almost biting, a continuation of their earlier struggle but in a completely different context. Richard responded eagerly, wrapping his arm around Michael's waist and pulling him close. Their bodies, still warm from the fight, pressed together, every touch sending sparks of desire shooting through them. Breaking the kiss, Richard whispered, "Wasn't expecting this when I walked into the motel tonight." Michael smirked, "Neither was I, but sometimes the unexpected is what we need."

They shared another heated kiss, both men now eager to explore each other further, the remnants of their fight serving as a reminder of the raw passion that had brought them together. The snowstorm outside raged on, but inside, a different kind of storm was brewing. As the night deepened, the two men's interactions shifted fluidly between bouts of gentle exploration and raw, aggressive passion. Both men fully explored the other's body. The rawness of their fight had now been replaced with the rawness of the pleasure and pain of exploration. Their previous fight, combined with the bottled-up tension and the unusual circumstances, had ignited a chemistry neither man had anticipated. Each touch, each caress was a testament to their newfound intimacy. Their fingertips roamed freely, discovering the curves, ridges, and textures of one another's bodies. Richard gently trailed kisses down Michael's neck, his hands grasping at the broad expanse of his back, pulling him closer. Michael responded by nipping lightly at Richard's earlobe, his own hands tracing the older man's toned arms, feeling the play of muscles underneath the skin. Their shared cigarette from earlier served as a symbol of their initial bonding, and now, with every shared breath, their connection deepened.

As dawn approached, they lay wrapped in each other's arms, the bed sheets tangled around them, a testament to their passionate night. The storm outside seemed to be letting up, but inside, the storm of emotions was still raging, both men unsure of what the new day would bring but content in the warmth of the present moment. The gentle light of dawn streamed through the crack in the curtains, casting a soft glow over the room. The storm had faded to a gentle snowfall, blanketing the world outside in a fresh layer of white. The distant sound of a snowplow could be heard, its monotonous rumble breaking the silence of the morning. Richard was the first to stir, gently disentangling himself from Michael's embrace. He quietly made his way to the bathroom, taking a moment to splash cold water on his face and gather his thoughts. The reflection staring back at him showed a man both exhilarated and confused by the events of the night.

Michael, meanwhile, gradually woke up, stretching and then sitting up in bed. The memories of the previous night washed over him, a mix of passion, aggression, and unexpected connection. He could still feel the lingering touch of Richard's hands, the heat of their shared breaths, and the aches from their tussles. He found his pants and began searching the pockets for his pack of cigarettes. Lighting one, he inhaled deeply, letting the nicotine calm his racing thoughts. Richard returned from the bathroom just as Michael was exhaling a plume of smoke. The older man paused for a moment, taking in the sight, then slowly approached, wordlessly taking the cigarette from Michael for a drag. The two sat in a comfortable silence, the only sound being the shared breathing and the distant noise of the outside world coming back to life. It was clear that they were both processing the unexpected intimacy they'd shared, trying to make sense of their feelings. Finally, Richard spoke, "I've never had a night like that." Michael nodded in agreement, "Me neither."

They shared a look, both men seeing the same mix of wonder and uncertainty in each other's eyes. While the storm outside had been a force of nature, the storm within them was just as powerful and unpredictable. With a reluctant sigh, Richard started to gather his things. "I guess we should be hitting the road soon." Michael nodded, "Yeah, before the next snowstorm hits." The two men dressed in silence, occasionally stealing glances at one another. As they made their way to the door, Michael hesitated for a moment. "Richard?" "Yeah?" "I don't know what last night was, but... thank you." Richard smiled softly, "Same to you, Michael." With a final shared look, the two men stepped out into the snowy morning, each heading in their own direction but forever changed by their unexpected night together.

RETIREMENT RUMBLE

At Sunset Meadows, a pristine retirement community nestled amidst manicured lawns and peaceful ponds, two residents, Joyce and Eileen, found themselves at odds. Both were widows and had always been fiercely independent, with a flair for the dramatic. Despite the serene backdrop, tensions had been brewing between the two since the day Eileen had accidentally taken Joyce's seat at a bingo night. It escalated when Joyce started spending more time with Eileen's close friend, Carol, drawing the latter away from her usual morning tea sessions with Eileen. "Come to my apartment after dinner," Eileen whispered to Joyce during a knitting circle, her voice laced with restrained fury.

At the appointed time, Joyce arrived, knocking softly on Eileen's door. Eileen had rearranged the furniture to create an open space in the middle. No words were exchanged. Both women understood the unspoken agreement: this would remain a private affair. The fight between Joyce and Eileen was a blend of strategy and raw emotion. Both women, despite their age, still had a spark of vigor in them, and this dispute brought out a side neither had shown in years. As they circled each other, Eileen took the first jab, her long fingers aiming for Joyce's cheek. Joyce, however, managed to dodge it, her shorter stature giving her an advantage in agility. In retaliation, Joyce aimed a quick succession of punches at Eileen's midriff. Eileen grunted with each blow, trying to shield herself with her arms. Eileen, trying to regain control, reached out and managed to grasp Joyce's wrist, using her height advantage to try and push Joyce off balance. But Joyce had other plans. She pivoted on her foot and sent a powerful uppercut towards Eileen's chin, making her stagger backward.

Eileen's tall frame wobbled but she steadied herself, eyes sharp with determination. She lunged at Joyce, aiming a right hook for her temple. The punch connected, and for a moment, it seemed as if Joyce would go down. But she shook her head to clear the daze and, with a growl, lunged back at Eileen. The two wrestled, their arms locked in a test of strength. Each tried to overpower the other, their grunts and the shuffling of feet the only sounds in the room. During the tussle, Joyce managed to land a sharp jab to Eileen's nose, causing her eyes to water. Seeing her moment, Joyce sent a flurry of punches, aiming for Eileen's chest and stomach, each one pushing Eileen further back. Eileen tried to block and dodge, but Joyce's onslaught was relentless.

Then, in a desperate move, Eileen tried a wild swing, hoping to catch Joyce off guard. But Joyce was ready. She ducked, and as Eileen's momentum carried her forward, Joyce sent a hard punch to her ribs, causing Eileen to lose her balance and stumble over. With Eileen down and momentarily winded, Joyce took the upper hand, pinning Eileen and landing a few more decisive blows to ensure her victory. It was clear that the fight had taken a toll on both women, but a victor had emerged. Both Joyce and Eileen lay panting on the floor amidst the disarray of the apartment. Their initial animosity had faded into mutual admiration and a realization that they had both underestimated the other. The tension of the fight had given way to another kind of tension - one laced with curiosity and possibility.

Eileen pushed herself to a sitting position, a sly smile forming on her lips. "I haven't felt this alive in years," she admitted, her eyes taking in the damage. "But we might want to find a more suitable venue if we're going to make this a regular thing." Joyce chuckled, pulling herself up to join Eileen. "I agree. Maybe we could rent out the community room. Put down some mats. Save the furniture." She reached out, placing a strand of Eileen's disheveled hair behind her ear, their eyes locking. "I am sure management will approve of that," Eileen replied. Eileen's eyes twinkled with mischief. "Perhaps we should lay some ground rules for our next bout," she suggested, her gaze drifting to Joyce's lips and back up. "And maybe discuss other... activities."

Joyce's heart rate, which had started to calm down after the fight, quickened again. "I think I'd like that," she murmured, the distance between them decreasing. Both women recognized the energy between them, a spark that neither had felt in quite some time. They left Joyce's apartment hand in hand, talking animatedly about their plans for a rematch and other newfound interests. Their evening fight had unexpectedly opened a door to something more profound and intimate.

TRAILER PARK CLASH

In the isolated environment of Redwood Trailer Park, there was no shortage of drama. But the most prominent of these was the bitter animosity between two heavy-set residents, Jenny and Brenda. Their mobile homes were situated right next to each other, and the walls, although thin, couldn't hide the deep-set grudges they held. It began over minor disputes: whose laundry was taking up space on the shared line, and who was playing music too loudly at ungodly hours. But as time went on, the disputes grew pettier and the clashes louder. One day, after a heated argument about a misplaced garbage can, Brenda yelled, "Enough! Let's settle this once and for all!" Jenny, never one to back down, agreed immediately. "Behind the maintenance shed, sunset. No audience, just you and me," Brenda declared. Jenny smirked. "Perfect. Prepare to get your ass kicked."

As the sun began its descent, casting an orange hue over the trailer park, Jenny and Brenda met at the designated spot. They sized each other up, their breathing heavy, eyes narrowed, fists clenched. Without a word, Brenda launched forward, swinging her hefty arm towards Jenny's face. Using her weight, Jenny charged, pushing Brenda against the wall of the shed. Brenda grunted but managed to free one arm, landing a sloppy punch on Jenny's side. Jenny retaliated with a punch that made Brenda's head snap to the side. The fight was messy, filled with grunts, slaps, and wild punches. It wasn't a well-choreographed fight but rather a raw display of pent-up rage. As the minutes wore on, their pace began to slow, fatigue setting in due to their hefty physiques and the energy they were expending. Brenda, using her slight height advantage, aimed a punch straight to Jenny's stomach. Jenny gasped, staggered, but didn't fall. She lunged at Brenda with surprising speed, and the two toppled to the ground. They rolled around, each trying to pin the other down. Dust, sweat, and blood mingled as their blows became less precise but no less powerful.

It was Jenny who finally managed to gain the upper hand. She pinned Brenda beneath her, using her weight as an advantage. With Brenda momentarily incapacitated, Jenny landed three successive punches to Brenda's face. Each blow landed with a dull thud, and by the third, Brenda was dazed and disoriented. Jenny, panting heavily, managed to pull herself up. "Had enough?" she spat, her eyes still blazing with fury. Brenda, blood trickling from her nose and a defiant look in her eyes, hissed, "Fuck you." Jenny, too exhausted to retort, simply turned on her heel and walked away, leaving Brenda lying in the dirt, battered but not broken. Their personal war was far from over.

Brenda had spent the past week nursing her wounds, both physical and emotional. The defeat stung, but more than that, it was the shame of losing in such a personal and private showdown. She might not have voiced it out loud, but in the tight-knit community of

Redwood Trailer Park, secrets had a way of getting out. Whispers had already started, and Brenda could feel the weight of pitying glances. But Brenda wasn't one to sulk for long. Revenge simmered in her mind. She remembered her sister, Marie, who had moved a couple of towns over after getting a job. Marie was taller, more athletic, and had been in her fair share of fights during her high school years. If anyone could help Brenda even the score, it was Marie.

One evening, Marie came over for a visit. The sisters shared stories, laughed over a bottle of cheap wine, and as the night deepened, Brenda poured out her tale of defeat. Marie, always protective of her younger sibling, was instantly on board with a revenge plan. The next evening, with the sun casting long, stretching shadows across the park, Brenda approached Jenny's trailer. She shouted a challenge, her voice loud and clear. Jenny, never one to back down, emerged with a smirk, ready for Round Two. But she stopped short when she saw Marie standing next to Brenda. "Two against one? Really, Brenda?" Jenny scoffed, clearly unprepared for this turn of events. Brenda sneered, "Just evening the odds."

Before Jenny could react, Marie lunged forward. Her first punch landed squarely on Jenny's jaw, making her stagger back. Jenny tried to retaliate but found herself outmatched by Marie's skill and speed. As Marie kept Jenny occupied, Brenda took her chance and tackled Jenny from the side. The two sisters were relentless. Every time Jenny tried to fend off one, the other would strike. It was evident that Jenny was outmatched and overwhelmed. Marie landed a particularly brutal punch to Jenny's midsection, making her keel over. Seizing the opportunity, Brenda delivered a swift uppercut, sending Jenny crashing to the ground. Jenny lay there, gasping for breath, her eyes darting between the two triumphant sisters. Brenda knelt beside her, her voice cold, "Remember this day, Jenny. You started this, but we're finishing it." Marie added with a smirk, "And don't even think of a rematch unless you have a sister hiding somewhere." The sisters walked away, leaving a defeated Jenny in the dust. The score was now settled, but in Redwood Trailer Park, grudges ran deep, and only time would tell if the feud was truly over.

HOTEL ROOM STAKES FIGHT (M/M)

In a hotel bar, Mark, a tall man with salt-and-pepper hair, took a seat beside Jason, a slightly more robust man of about the same age. Both were in town for a business conference, and after a long day of meetings, they were looking for a moment of relaxation. Mark took a sip of his whisky and commented on the intensity of the day's sessions. Jason nodded, agreeing, and began sharing a story from his youth when he was part of his high school's wrestling team. Mark's eyes lit up with interest, "Really? I used to wrestle too in college!" They laughed about the similarities in their backgrounds and began swapping tales of their old matches, relishing the memories of the adrenaline and the camaraderie. As the night wore on, the conversation turned more personal. Jason mentioned how he missed the physicality of those days, not just the wrestling, but even the playful body punches he and his teammates would exchange. Mark raised an eyebrow, "You know, I thought I was the only one who missed that. There's something exhilarating about a good body punch. Sort of... reconnects you to your physical self, doesn't it?" Jason nodded with a smirk,

"Exactly! It's not about the pain, but more about the shock and the connection."

They continued discussing the rush they felt from the sport and the unique bond it created. By the end of the evening, they'd agreed to meet up the next day for a friendly sparring session, a chance to relive those cherished memories and maybe even start a new tradition on future business trips. As the conversation grew more animated, Mark gestured to his pack of cigarettes, "Care for a smoke?" Jason nodded, "I could use one, actually." They both made their way outside, the cool night air hitting them as they stepped into a quiet alley beside the hotel. The sounds from the bar became muffled, replaced by the distant hum of traffic. Lighting up, they took a moment to enjoy the sensation, letting the nicotine calm their nerves. The glow from their cigarettes illuminated their faces intermittently as they puffed away. "You know," Jason began, exhaling a plume of smoke, "there's something about wrestling and body punching that's just... primal. Even just talking about it brings back that rush." Mark chuckled, "Yeah. There's this raw physicality to it. It's like a dance, but with more force. It reminds you that you're alive."

The two of them continued chatting, leaning against the brick wall of the hotel. They shared stories of their favorite matches, the opponents they remembered, and the places their sports journey had taken them. By the time they stubbed out their cigarettes, they had forged a surprising bond, two middle-aged men rediscovering a mutual passion from their youth. The evening had turned into a memorable encounter, with plans to meet the next day and, perhaps, rekindle that feeling of being truly alive once more. Mark hesitated for a moment, taking another cigarette from his pack and lighting it. "You ever... meet someone and just... fight? You know, in a hotel room, no audience, just testing each other out?" Jason, lighting up his own cigarette, exhaled slowly before meeting Mark's gaze. "Actually, yes. Met a guy about a year ago during another business trip. We both found ourselves in adjacent hotel rooms. Had a few drinks, talked about the old days, and well... decided to see who still had the upper hand." Mark smiled, "Funny you should mention that. I had a similar encounter a few months back. It was with an old college friend. Was unexpected but... exhilarating."

As the night enveloped them, the orange glow from their cigarettes was the only thing cutting through the darkness. The two men were now standing closer than before, the atmosphere between them heavy with intrigue. "You know," Jason began, looking at the hotel looming above them, "we both have rooms here, and we've been talking about this all evening..." Mark, taking a final drag from his cigarette, said, "Why not see if the talk lives up to the real thing?" Jason smirked, "My thoughts exactly." There was a charged silence between the two. The evening had taken an unexpected turn, and both were excited to see where it would lead.

Once back inside the bar, the ambience seemed even more muted compared to their intense conversation outside. Pop music playing in the background and the clink of glasses provided a comfortable backdrop as they took their seats. Taking a sip from his drink, Mark ventured, "So... outside of the business world and our shared... interests, tell me about yourself.

Single? Married?" Jason hesitated for a moment before answering, "Divorced, actually. About two years now. And you?" "Single," Mark replied with a half-smile. "Was in a long-term relationship, but it ended a few years back." They both took a moment, sipping their drinks, feeling the weight of past relationships. Jason then asked, tentatively, "So, in terms of... preferences, where do you stand? I mean, I've always identified as bi." Mark nodded, appreciating the honesty. "Same here. Always felt a connection to both genders, although I've mostly been with women in the past." The disclosure seemed to lift a weight off their shoulders, allowing them to navigate their newfound attraction with a sense of clarity. Both men realized that their conversation was breaking barriers, not just about their shared passion for wrestling, but also about understanding themselves and each other better.

As the night deepened and the bar's atmosphere became more intimate, Mark cautiously broached another topic. "You mentioned private matches in hotel rooms before... ever had any that got a bit too intense? You know, going beyond just the usual wrestling?" Jason paused, swirling the liquid in his glass before answering. "A couple of times, yes. Sometimes the adrenaline, the proximity, and the mutual understanding can take things to another level. It's not necessarily about aggression, but rather the intensity and vulnerability of the moment." Mark nodded, remembering a similar experience. "I had a match once where things got... heated. It started as friendly competition, but emotions and physicality intertwined, and boundaries blurred." There was a reflective silence between the two, each lost in their own memories. Jason finally added, "It's not something

I actively seek out, but when you're in the moment, and there's mutual trust, it can be... transformative. It's a mix of raw emotion, physical exertion, and connection." Mark agreed, "Exactly. It's not for everyone, and it doesn't happen every time, but when it does, it's memorable." Jason laughed, taking another sip from his drink, "You know, as much as I enjoy a good wrestle, there's something about gut punches. There's a thrill in receiving them, almost as much as giving them. It's hard to explain."

Mark raised an eyebrow, intrigued. "Really? I've always felt the same way. There's this exhilarating sensation, a mix of vulnerability and strength. But I steer clear of anything that might leave a mark, especially on the face. After all, I've got meetings to attend and a professional image to uphold." Jason laughed, "Exactly! It's a strange kind of thrill, isn't it? To walk into a meeting the next day, knowing what you've experienced, and no one is any the wiser." Mark nodded, "It's our little secret. The hidden side of us that most people never get to see." Their candid confessions led to a deeper understanding between the two. It was rare to find someone who shared such a niche interest, let alone someone willing to openly discuss it. Mark leaned in slightly, the hum of the bar providing a backdrop to their intensifying conversation. "You know, Jason, some matches I've been in had predetermined stakes. Given what you mentioned about being bi... how about adding a twist? Maybe the winner gets to... have a bit more fun with the loser?" Jason, looking both thoughtful and intrigued, took a sip from his drink. "Interesting proposition. So, let's say, for example, a nice blowjob for the winner, or maybe more? It does make the competition a little more real, doesn't it?"

Mark's smirk grew wider, "Exactly my thought. It's not just about the fight anymore, but the tantalizing reward awaiting the victor. And if the mood is right and the chemistry's there... who knows where the night might lead?"

They agree to take this meeting to one of their rooms. They fight until one pleads for the other to stop. They fight until there is a winner. No ties. They also briefly discuss the post-fight stakes. The conversation was turning the two on. They need to step outside once more, each lighting up another cigarette as the cool night air enveloped them. The atmosphere was thick with anticipation. Mark exhaled a plume of smoke, starting the discussion. "Alright, so we're clear on the rules? Gut and body punching, not holding back, but nothing to the face. If one of us breaks that rule, it's game on for face shots." Jason nodded in agreement, "That's fair. And we fight until one of us pleads to stop. I don't want any ambiguity. We go until there's a clear winner." Mark tilted his head, thinking, "And post-fight stakes? I think giving the winner a choice is the best way to go. Be it a blowjob, penetration... whatever the winner desires at the moment." Jason took a long drag from his cigarette. "Agreed. Winner's choice. It makes the stakes real and the competition fierce." They both stood in silence for a moment, letting the gravity of their arrangement sink in. The blend of competition and intimacy had transformed their casual bar encounter into a night neither would forget. The thrill of the unknown, combined with the allure of the stakes, created an electric atmosphere between them.

The thought of a safe word came up. Mark took

a moment to consider, the smoke from his cigarette swirling around him. "Do we want a safe word? Or do we trust each other enough to let the winner decide when it's over?" Jason looked thoughtful, "There's a certain thrill in not having a safe word, letting the competition run its course until the winner feels it's done. But it also requires immense trust." Mark nodded, "Exactly. It's a higher level of vulnerability. But if we're both up for it, we can forgo the safe word." Jason took a final drag from his cigarette, crushing it under his shoe. "Let's do it then. No safe word. We fight until one of us emerges as the clear victor, and that person decides when it ends." Mark extended his hand, and Jason took it, sealing their agreement with a firm handshake.

Once inside one of their spacious hotel rooms, Mark moved over to the window, glancing briefly outside before pulling a cigarette from his pack. Jason raised an eyebrow, a smirk forming on his lips. "You know this is a no smoking room, right?" Mark lit the cigarette, taking a deep drag and exhaling the smoke. "Yeah, I know. But fuck it. I'll pay the cleaning charge. After tonight's stakes, that seems like a small price to pay." Jason chuckled, loosening his tie. "You're a bold one. I like that." Jason smirked, reaching into his pocket for his own pack of cigarettes. Lighting up, he inhaled deeply, then set his cigarette on the edge of a water-filled glass, makeshift ashtray style. Mark removed his blazer and tie. He began unbuttoning his shirt, revealing a hairy gray chest underneath. "Well, if we're going to do this, might as well get comfortable." Jason followed suit, his eyes never leaving Mark as he slowly began to shed layers. "Agreed. These business suits weren't made for what we have in mind." Piece by piece, they discarded their formal attire: ties tossed carelessly onto a chair, shoes kicked off to the side, shirts and trousers folded neatly on a table. They stood facing each other, only in their underwear, the full extent of their physiques on display. Mark broke the silence, "So, shall we get started?" Jason nodded, the glint in his eyes evident, "Absolutely."

Jason, with a smirk and a confident glint in his eyes, hooked his fingers into the waistband of his underwear and smoothly slid them down his legs, stepping out of them with a deliberate slowness. Standing unabashedly in his full glory, he quipped, "Just so you know what your ass can expect." Mark, despite his attempt to keep a stoic face, couldn't help but raise an eyebrow in appreciation. "Confident, aren't we?" Jason shrugged with a sly grin, "Always good to give a preview of the stakes." Mark, taking Jason's lead, also slid off his underwear, standing in a contrasting yet similarly exposed state. Jason's eyes roamed over Mark's figure. Mark's build was consistent with that of a middle-aged businessman: a physique once firmer in youth but now softened by the comforts of professional success and years seated behind a desk. His chest was broad, not from the gym but from age and a relaxed lifestyle. The contours of his abdomen were gentle, without any defined muscles but with a soft padding indicative of occasional indulgence and fewer visits to the gym. The gray and black hairs that peppered his chest grew thicker around his midsection. Mark's legs were sturdy, but without the toned definition of regular exercise.

Mark's gaze traveled over Jason in return. Jason's frame was similar, though perhaps a touch leaner. His shoulders were still broad, hinting at a past where he might have been more active. His midsection, like Mark's, bore the comfortable roundness of middle age, a soft paunch that spoke of business lunches and a penchant for good wine. His chest, lightly peppered with gray amidst the black, had a softness to it, lacking the tautness of rigorous workouts. His legs, while long, had the same relaxed appearance as the rest of him. Both men, in their vulnerability, represented the average middle-aged businessman — comfortable in their own skin, bearing the natural effects of age and a life focused more on professional pursuits than physical fitness. Their appearances spoke of contentment, experience, and the natural progression of time. They stood, unashamed and genuine, each man a reflection of the other's reality.

The final puffs of their cigarettes fill the air, each man taking one last inhale before extinguishing them in the makeshift ashtray. As the last trails of smoke drift away, Mark, with a mischievous glint in his eyes, reaches out to grasp Jason's cock, giving it an appreciative squeeze. "Very nice," he comments, his voice low and teasing. Jason, always game for a challenge, reciprocates by taking hold of Mark's cock, mirroring the gesture. Their eyes lock. With their most intimate parts clutched in each other's hands, they find themselves at close range, the stakes of their prior agreement evident. Mark makes the first move, landing a punch squarely on Jason's abdomen. The sound of the impact echoes slightly in the room. Jason grunts, feeling the sting, but the close proximity means he has little room to maneuver away. Instead, he retaliates with a punch of his own, aiming for Mark's side, making Mark hiss in response.

Their grip on each other ensures they stay in close

quarters, the battle becoming one of endurance rather than skill. Every punch is felt keenly, the tight space preventing much dodging or strategic movements. Mark, using his slightly larger frame, tries to land successive body shots on Jason, targeting his ribs and abdomen. Jason counters by aiming his punches towards Mark's soft midsection, trying to wind him. The atmosphere is thick with exertion, each man's breathing growing more labored with every strike. Jason manages to land a particularly forceful punch on Mark's side, causing him to momentarily lose his grip. But Mark recovers quickly, tightening his hold on Jason and retaliating with a series of punches to Jason's lower abdomen. The intensity of their unique combat, combined with the trust and vulnerability of their mutual grip, creates a scene of raw emotion and physicality. It's clear that this is not just about winning but about proving something to themselves and each other. The room is filled with the sounds of grunts, thuds, and heavy breathing as they continue their contest, waiting to see who will emerge as the victor.

As the struggle continues, the line between pain, dominance, and pleasure becomes increasingly blurred. The raw intimacy of their unusual combat is undeniable. With each well-placed punch, their arousal becomes more evident, their bodies betraying the mixed sensations they're experiencing. After a particularly strong jab from Jason to Mark's side, Mark gasps, momentarily losing his concentration. In that split second, his grip on Jason's now erect penis falters and loosens. Jason notices immediately, a triumphant smirk forming on his lips, even as Mark quickly tries to regain his hold. However, the damage is done. The brief release, combined with their evident arousal, changes the dynamic. Both men, though erect and flushed with adrenaline, are acutely aware of the sexual tension that's been underpinning their bout from the start. The question now becomes not just who will win their physical contest, but how the night will continue to unfold. Jason, sensing an advantage, tightens his grip on Mark's erection and deliberately lifts it upwards. The sudden, unexpected motion sends a jolt of sharp pain through Mark, making him gasp out loud. His eyes widen in surprise and discomfort, his focus entirely redirected by Jason's bold move. "Enough," Mark manages to utter, gritting his teeth against the mix of pain and arousal. Jason, feeling the upper hand but not wanting to overstep the boundaries of their mutual respect, releases his grip shortly after, allowing Mark some relief. The intensity between them is palpable; they're both breathing heavily, flushed and sweating.

Jason smirks, "Got you off guard there, didn't I?" Mark, catching his breath, responds with a smirk of his own, "You certainly did. Well played." With Mark momentarily off-kilter from the sudden move, Jason's confidence surges. He remembers their agreement – no safeword, meaning the fight would end only when one of them deemed it over. Locking eyes with Mark, Jason's voice drops, low and commanding, "Remember, Mark, it's enough only when I say it's enough." Before Mark can react or respond, Jason throws a punch directly at Mark's midsection. The impact forces the air out of Mark's lungs, leaving him momentarily breathless and stunned. The clear power dynamic, with Jason currently in control, adds an additional layer of tension and intrigue to their unique contest. With Jason's clear assertion of dominance, the dynamic of their tussle shifts. Mark, determined not to be outdone, rallies quickly, pushing past the momentary discomfort from the punch. He lunges at Jason, trying to close the distance and take away any range advantage. Mark manages to land a hard punch to Jason's side, causing a grunt of pain. Jason counters by driving his fist into Mark's ribs. They move in a dance of controlled violence, each trying to gain the upper hand.

The room becomes a whirlwind of motion. Punches are thrown in rapid succession, some landing with solid thuds while others are deflected or missed entirely. The confined space of the hotel room only adds to the intensity, with each man trying to maneuver the other into a corner or against a wall. As they wrestle, their previous state of undress and the physical exertion causes their bodies to glisten with sweat, making holds and grips harder to maintain. Mark manages to pin Jason briefly against the wall, landing several quick punches to his abdomen before Jason uses his legs to push Mark off and regain his footing. With every blow dealt, the two men grow more tired, yet neither is willing to give in. Their breaths come in ragged gasps, the strain showing on their faces, but their determination is unwavering. In one particularly intense moment, Jason feints a move to the left, causing Mark to misstep. Capitalizing on the mistake, Jason sweeps Mark's legs out from under him, sending him crashing to the floor. But Mark is quick to recover, grabbing Jason's leg and pulling him down as well.

Now on the floor, their fight becomes even more primal. They roll, each trying to gain the dominant position, landing punches and grappling with fervor.

Their exertions cause the room to fill with the sounds of heavy breathing, grunts, and the occasional groan of pain. It's a testament to their stamina and willpower that the fight continues for as long as it does. Both men, despite their age and the physical toll of the battle, seem driven by a mix of pride, adrenaline, and the charged atmosphere of their unique confrontation. The intensity of their battle on the floor, mixed with the undeniable sexual tension, adds an almost surreal edge to their contest. Their erections rub against one another as they wrestle, adding another layer of sensation to their mixed emotions of pain, dominance, and arousal. In the heat of the moment, with punches being thrown and their intimate parts being used for leverage, Mark, in a bid to unbalance Jason, slips a finger towards Jason's asshole. The sudden intrusion catches Jason off guard, his eyes widening in surprise.

Jason's immediate reaction is a mix of shock and arousal, and in that split second of distraction, Mark lands a solid punch to his midsection, taking advantage of the momentary lapse in Jason's defenses. However, in the ensuing scramble and with emotions running high, Jason's hand, in a reflexive motion, comes dangerously close to Mark's face. It's not a direct punch, but the implication is clear – in the heat of their passionate fight, the previously established rules are at risk of being forgotten. Mark, feeling the near-miss, locks eyes with Jason, a silent warning passed between them. They both recognize the line they're toeing and the potential for things to escalate beyond their initial agreement. The fight continues, but there's a heightened awareness now, a mutual understanding that they must be cautious not to cross the boundaries they set, despite the overwhelming mix of emotions and sensations they're experiencing. The blend of aggression, competition, and arousal makes every move, every touch, every punch charged with significance. The sudden punch from Jason echoes sharply in the room, the sound an immediate contrast to the muffled thuds of their previous blows. It lands with precision on Mark's face, the sting immediate and intense. Mark's eyes widen in surprise, his cheek turning a shade redder from the impact. It was a clear deviation from their agreed-upon rules. It was also an invitation, a subtle nudge for them to raise the stakes. Jason's gaze remains locked onto Mark's, searching, challenging, and perhaps even enticing. Mark's face displays a myriad of emotions: anger for the punch, confusion for the breach of their agreement, but also understanding, recognizing the subtle invitation Jason was extending. The boundaries they had set were now being tested, potentially leading to a more intense and unrestrained encounter.

The silence in the room is almost palpable, broken only by their ragged breaths. Jason, with a hint of defiance and perhaps expectation, waits for Mark's response. Mark, after a tense moment, retaliates, sending a slap back towards Jason's face. The contact is just as sharp, just as loud, echoing the challenge. It wasn't merely a response but an acknowledgment — a silent agreement that their initial boundaries could be pushed further. With the unspoken rules now evolving, their battle intensifies. The atmosphere is charged with an even greater sense of anticipation and unpredictability. The blend of pain and pleasure, dominance and arousal, grows more profound, making every subsequent move between them heavy with implication and uncertainty.

The newfound freedom to target the face adds another layer of intensity to their already fervent battle. With this new rule in play, their movements become more strategic, and their defenses more guarded.

Jason, trying to capitalize on his earlier momentum, throws a swift jab towards Mark's jaw. Mark, anticipating the move, ducks to the side, narrowly avoiding the punch. He retaliates with a hook aimed at Jason's temple, but Jason blocks it with a well-timed forearm. The close proximity of their wrestling match on the floor now evolves into something akin to a boxing bout, albeit one without gloves and with the added dimension of their other intimate tactics. They circle each other warily, darting in and out of range, both seeking an opening while trying to defend their newly vulnerable faces. Mark lands a glancing blow to Jason's cheek, making him stumble back slightly. Seizing the moment, Mark tries to follow it up with an uppercut, but Jason sidesteps, narrowly avoiding the powerful swing. The rhythm of their fight changes noticeably. Whereas earlier their tactics were grounded in wrestling and body punches, they're now using footwork, feints, and head movement, akin to trained fighters. The difference, of course, is the deep undercurrent of intimacy and the heightened stakes of their personal contest.

Despite the aggressive nature of their fight, there's a clear understanding between them. While the face is now a viable target, neither wants to inflict lasting damage. Their punches, while firm and intended to show dominance, are not thrown with full force. As they continue, their faces bear the marks of their skirmishes – reddened areas from slaps, slight swellings from the more solid punches, sweat streaming down, mixing with the occasional wince of pain. As their skirmish continues, it becomes evident that one of the men is gaining an advantage. The intricate dance of footwork and feints starts to favor Jason. Using his slightly superior strength and momentum, he manages to push Mark aggressively against the wall. The sudden move forces them chest to chest, their erections pressed firmly against one another in a provocative juxtaposition of their ongoing battle. Mark's back is pressed against the cold, hard surface, momentarily taking his breath away. Jason uses this chance to land a few rapid body punches to Mark's midsection. Each blow pushes them closer together, intensifying the sensation of their bodies in close contact. As Mark tries to gather his bearings, Jason's hands, which were initially pinning Mark's wrists, slide down to his lower back. They inch closer, venturing daringly to Mark's rear. Jason's fingers brush against the curvature of Mark's buttocks before slipping further down, teasingly probing the more intimate areas. The touch, although unexpected, sends a shiver up Mark's spine, further blurring the line between pain, dominance, and arousal. This mix of aggression and intimacy holds them both in a tight embrace, their heavy breaths mingling, faces just inches apart. The dynamic between them is changing once again, and it's unclear where this renewed intensity will lead them next.

The heightened intimacy seems to momentarily distract both men from the primary objective of their fight. Their breaths come in ragged synchrony, and the energy in the room shifts from pure aggression to a complex blend of dominance, competition, and desire. Mark, sensing an opportunity and driven by a mix of instinct and strategy, uses the wall for leverage. Pushing against it with his feet, he tries to reverse their positions. But Jason, anticipating the move, manages to thwart the attempt, pressing his advantage and landing a solid blow to Mark's ribs. The impact makes Mark gasp, the pain sharp and immediate. But rather than buckling, it ignites a renewed determination in him. He counters with a swift knee aimed at Jason's midsection, forcing him to momentarily double over. Seizing this advantage, Mark manages to slip from Jason's grasp, quickly maneuvering behind him. He locks an arm around Jason's neck, attempting to restrain him in a chokehold. Jason struggles, his face reddening from the pressure, but Mark's grip is firm. Despite the discomfort, Jason refuses to yield. With a burst of strength, he pushes backward, pinning Mark once more against the wall, this time with added force. The move breaks Mark's hold, allowing Jason to land several rapid punches to his opponent's torso.

Mark, though winded, tries to counter, but his moves are now slower, the exhaustion evident in every motion. Jason, sensing Mark's weakening defenses, delivers a couple of firm body shots, causing Mark to slump slightly, his breathing labored. Finally, with a mix of fatigue, pain, and perhaps even a hint of satisfaction, Mark murmurs, "Enough," signaling his submission. Both men, sweat-soaked and breathing heavily, disengage. The intensity of the fight, the blurring of boundaries, and the undeniable connection they shared throughout the battle hangs heavily between them. The culmination of their unique contest has left them both physically drained and emotionally charged. The room is thick with tension, but now it's of a different sort, one that ponders what comes next after such a heated encounter.

After Mark's murmured submission, Jason wasn't quite ready to let go of the moment. The lack of a safe word had set the tone for an encounter where boundaries could be pushed, and Jason intended to do just that. With Mark still trying to catch his breath, Jason, in a swift move, pushed him down onto the floor. Taking advantage of Mark's weakened state, he straddled him, effectively pinning him beneath his weight. Before Mark could fully register what was happening, Jason began landing a series of soft punches on his face. They weren't meant to injure, but to assert dominance, to remind Mark who was in control. Mark's eyes widened in surprise, not having anticipated this extension of their bout. Every punch, though light, emphasized Jason's position of power, making Mark feel more vulnerable than before. The punches continued, with Mark's protests growing more and more desperate. "Enough, Jason! I conceded!" he gasped out, trying to shield his face. But Jason, holding true to their earlier agreement, responded tersely, "It's over when I say it's over." After a few more deliberate punches, Jason finally seemed satisfied. He paused, looking down at Mark's flushed and slightly bruised face, their heavy breaths filling the room. The aftermath of their battle laid bare in their exhausted expressions, the raw emotions, and the power dynamics that had played out.

Eventually, Jason leaned in, his face inches from Mark's, whispering, "Now it's over." He then slowly lifted himself off Mark, allowing both men to fully absorb the intensity of what had transpired between them. Mark's face contorted with a mixture of pain and frustration as he slowly sat up from the floor. The post-battle weariness was evident in his movements, but it was his eyes that held the most emotion. While the unexpected extension of their bout had taken him by surprise, upon reflection, he recognized the raw hunger for dominance in Jason's actions. It was the very same drive he himself possessed. Pushing himself into a seated position, Mark exhaled deeply, "That was uncalled for, Jason," he said, rubbing his reddened face. But then he added with a rueful smirk, "Though I'd probably have done the same if our positions were reversed."

Jason, already by the room's minibar, poured himself a glass of water, taking a long gulp. "It's the nature of our agreement," he replied, his voice slightly hoarse from the exertion. "No boundaries, remember?" Mark just nodded, understanding the primal urge that had taken over both of them. The unique terms of their encounter had allowed them to push boundaries, both their own and each other's. Jason then reached for his cigarette pack, pulling one out and lighting it. The first drag was long, the smoke curling upwards in a thin stream. He turned to look at Mark, an unspoken acknowledgment passing between them. Their fight had taken them on a wild journey of emotions and physicality, and while there might have been moments of disagreement, there was also a deep mutual understanding of the boundaries they had both chosen to explore.

Mark's muscles ached as he began to rise from the floor. He felt Jason's gaze on him, heavy and full of intent. As Mark extended his hand to take the offered cigarette, Jason suddenly spoke up, "No need to stand. On your knees will be fine." The words carried a weighted implication, and Mark paused, processing their meaning. There was a momentary flash of resistance in his eyes, but he quickly accepted the situation. After all, they had agreed on certain consequences for the loser, and he knew what was expected. Jason, taking note of Mark's brief hesitation, felt a thrill of dominance. The power dynamics from their earlier fight were still very much at play. He lit another cigarette for himself, watching Mark intently as the smoke curled around his head. Inside, he reveled in the control he held over the situation, keenly aware of the intimate turn their encounter was about to take.

Mark, meanwhile, was processing a whirlwind of emotions. The defeat was still fresh, but this next step was something altogether different. He felt a combination of vulnerability, anticipation, and even a hint of excitement. These conflicting feelings were muddled by the weariness from their physical skirmish, making the entire scenario feel almost dreamlike. He took a deep drag from the cigarette, the familiar taste and sensation grounding him. Then, exhaling, he carefully lowered himself to his knees, ensuring he maintained eye contact with Jason. The act was both one of submission and a silent acknowledgment of the pact they had made. Jason's voice broke the thick silence. "Here," he said, extending a glass of water towards Mark. The gesture, though simple, was laden with meaning, further solidifying the shifting power dynamics. As Mark took the glass, both men were keenly aware of the profound intimacy and understanding they now shared. Despite the intensity of their earlier skirmish and the emotions swirling in the room, both Jason and Mark were still visibly aroused. The unique mix of competition, dominance, and submission had kept them in a heightened state of anticipation.

Placing his cigarette pack beside Mark, Jason's voice carried a new kind of command, "I want a smoky blowjob." The statement, provocative and explicit, heightened the already charged atmosphere. Mark's eyes flickered with a blend of surprise, intrigue, and readiness. The request was unusual but, given the night's events, nothing seemed off the table. Jason, reading the subtle cues in Mark's expression, gently grasped the back of Mark's head, guiding it towards his erect cock. The guiding motion was both assertive and encouraging, meant to embolden Mark in this next step of their shared experience. Mark, still holding the cigarette, took another drag. The warmth of the smoke filled his mouth just as he began to fulfill Jason's request. The smoky texture added another layer of sensation for Jason, who inhaled sharply, a mix of pleasure and the thrill of command.

Both men, lost in the moment, allowed themselves to be fully consumed by the unique blend of sensations, pushing boundaries and exploring desires in ways neither had anticipated. Their earlier fight had set the stage, but it was this unexpected intimacy that truly tested their limits. As Mark continued with the act, Jason found himself consciously regulating his breathing and focusing his thoughts. The combination of the smoky sensation and Mark's technique was electrifying, and Jason had to summon considerable willpower to keep himself from exploding. Every touch, every subtle movement was intensifying his pleasure, but Jason had something else in mind. He wasn't ready for this to be the grand finale.

His hand gently rested on the back of Mark's head, not pushing, but softly guiding. It was a subtle message to Mark, an indication of his intent to prolong their encounter. Jason's thoughts were already on the plush hotel bed that awaited them, where he envisioned an even more intense culmination of their shared experience. Mark, sensing Jason's restraint, adjusted his pace. It was clear that Jason was directing the rhythm of their evening, and Mark was willing to follow the lead. The energy between them was an intricate dance of control, submission, and mutual understanding. Jason's pacing was a testament to the depth of their connection — not just about immediate gratification, but a desire to explore every facet of their newfound intimacy. As the moment continued, both men were acutely aware of the profound journey they had embarked upon together.

Jason's sudden change in demeanor caught Mark slightly off guard. One moment he was savoring the intimate act, and in the next, a strong hand had gripped his hair, pulling him upwards. Mark's cigarette tumbled from his lips, and Jason deftly caught it, extinguishing it in the makeshift water glass ashtray. With a firm push from Jason, Mark found himself propelled towards the bed. The command was clear, and Mark quickly maneuvered himself onto his belly, the cool sheets a stark contrast to the warmth of his flushed skin. Mark could feel Jason's weight as he mounted him. While their earlier interactions had hints of tenderness, there was a definite shift now. Jason's movements were more deliberate, insistent, and powerful. Each deep thrust elicited a groan from Mark, a mixture of surprise, pleasure, and the intensity of the moment. The bed beneath them creaked and shifted with their movements, bearing testament to the fervor of their connection. Jason's earlier restraint was now replaced with an unleashed passion, and Mark, though taken aback by the sudden shift in intensity, surrendered to the experience. Every sensation, every sound was heightened, and both men were completely immersed in the raw, unbridled intimacy of the moment.

Mark's body was a torrent of sensation. With each powerful thrust from Jason, a deep-seated, primal feeling surged through him. There was a mix of pain and pleasure, the sharp sting of unexpected force intertwined with the intoxicating warmth of intimacy. The groans escaping his lips weren't just from the physical act; they were expressions of his emotional and psychological state. There was vulnerability in being so exposed, in surrendering control to another. And yet, amidst that vulnerability was a rush of exhilaration. Every time he felt Jason push into him, he was reminded of the pact they'd made, the mutual trust they had established. His cries grew more fervent, echoing the intensity of the act. With each subsequent thrust, Mark felt both the weight of Jason's desire and the depth of his own longing. There was an aching need, an urgency that was powerful between them.

And as Jason moved closer to his climax, Mark could feel that energy building. There was a rising crescendo, a mounting tension that seemed to electrify the air around them. Jason's movements became more frantic, his breathing more ragged. And Mark, responsive to every shift, every nuance, felt himself being drawn into that whirlwind of passion. When Jason finally reached his explosive end, Mark felt it as deeply as if it were his own. The world seemed to narrow to that one singular moment, where two individuals, lost in a sea of sensation and emotion, found a profound connection unlike any other. The room was filled with the aftermath of their intense encounter, the air thick with a blend of sweat, satisfaction, and the remnants of their previous smoky indulgences. The two lay side by side, catching their breath, the tension from before now replaced with a more mellow energy.

Reaching over to the bedside table, Jason pulled out a cigarette, lighting it with a relaxed hand. He offered it to Mark first, who took a deep drag, allowing the familiar nicotine to calm his racing heart. They passed it back and forth between them, the shared cigarette acting as a symbolic gesture of their mutual experience. The soft glow of the burning tip illuminated their faces in the softly lit room. Jason, with a sly grin, decided it was Mark's turn to receive some pleasure. "You did good," he murmured, his voice low and teasing, "I think you've earned a little something." Without waiting for a response, Jason made his intentions clear, leaning down to give Mark the same intimate attention he'd received earlier. Mark's initial surprise quickly melted into appreciation, his body responding readily to Jason's skilled touch as he took Mark's full erection in his mouth. The journey to Mark's explosive climax was a mixture of gentleness and fervor, mirroring their earlier escapades. The room was filled with soft moans, punctuated by the occasional deep inhale from the dwindling cigarette.

By the end, both men lay spent, sated, and content. Their initial competition had evolved into an evening of mutual exploration and pleasure. In this game, both had emerged as winners, discovering new aspects of themselves and each other in the process. After the heightened emotions and physical exertions of their intense encounter, both men took a moment to assess the aftermath on their bodies. Jason's upper torso displayed several reddish marks, the evidence of Mark's fervent body punches. Some would turn into bruises over the next couple of days. There was a minor scrape on his elbow, likely from the friction against the carpet during their tussle on the floor. His lips felt a bit swollen, a testament to the passionate exchanges they had shared. Overall, while Jason had been the more dominant of the two in their physical contest, he hadn't come away unscathed. His body would bear the marks of their encounter for a few days, but he felt they were well worth the experience.

Mark's face had a faint redness from the soft punches and slaps he'd received. Luckily, no bruises, but there would be some tenderness when he touched those areas. His torso, especially the gut area, bore the most evidence of their roughhousing. There were various shades of red and purple, the outcome of Jason's powerful punches. His wrists displayed faint red marks, possibly from being held down at certain points during their intense session. A few superficial scratches on his back, likely from the friction against the bed linen during their more passionate moments. The most profound feeling was a deep soreness in his ass, a direct result of Jason's intense climax. It was a sensation that Mark knew would remind him of the evening for a day or two. Both men understood that their bruises and marks were temporary, a physical testament to the raw intensity they had shared.

As the first light of dawn crept into the hotel room, Jason and Mark lay side by side, their breathing synchronized in the stillness of the early morning. The room bore silent witness to the night's events: the tousled bed linens, discarded clothing, empty cigarette packs, and the makeshift water glass ashtray. While the physical marks of their encounter would fade in a few days, the emotional and psychological impact would stay with them. They had ventured into uncharted territory, testing boundaries and building trust. It was a night neither would forget. As the two businessmen prepared to return to their professional lives, they shared a knowing look, a bond forged in the crucible of shared vulnerability and passion. They exchanged contact information with the promise of staying in touch, an understanding that this might not be their last encounter. The business trip came to an end, and they returned to their respective homes and routines. However, the connection remained. They would occasionally chat, sharing updates about their lives, the challenges of their jobs, and, sometimes, reminiscing about that fateful night. The encounter had awakened something in both of them, a deeper understanding of themselves and the possibilities of human connection. It had been a night of extremes, of pushing boundaries and discovering new facets of their identities. And while life went on, with its usual mix of highs and lows, the memory of that night remained, a testament to the unpredictable, often profound connections that can be forged between two people.

JO'S LITTLE SECRET

Mae and Jo were in bed, the soft glow of their cigarettes illuminating the room after an incredible sexual encounter. They lay in silence for a while, enjoying the afterglow and the warmth of each other's presence. But as the last wisps of smoke drifted towards the ceiling, Mae suddenly straddled Jo. Jo's eyes met Mae's, expecting another round of passionate lovemaking. Instead, Mae's gaze was hard and serious. "Tell me about this Karen," she demanded, her voice cold. Before Jo could even process the question, a stinging blow landed on her lips. Mae had punched her squarely in the mouth. Jo, stunned and bleeding, gasped, "What the fuck, Mae?" "You think I wouldn't find out? That I didn't know?" Mae's voice trembled with fury. Jo's mind raced, trying to find the link between their intimate moment and this sudden rage about Karen. "Mae, what on earth are you talking about?" Mae throws another punch into Jo's cheek. "Don't play games!" Mae snapped, her fingers digging into Jo's wrists. "The messages, the calls, the secrets, all with Karen." With Jo's leg slightly spread, Mae delivers a hard knee into Jo's unprotected pussy. Jo cries out in pain.

Suddenly, it clicked for Jo. "Mae," she said, her voice filled with both pain and realization, "Karen is my sister. We've been planning a surprise birthday party for you. I didn't want to spoil the surprise. Please stop; you're hurting me." Mae's face drained of color as the weight of her misunderstanding crashed down on her. Her grip on Jo's wrists slackened. "Your sister?" she murmured, tears filling her eyes. "Yes," Jo replied, touching her bleeding lip, "Trust, Mae. I though you trusted me." The bedroom air was thick with tension as Mae's guilt-ridden eyes sought out Jo. "I'm so sorry, Jo," she whispered, her voice choked with regret. "Can you ever forgive me?" Jo gingerly touched her swollen lip, feeling a sense of satisfaction at Mae's remorse. She retreated to the bathroom, using the moment to light another cigarette. The smoke curled up as Jo examined herself in the mirror. Her reflection showed a woman skilled in the art of manipulation, and the lie she had just spun was one of her finest.

"Mae," she called out, voice dripping with feigned hurt, "I can't believe you'd jump to conclusions like this." The door muffled her words, but Jo knew Mae could hear the disappointment in her tone. From the other side, Mae's voice was shaky. "I trust you, Jo. I should've never doubted you. I am so sorry." Jo privately smirked, inhaling deeply. Mae's trust was her greatest weapon. It allowed Jo the freedom she desired while still enjoying the lavish lifestyle Mae provided. Returning to the bedroom, Jo met Mae's remorseful gaze. "It's okay," she said softly, making sure her eyes looked hurt but forgiving. "I understand why you might've been worried." Mae hesitated, then whispered, "I just... I love you so much, Jo."

Jo smiled sweetly, wrapping her arms around Mae, "I love you too." It was a lie she had perfected over time. The truth was that Karen, hidden away from Mae's knowledge, was the one Jo desired and who she had been seeing behind Mae's back for some time now. But

Karen didn't have the wealth and luxury Mae offered. Jo had always been good at playing both sides, extracting what she wanted from each relationship. As the night deepened, Jo felt a rush of adrenaline. The thrill of lying, the excitement of having two lovers, and the luxury that Mae provided all fed into her manipulative game. For now, she was winning, but deep down, she knew that every game had its risks. She was prepared to face the moment of truth when that time occurred; but tonight was not the night.

The intricacies of Jo's lies became a delicate dance she expertly maneuvered. As weeks turned to months, she spun tales of imaginary family gatherings, sudden emergencies, and late-night work commitments – all fabrications designed to buy her time with Karen. However, Mae, with her inherent trust and love, began picking up on inconsistencies. Once, she had called Jo's workplace only to find out she'd taken the day off when Jo had claimed she was working late. Another time, Mae bumped into a mutual acquaintance who unknowingly revealed that they had seen Jo out at a restaurant when Jo had claimed she was visiting her non-existent sister. Mae's confusion and concern grew with each discrepancy. When she would tentatively approach Jo with her doubts, Jo's response was always fiery defensiveness. "Why are you always doubting me?" Jo would snap, turning the conversation into a blame game.

On more than one occasion, these confrontations escalated beyond heated words. Jo, using her manipulative nature to shift blame, would lash out physically at Mae. And every time, in a twisted cycle of guilt and dependence, Mae would end up apologizing, feeling that she was at fault for doubting Jo and causing the discord. Their relationship dynamics became a toxic dance of suspicion, deflection, and regret. Jo grew more audacious in her lies, while Mae became increasingly insecure, second-guessing her every thought and feeling. Deep down, Mae knew something wasn't right. Her instincts told her that Jo's stories didn't add up, but the emotional manipulation and occasional violence left her feeling disoriented, doubting her own judgment. The luxurious gifts and experiences Jo provided with Mae's wealth served as a temporary salve, but they couldn't mask the growing rift between them.

Mae, despite her feelings of guilt and insecurity, couldn't ignore the nagging sensation that something was awry. She decided to take matters into her own hands and gather undeniable proof. It wasn't a decision she took lightly, knowing it could forever alter the course of their relationship.

Mae, having grown desperate, placed a small hidden camera in their shared living space.
The footage from the hidden camera was more agonizing for Mae than any physical pain she'd ever felt. The intimacy between Jo and Karen on Mae's own bed was a severe betrayal. However, what cut even deeper were their callous words. Mae's hands trembled as she watched Jo lean into Karen, whispering something that made both women break into laughter. "Mae really believes this whole charade," Jo chuckled. "Can you believe it?" Karen snorted, tossing her head back with amusement. "She's so pathetically gullible. Sometimes I wonder how someone can be so dense." The camera captured Jo's smirk clearly. "Every time I feed her one of my sob stories about a

'family emergency' or a 'late work night', she laps it all up. It's like stealing candy from a baby." Karen, mimicking a childish voice, teased, "Oh, Jo, I trust you. You'd never lie to me." They both broke into peals of laughter, clearly enjoying their cruel game. "They say love is blind," Jo sneered, "but in Mae's case, it's also deaf and dumb." As their laughter filled the room, Mae felt a mixture of emotions — from anger to heartbreak to disbelief. Each derogatory name they threw at her, each snide remark, was a sharp reminder of the deception she'd fallen victim to. The pain of the affair was one thing, but the blatant disrespect and mockery were unbearable. Karen laughed even harder. "And the best part? We're doing all of this right under her nose, in her house, on her bed." Jo, playfully poking Karen, added, "Using her money, too. She's just a little piggy bank for us."

The sting of betrayal had left Mae burning with anger and a need for vengeance. The repeated images of Jo and Karen on her bed, their cruel laughter echoing in her mind, fueled her resolve. While confronting Jo was inevitable, Mae knew that to truly hurt Jo, she needed to target Karen first. Mae had resources and contacts; it wasn't difficult for her to track Karen's routines. She learned about her favorite places, where she hung out, even her late-night excursions. With each detail she gathered, her plan crystallized. One evening, Mae followed Karen discreetly as she left a local bar. The alleyway next to the bar was dimly lit, providing the perfect setting for Mae's confrontation. The night air was thick with tension as Mae approached Karen in the alleyway. As Karen fumbled for her car keys, she became aware of a shadow looming behind her. Turning, she came face-to-face with a furious Mae, eyes ablaze with anger and determination.

For a split second, there was a standstill. Both women sizing up each other, knowing that the confrontation was inevitable. Karen's eyes darted, looking for an escape, but Mae was quicker. Launching forward, Mae threw a right hook at Karen's jaw. The force caught Karen off guard, causing her to stumble back into her car. Recovering quickly, Karen tried to raise her arms to shield herself, but Mae was relentless. She jabbed at Karen's midsection, forcing the wind out of her. Karen gasped, but there was no reprieve. Mae's anger was evident in every blow she landed — each one a testament to her sense of betrayal. But Karen wasn't going down without a fight. Pushing herself off the car, she lunged at Mae, trying to grapple her to the ground. The two women crashed onto the cold asphalt, the scuffle causing dust to rise. Locked in a tight embrace, Karen managed to land a few punches on Mae's ribs. Mae grunted in pain but quickly retaliated, her fingers searching for Karen's hair. Yanking it hard, Mae rolled, pinning Karen beneath her. Their faces were inches apart, and for a moment, the intensity of Mae's gaze threatened to overpower even the physical pain she was inflicting. However, Karen was not done. Using her legs, she kicked at Mae's abdomen, creating just enough space to free herself. She scrambled to her feet, her eyes scanning the alley for anything she could use as a weapon or a means of escape. But Mae was on her feet just as quickly, and the two circled each other like predators. There was no more taunting, no words, just the heavy sound of breathing and the occasional grunt of exertion.

Suddenly, Karen lunged forward, trying to tackle

Mae. But Mae sidestepped, using Karen's momentum against her and pushing her hard into the brick wall of a nearby building. Mae threw numerous punches that into Karen's midsection, side, ribs and face. One final punch from Mae had Karen's back sliding down the brick wall onto the ground. After what felt like an eternity, Mae took a step back, her breathing heavy. Karen was on the ground, dazed and hurting. Leaning down, Mae whispered, "Tell Jo this was just a preview. She's next." With that, Mae left the scene, leaving Karen in the dark alley to contend with both her physical pain and the realization that their secret was out.

Jo's heart raced as she parked her car outside her shared home with Mae. The news of Karen's beating had hit her like a ton of bricks. Panic had gripped her initially, but as she approached the house, a simmering anger began to replace her initial shock. The front door was slightly ajar, a sign that someone was waiting inside. She pushed the door open cautiously and stepped into the dimly lit living room. There, in the soft glow of a solitary lamp, was Mae. She sat poised on the sofa, one leg crossed over the other, a lit cigarette held elegantly between two fingers. The TV screen was paused on an all-too-familiar frame: her and Karen, in Mae's bed. Their eyes locked. The atmosphere was thick with tension, the air punctuated only by the soft exhale of Mae's smoke. "So," Mae began, her voice icy, gesturing towards the screen, "Recognize this?"

Jo swallowed hard. She tried to maintain a neutral expression, but her eyes betrayed her shock and anger. "What did you do to Karen, Mae?" Mae took a drag from her cigarette, letting the smoke curl out slowly. "I taught her a lesson." The anger in Jo's voice was undeniable. "You had no right! No matter what happened between us, Karen didn't deserve that." Mae leaned forward, grabbing the remote and pressing play. The room filled with their mocking laughter and derogatory remarks about Mae from Karen. "Did you really think you could mock and betray me without consequences, Jo?" For a moment, the room was silent. The weight of their shared history, the love and now the betrayal, hung heavily between them. Jo's voice quivered with emotion. "This isn't just about Karen, is it?" Mae smirked, her eyes sharp. "No. It's about us, too." Jo took a step closer, her eyes never leaving Mae's. "And what now? You've made your point. Karen's hurt, and we're broken." Mae rose from the sofa, standing tall, placing her cigarette in an ashtray. Their faces were mere inches apart. "Now," Mae whispered, her voice laced with venom, "you're going to understand the pain of betrayal. Just like I did."

The tension in the room was thick. Mae, with her unwavering gaze, looked deeply into Jo's eyes. "Jo," she began, her voice firm but controlled, "I'm not going to kick you out. You can stay, live under my roof, and enjoy all the comforts my money affords. But things are going to be very different." Jo shifted uneasily, the weight of the situation pressing down on her. She swallowed hard, trying to anticipate what Mae might say next. Mae continued, "You've used me, played games with my emotions, and enjoyed every luxury I provided. If you choose to stay, it will be on my terms." She paused for emphasis, leaning in slightly, "I own your ass. Every decision, every move, every word... will be under my watchful eye. No more games, no more lies. Your freedom, as you've known it, is over." The air grew thick,

Jo's heart pounding loudly in her chest. The gravity of her actions and the consequences now facing her became clear. She was cornered, trapped by her own deceit.

Jo's mind raced. She could leave, start anew somewhere else, far from the comforts and luxuries she had grown accustomed to. But she also knew the financial and emotional challenges that awaited her. On the other hand, staying with Mae meant a life of surveillance, servitude, and a loss of the independence she had once taken for granted. Lighting a cigarette, Mae patiently waited for Jo's response. Finally, Jo spoke, her voice barely above a whisper, "I'll stay." The words felt heavy, sealing her fate. Mae raised an eyebrow, taking a deep drag from her cigarette. The cold smile still playing on her lips. "And?" she prompted. Jo hesitated for a moment, gathering the shreds of her pride. Then, swallowing hard, she finally conceded, "And... you own my ass. I'll follow your rules." Mae stepped back; satisfaction evident in her posture. "That's what I wanted to hear." The room's atmosphere shifted from tense confrontation to a new, uneasy equilibrium, with Mae holding all the cards. Mae smiled, a cold, calculated smile, "I thought you might. From now on, you'll remember your place."

Mae's voice was composed, but the fire in her eyes spoke volumes. "You need to be punished, Jo. And you're going to have a say in how it happens." She took a step closer, ensuring Jo was listening to every word. Mae began to lay out the options. "One, I can take off my belt and give you a whipping you won't forget for a long while." She paused, allowing the weight of the option to sink in. "Two, I can punch you until you're on your knees, begging for me to stop." Jo shifted uneasily, her eyes darting as she weighed each option. But Mae wasn't finished. "Or three," Mae continued, her voice taking on a dangerous edge, "we can have a proper fight. You can fight back, defend yourself, and maybe even land a few blows of your own. But remember, Jo, it'll be no holds barred. Anything goes." The room seemed to grow even colder. Jo gulped audibly, torn between the horrifying choices presented to her. The idea of a whipping was terrifying, but the notion of being punched repeatedly until she was forced to her knees was equally daunting. Yet the third option, a full-blown fight, held its own risks and potential injuries.

Finally, after what felt like an eternity, Jo found her voice. "I'll fight," she whispered, her tone filled with a mix of defiance and fear. "If I'm to be punished, I'd rather face you head-on." Mae smirked, impressed by Jo's bravery or perhaps foolishness. "Very well," she said with a chilling calmness. "Prepare yourself."

The atmosphere in the room intensified as Mae lit another cigarette and began to unbutton her blouse, eyes never leaving Jo's. With a deliberate slowness, she slid the fabric off her shoulders, placing it neatly on the back of a chair. The tension only grew as she unzipped her skirt, letting it fall to the floor, standing confidently in her bra and panties. The stark contrast of her underwear against her skin, combined with the dangerous glint in her eyes, made for an intimidating sight. Mae had the physique of someone who took care of herself, toned muscles hinting at hidden strength. She pointed a commanding finger at Jo. "Your turn. Strip." Jo hesitated, taken aback by the unexpected directive. But one look at Mae's unyielding expression was enough to convince her that resistance would be unwise. Trying to match Mae's calm demeanor, Jo also lit a cigarette and began to undress, her movements more hesitant and self-conscious. Soon, she too stood in only her bra and panties, her vulnerability evident. The two women locked eyes, the electricity between them undeniable. What was to come was not just about physical prowess but also a battle of wills and emotions. The stakes were higher than ever, and both knew that this confrontation would shape the trajectory of their relationship.

Mae and Jo circled each other, feet padding softly on the floor, both searching for any sign of weakness in the other. The stillness was suddenly broken by Jo lunging forward, throwing a right hook to Mae's face. The punch rocks Mae back, but she counters with a swift jab to Jo's midsection. Jo grunted from the impact but retaliated with a series of punches. Some Mae easily parried; others found their mark. But for every successful hit Jo managed, Mae delivered two in return, her hits harder and more precise. Mae's experience and strength began to show. She moved with purpose, her footwork impeccable, dodging Jo's increasingly desperate swings while landing her punches with devastating accuracy. Jo's face reddened from the blows, her eyes swelling, lips split. Despite the odds, Jo didn't relent. She was determined, driven by a mix of regret, fear, and pride. But no amount of determination could make up for the difference in skill and power. Mae seized an opportunity when Jo left herself open after a poorly aimed haymaker. She unleashed a rapid combination, striking Jo's face, chest, and stomach. Jo stumbled back, gasping for air, the force of Mae's blows pushing her off-balance. In the end, Mae landed a solid uppercut, lifting Jo slightly off her feet and sending her crashing to the floor. Jo lay there, disoriented and panting heavily, her body a testament to the severity of the beating she'd received. Mae, breathing hard but still standing, looked down at her with a mix of pity and anger. "It's over," she declared, her voice stern, leaving no room for argument. Jo, battered and defeated, could do nothing but nod in agreement from her prone position on the floor.

Mae, with a mixture of exhaustion and triumph evident in her posture, gracefully sunk into the soft cushions of the sofa. She pulled out a sleek silver cigarette case from the nearby coffee table, selected a cigarette, and lit it, drawing in the smoke deeply, allowing it to momentarily cloud her thoughts. Jo, still nursing the physical reminders of their confrontation, hesitantly moved towards the sofa, her movements betraying the pain she felt. Mae, without looking, extended the case towards her, an unspoken invitation. Jo took a cigarette, lit it, and inhaled deeply, the familiar burn providing a brief distraction from the aches and throbbing. The two women sat side by side, a tangible tension hanging in the air, broken only by the periodic exhales of smoke. The events of the evening had irrevocably altered the dynamics of their relationship. There was a new understanding, a painful acknowledgment of the undercurrents that had always existed between them.

Mae's love for Jo was undeniable. Every action, even the fight, had been colored by her profound sense of betrayal and an underlying need to reestablish the trust and intimacy they once shared. But the question that lingered like the smoke in the room was Jo's intentions. Jo had been drawn to Mae's opulence, to the allure of a life she had never known. The money, the gifts, the lavish experiences, all were intoxicating. But as she sat there, nursing her wounds, Jo was forced to confront her own feelings. Did she truly care for Mae, or was she merely infatuated with the lifestyle Mae offered? Their future seemed uncertain. While Mae's love provided a foundation, the question was whether Jo could, or would, genuinely reciprocate those feelings beyond the material gains. If she couldn't, their relationship was bound to be a series of tumultuous encounters, always on the brink of another explosion. But if she could find genuine affection and commitment for Mae, there might be a chance for them to rebuild, to find a deeper, more authentic connection amidst the chaos they'd wrought.

THE REDEMPTION

A week ago, Sue's laughter had echoed throughout her home, filling the rooms with warmth and joy. Now, as she nursed her bruises, she bore the weight of betrayal. She was resilient, though the raw marks on her skin were painful reminders of the ambush by Karen and her accomplice. Sue had considered Karen a close friend for years. Their bond was apparent in the framed pictures on Sue's walls. But something had gone sour, and Sue was left grappling with the whys and hows of the sudden treachery. When Tammy, another friend of Sue's, learned of the altercation, anger surged within her. Sue was not just a friend; she was like a sister to Tammy. The thought of Karen taking advantage of Sue, especially with another's aid, was too much to bear. Tammy decided she would make sure Karen wouldn't hurt Sue or anyone else ever again.

Standing at Karen's doorstep, Tammy's knock was firm and resolute. The door creaked open, revealing a seemingly surprised Karen. "Tammy?" she queried. "I have some papers for you," Tammy said curtly, holding out the envelope as a pretense. As Karen reached out to take them, Tammy swiftly moved past her, stepping inside. Without giving Karen a chance to respond, Tammy's voice was icy as she uttered, "This is for Sue." In the split-second that followed, both women sized each other up, understanding that what came next was a physical showdown neither had anticipated. Karen was the first to act, launching herself at Tammy with a wild right hook to her face. Tammy lunged, trying to knock Karen off balance with a quick push. But Karen was agile and managed to sidestep, swiftly retaliating by attempting to sweep Tammy's legs from beneath her. As Tammy stumbled backwards, Karen followed up with a knee aimed at Tammy's midsection. Twisting her body to the side, Tammy avoided the brunt of the blow, using the momentum to punch Karen in the ribs.

Gasping from the pain, Karen clutched her side and staggered backwards, knocking a vase off a hallway table. The crashing sound seemed to escalate the intensity of their duel. With narrowed eyes, Karen lunged again, her fingers aiming for Tammy's eyes in a desperate attempt to blind her temporarily. But Tammy was prepared. She grabbed Karen's wrists, pulling them downwards while pushing her knee upwards, catching Karen in the stomach. As Karen doubled over, Tammy attempted to subdue her with a chokehold, her forearm pressing against Karen's throat. The two fought, their struggles causing them to bump into walls and knock over picture frames. The scuff marks of their shoes on the wooden floor bore witness to the fierceness of their fight. Karen, feeling the pressure around her neck, summoned all her remaining strength to elbow Tammy in the side. This forced Tammy to release her grip momentarily. Both women, now panting heavily, circled each other, eyes locked, each waiting for the other to make a move.

With a sudden burst of energy, Tammy closed the distance, tackling Karen to the floor. The two wrestled, rolling over and over, each trying to gain the upper hand. But in the end, it was Tammy's sheer determination and the weight of her resolve that pinned Karen beneath her. With Karen subdued and clearly defeated, Tammy's heavy breathing was the only sound that filled the house for a few moments before she spoke her final warning. In the heat of their skirmish, Tammy's memories of Sue's injured face fueled her with a righteous fury. With Karen momentarily dazed from their tussle, Tammy seized the upper hand. Her right fist clenched, she delivered a sharp punch to Karen's left cheek, immediately leaving a red imprint. Karen tried to protect her face, her arms flailing, but Tammy's onslaught was relentless. Another punch landed on Karen's nose, causing a painful crunching sound and an immediate flow of blood. Karen's eyes welled up, both from the pain and the humiliation of the moment. Not stopping there, Tammy took a moment to aim and delivered two more punches in quick succession to Karen's right eye. The impact caused an instant swell, darkening by the second, ensuring it would be a deep purple bruise in no time - a mirror to Sue's own injury.

The force of the punches drove Karen's head back against the wooden floor of the hallway, disorienting her. Each hit was a message, a declaration that the pain inflicted upon Sue was neither forgotten nor forgiven. With Karen's resistance waning, Tammy finally stepped back, her own hands throbbing from the intensity of her blows. There was a stark contrast between the two women now. Tammy, standing tall and breathing heavily, eyes ablaze with triumph and justice, while Karen lay on the floor, her face bloodied and bruised, a clear reflection of her treachery. With Karen groaning on the floor, her face a patchwork of pain, Tammy leaned down, her eyes cold but determined. Their faces were inches apart, and in a steely whisper that promised consequence, Tammy said, "You might have outnumbered Sue, but she's not alone. If you so much as think of hurting her or anyone else again, remember this moment. Remember that there are consequences, and I won't hesitate to remind you of them." Karen's swollen eye met Tammy's fierce gaze, and she swallowed hard, pain evident not just from the physical beatdown but also from the weight of the warning. Without another word, Tammy turned and strode out of the house, leaving behind a scene that would remain etched in Karen's memory for a long time.

INSIDE THE BIG RIG (M/M)

The night was thick with tension, and the desolate hum of the truck stop seemed to accentuate it. The vast expanse of parked rigs and dim streetlights painted a scene straight out of an old noir film. Mitch stood leaning against his rig, an orange ember glowing at the end of his cigarette. He eyed the darkened corner where Jake was expected to emerge. Sure enough, the figure of Jake appeared, the glow from his cigarette announcing his presence. "Mitch," he grumbled, the smoky haze that surrounded him seeming to match the mood. "You really want to do this shit?" Mitch smirked, taking one last drag before flicking his cigarette away. "I've been waiting, haven't I?" He reached behind him, yanking open the door to the refrigerated section of his trailer. The hum of the cooling units created an isolating barrier, muffling sounds from the outside. "In here. We can settle this without an audience." Jake eyed the open space, a cold gust wafting out. "Fitting. Our hot-blooded history, now playing out in the cold." He stepped up, heading into the refrigerated chamber. Mitch followed suit, closing the door behind them. Inside, their breaths materialized, and the walls echoed every sound. The confinement added an extra layer of intensity to an already heated moment.

Jake took the first swing, a powerful right hook aimed at Mitch's jaw. The impact sent Mitch stumbling backward, but he quickly regained his footing, lunging forward with a ferocious counterattack. His target was Jake's eyes, wanting to ensure that for the next few days, every time Jake looked in the mirror, he'd be reminded of their encounter. Jake winced as Mitch's knuckles contacted the area below his eye, feeling the immediate sting and knowing a bruise would soon form. But it only seemed to fuel his fire. He charged, tackling Mitch to the ground. They grappled, their bodies writhing and twisting as they each tried to gain the upper hand. The proximity, the raw physicality of their struggle, had an undeniably electrifying undercurrent. Their shared intimate past and the emotions of the present intertwined, transforming their fight into something deeply primal.

Mitch managed to get on top, straddling Jake. He landed a few more blows, each calculated — forceful enough to hurt, but with a restraint that showed he didn't want to cause lasting harm. Jake's face was now a mosaic of reds and purples, but he fought back with renewed vigor, landing a solid punch to Mitch's midsection. The blow winded Mitch, allowing Jake to reverse their positions. Now on top, Jake unleashed a flurry of punches, focusing on Mitch's face, especially around his eyes. With each strike, he remembered the times Mitch had looked at Lila, a truck stop waitress that was their shared object of affection. If he had his way, Mitch wouldn't be looking at her — or anyone else — without the reminder of this encounter. Finally, exhaustion began to take its toll. Their punches grew slower, their movements more labored.

Their bodies ached from the impact and the cold, and yet, amid the pain and exhaustion, there was an undeniable connection, a potent mix of anger, passion, and raw desire. Lying there in the frosty chamber, battered and bruised, they both knew they had reached a threshold. The fight was brutal, but it was also cathartic, a physical release of all the tension and emotions that had built up over the years. Both men had come to a point that they need a break. They both moved apart.

Mitch, his breathing heavy from the fight, fumbled with his shirt pocket, trying to get a cigarette. When he pulled out the pack, it was crushed — a testament to the ferocity of their brawl. He let out a string of expletives, his frustration evident. "Give me a fucking cigarette," he snapped at Jake, his voice gravelly from the exertion. Jake smirked, reaching into his own pocket. He pulled out two cigarettes, lighting them simultaneously with a single flick of his lighter. But just as he was about to hand one to Mitch, Jake's fist came out of nowhere, connecting sharply with Mitch's already-bruised cheek. Mitch grunted in pain, staggering back a step, eyes flashing with anger and surprise. "Here, fucker," Jake said, a devilish grin on his face, as he extended the lit cigarette to Mitch. Mitch took it, inhaling deeply, the smoke helping to soothe his battered nerves and body. He shot Jake a seething look, but there was also a hint of begrudging respect. The two of them were a tangled mess of emotions, and every interaction — whether a punch or a shared smoke — was laced with layers of history and intensity.

Jake's eyes widened in surprise as Mitch's hand shot out, grabbing him by the crotch with a vice-like grip. The force of Mitch's hold made Jake's back meet the cold wall of the refrigerated unit, trapping him. He grunted, both from the unexpectedness of the gesture and the mixture of pain and pleasure that surged through him. Mitch leaned in, his face inches from Jake's, his breath visible in the cold air. He smirked, feeling the undeniable hardness of Jake's cock. "You fucker," Mitch whispered, voice laced with a mix of amusement and arousal, "you're hard as a rock." But just as suddenly as the intimate touch began, it ended. Mitch released his grip, and with a swift motion, punched Jake square in the gut. Jake doubled over, gasping for breath, the contrasting sensations leaving him dazed and disoriented. Their interactions were a volatile mix of aggression and attraction, each move oscillating between passion and rage.

Mitch took a deep drag from his cigarette, the glowing ember briefly illuminating the tense atmosphere in the cold chamber. He exhaled, watching the smoke curl upwards before dissipating into the frigid air. The raw physicality of their brawl had brought them to a point of undeniable arousal, and it hung heavily between them, an unspoken challenge that neither man seemed willing to address directly. Breaking the silence, Mitch's raspy voice held a mix of challenge and curiosity. "So," he began, nodding toward their evident arousal, "you think we're gonna stand here like a couple of teenagers, or you got a plan to deal with... this?" He tilted his head, indicating both their erections. Jake took a slow breath, his eyes locked onto Mitch's, searching for something. A decision, an acknowledgment, perhaps just an understanding of the complex emotions they shared. "You always did have a way of pointing out the obvious," Jake replied, his voice laced with sarcasm but also a hint of amusement. He looked down briefly at their mutual state of arousal, then back up, a smirk forming. "Maybe it's time we address this... distraction." He stepped closer, reducing the space between them, his voice dropping to a whisper. "After all, we've always been good at multitasking, haven't we?" The statement, though spoken in jest, held layers of meaning from their shared history, and Jake's eyes sparkled with a mix of challenge and anticipation.

With the cigarette perched precariously between his lips, Jake's hands moved with a practiced confidence towards Mitch. The smoke curled upwards, grazing his eyes and causing them to narrow slightly, but his focus remained unwavering. Each movement was deliberate, as his fingers began working on the top button of Mitch's worn jeans. The familiar texture of the denim, rough against the pads of his fingertips, was a stark contrast to the warmth he could feel emanating from beneath. The subtle noises of the surrounding refrigerated unit, the hum of the machinery, and their shared, slightly ragged breaths created a backdrop to this intimate act. With each button that Jake undid, the tension between the two men seemed to increase, building in anticipation. Mitch watched intently, the cigarette smoke from Jake's lips caressing his face, the scent mingling with their shared adrenaline and the underlying aroma of motor oil and leather from their earlier scuffle. By the time Jake had finished with the last button, the weight of their shared history and the present intensity hung thick in the air, challenging them to confront the complexity of their relationship once again.

The atmosphere inside the refrigerated unit was already thick with tension, but as Mitch's actions took a sudden turn, it escalated to an entirely new level. With a swift motion, Mitch plucked the cigarette from Jake's lips, placing it between his own. The ember glowed brighter as he took a deep drag, exhaling with a mix of relief and determination. With practiced ease, Mitch began to unthread the belt from his jeans, its leather sliding smoothly through the loops. Jake watched, an underlying anticipation evident in his eyes. The two of them had been down this road before, familiar with the dance of dominance and submission that intertwined with their complex relationship. Before Jake could react, the belt was looped around the back of his neck. Mitch held one end firmly in each hand, securing Jake in a grip that was both restrictive yet oddly familiar. The tension on the belt determined Jake's posture and movement, an unspoken communication passing between them.

Jake's face was brought closer to Mitch, the proximity removing any semblance of personal space. As Mitch's grip on the belt tightened, Jake found himself in a compromising position, with Mitch's cock filling his mouth. The cigarette remained clenched between Mitch's teeth, its smoke swirling around them, adding to the heady mix of adrenaline, desire, and power dynamics. Every movement, every breath, and every touch was a testament to the raw, complicated bond they shared. Despite the constraining grip and the precarious position he was in, Jake's expertise was immediately evident. His lips sealed seamlessly around Mitch, applying just the right amount of pressure. It was an act that had taken place many times before, with Jake taking the lead this time. Jake's tongue worked with a precision that only comes from experience, moving in ways that had Mitch biting down harder on the cigarette, trying to stifle the groans that threatened to spill out. Every nuanced movement was intentional, from the way he swirled his tongue to the gentle suction he applied, drawing out the sensations and driving Mitch closer to the edge. Even under the restrictive pull of the belt, Jake managed to maintain a rhythm that was both tantalizing and torturous for Mitch. The juxtaposition of their aggressive confrontation and this intimate act only heightened the intensity of the moment. The cold air of the refrigerated unit seemed inconsequential compared to the fiery heat of their connection. Mitch's fingers tightened on the belt instinctively, responding to the waves of pleasure coursing through him. The grip was a reminder of their power dynamic, a blend of dominance and submission that underlined the very essence of their relationship. Throughout it all, the one constant was Jake's undeniable skill, proving once again that, even in the most challenging of situations, he was a master at his craft.

As the sensations built and the atmosphere in the refrigerated unit thickened with tension, Jake's survival instincts began to kick in. Amidst the pleasure and power play, he suddenly threw a punch to Mitch's side, a quick jab that was meant to both surprise and alert. Mitch grunted in response, the sting of the blow bringing a rush of emotions. Almost instinctively, his grip on the belt tightened, constricting Jake's movements and breathing. The leather bit into the back of Jake's neck, a stinging reminder of the control Mitch held. Jake managed to land another punch, this one slightly harder, aiming for the same spot on Mitch's side. The response was immediate: Mitch tightened his grip on the belt even more, the leather becoming a vice around Jake's neck. The sudden restriction caused Jake to gag, his eyes watering as he struggled to maintain composure.

The atmosphere in the refrigerated unit was intense. Mitch's fingers, which had been clenching the belt so tightly, finally relented, letting the leather fall slack around Jake's neck. As he released his grip, he took a deep drag from the cigarette, the ember burning brighter with his inhalation. The combination of the physical exertion, Jake's undeniable skill, and the heightened emotions from their altercation culminated in an intense moment for Mitch. With the cigarette smoke still swirling from his lips, he reached his peak, surrendering to the sensations that Jake had expertly brought forth. For a few seconds, the only sounds in the unit were their heavy breathing and the muted hum of the machinery around them.

Jake, gasping for breath after the constriction of the belt and the intensity of the moment, immediately spat out what Mitch had deposited in his mouth. The thick liquid landed on the cold metal floor of the refrigerated unit, slowly being absorbed into a wet spot. Mitch, still trying to catch his breath from the climax and the weight of their actions, looked down at the spot and then back up to Jake. Their eyes locked, a myriad of emotions flashing between them: challenge, satisfaction, regret, and a hint of defiance from Jake. For a moment, neither said anything. The act of spitting, simple yet symbolic, was Jake's way of reasserting some semblance of control and individuality after the intense power play they had just navigated.

Mitch's reaction was swift and visceral. The act of Jake spitting out what Mitch had given him felt like a direct challenge, a slight against the dominant-submissive dance they'd been engaged in. With adrenaline and emotion still coursing through his veins, Mitch's hand shot out, grabbing a fistful of Jake's hair, yanking his head back to expose his face. "My load not good enough for you?" Mitch said. Before Jake could react or utter a word, Mitch's other hand swung forward, landing a solid punch to Jake's face. The impact made a sharp sound that echoed in the enclosed space of the refrigerated unit, reverberating off the cold metal walls. Jake's head snapped to the side, pain flashing in his eyes. Mitch, breathing heavily, his voice dripping with a mix of anger and arousal, growled, "That's for not swallowing, bitch." The harsh fluorescent lights overhead cast a cold glow over the scene, highlighting the reddening mark on Jake's face and the fierce determination in Mitch's eyes.

Jake, still reeling from the punch and the aggressive pull on his hair, tried to regain his composure. He blinked hard, the taste of blood evident in his mouth. Jake stands up in front of Mitch, answering his previous punch, Jake delivers a hard punch to Mitch's gut. "Time to stretch that ass," Jake said, his voice gravelly and low, a promise of what was to come. Mitch swallowed hard. Their relationship had always been a complex tangle of emotions, dominance, submission, pain, and pleasure. Tonight was no different. Mitch's smirk grew wider, his eyes glinting with mischief. "Remember the last time you tried taking charge, pencil dick?" His words dripped with condescension and a hint of playfulness, a throwback to an old nickname and perhaps an old argument or jest between the two. Jake's face reddened, a combination of anger and embarrassment. That nickname had always been a sore spot for him, a jab from their past, when their banter would sometimes cross the line from playful to hurtful. "Oh, you're really asking for it now," Jake retorted, trying to mask the sting of the old insult with a show of bravado.

In one swift motion, Jake's arm snaked around Mitch's neck, pulling him in close. Their bodies pressed together, the cold of the refrigerated unit contrasting with the heat radiating off them. With Mitch momentarily immobilized by Jake's hold, Jake seized the opportunity. His free hand launched a series of rapid-fire punches into Mitch's midsection. Each impact landed with a thud, the sound echoing within the confines of the metal chamber. Mitch grunted with each blow, the wind knocked out of him repeatedly, his body instinctively trying to double over but restricted by Jake's grip. The punches were driven not just by physical strength but also by the pent-up emotions, frustrations, and the complexity of their relationship. Each hit was a manifestation of their tumultuous bond, a mix of anger, passion, and dominance. After what felt like an eternity, Jake finally released his grip, letting a gasping Mitch stumble back.

Jake's hands moved to Mitch's waist, removing his jeans. Mitch offered no resistance as Jake tugged the fabric down, revealing Mitch's hardened arousal. Their eyes met briefly, a wordless acknowledgment passing between them. Using the cross bar for leverage, Mitch leaned into it, presenting himself in anticipation. Jake didn't waste any time, positioning himself just right, and with a firm hand on Mitch's hip, he began to thrust. The cold, metallic surroundings contrasted starkly with the warmth and intensity of their connection. Each movement was filled with raw emotion, a mingling of desire, dominance, and submission. The rhythmic sounds of their union echoed within the refrigerated unit, punctuated by the occasional grunt or moan. Jake's grip on Mitch tightened as he drove into him with force, ensuring that every thrust was deeply felt. Mitch held onto the cross bar, his knuckles white, the sensations coursing through him both overpowering and intoxicating.

Each thrust was punctuated by Jake's coarse language, a raw expression of the tumultuous emotions and passions coursing through him. "You like that, huh?" Jake growled, his voice dripping with lust and aggression. "Take it, Mitch. Fucking take it." Mitch, holding onto the crossbar for dear life, could only respond with gasps and grunts, each exclamation a testament to the intensity of their union. The cold of the refrigerated unit seemed to disappear, replaced by the heat generated between them. "You think you're so tough," Jake hissed, driving into Mitch with renewed fervor. "But you're mine, right now. All fucking mine." The combination of Jake's aggressive words and actions sent waves of sensation through Mitch, blurring the line between pleasure and pain. The air was thick with tension, punctuated only by the sounds of their physical connection and Jake's guttural curses.

With his free hand, Jake reached around Mitch's waist, seeking out Mitch's hardening cock. The moment his fingers made contact, Mitch let out a sharp intake of breath. Jake, still thrusting from behind, began to work Mitch with a practiced rhythm, milking him with a firm grip that matched the intensity of their union. Mitch's reactions grew even more fervent. Every touch from Jake, every thrust and squeeze, seemed to magnify the sensations coursing through him. The combination of being taken from behind while simultaneously being pleasured from the front was overwhelming. Jake's whispered curses and aggressive coaxing only added to the moment, pushing them both closer and closer to the edge. Their rhythm synchronized, each movement building on the previous one, driving them towards an intense climax that seemed inevitable. The confines of the refrigerated unit seemed to disappear as they lost themselves completely in the raw, passionate connection they shared.

The intensity between the two men reached a fever pitch. Jake's movements grew even more frenzied, his grip on Mitch tightening. With a guttural groan, he reached his climax, releasing deep inside Mitch in a surge of warmth and passion. Mitch felt every pulse of Jake's release, pushing him closer to his own edge. Jake's hand continued its rhythmic motion, milking Mitch with precision. Even as he felt the aftershocks of Jake's climax, Mitch was teetering on the brink.

A few more deliberate strokes from Jake, combined with the overwhelming sensations from their union, were all it took. With a shuddering moan, Mitch reached his own climax, his release spilling over Jake's fingers in heated waves. The two men remained connected for a moment longer, riding out the aftershocks of their intense union. The sounds of their heavy breathing and the occasional sigh filled the refrigerated unit, a testament to the raw passion they'd just shared.

In the aftermath of their intense encounter, Jake and Mitch slowly gathered themselves, dressing in a companionable silence, each lost in his own thoughts. The cold of the refrigerated unit, which had seemed so inconsequential during their heat-filled moments, now made itself known, causing them both to shiver. Mitch was the first to break the silence, lighting up a cigarette and taking a long drag. "We can't keep doing this," he said softly, smoke escaping his lips as he exhaled. Jake leaned against the cold metal wall, rubbing his temple. "I know. Every time we say it's the last time. Yet here we are." Mitch looked over, the corners of his lips quirking up in a half-smile. "It's complicated." Jake chuckled, "That's an understatement. But yeah, it is." He sighed, "Look, about the waitress..." Mitch waved it off, "Forget it. Old scores, new scores, it's all the same. We're just... us." Jake nodded, pausing for a moment before adding, "There's something between us, Mitch. Maybe we should try to figure it out rather than hiding behind fights and other distractions." Mitch raised an eyebrow, "You suggesting we, what? Fucking date?" Jake shrugged, "I don't know. Talk? Really talk? Without fists or... other things getting in the way." Mitch took another drag, blowing out a smoke ring. "Maybe. But not tonight."

ABOUT LIZ EDON

Liz Edon is a provocative voice in the world of erotic literature, penning tales that revolve around empowered, mature women with a penchant for smoking and fierce competition. Her stories often culminate in intense face-offs, where sensuality meets dominance, and where tension is released in fervid physical skirmishes.

Deeply influenced by the allure of confident women, Liz's narratives push the boundaries, daring to explore the edgier side of life. While her tales are fictional, they're woven with threads from her own experiences, granting her a unique perspective into the worlds she creates. This blending of reality and fiction provides a depth and authenticity that her readers cherish.

The realm of erotic literature is vast and varied, with many works catering to smoking fetishes or to the thrill of catfights. However, Liz's unique craft lies in melding these two passions. Her characters are as passionate about their cigarettes as they are about their battles, often indulging in both simultaneously. This distinctive combination sets Liz Edon apart, making her a cherished author for those seeking a blend of these exhilarating worlds.

Printed in Great Britain
by Amazon

46468223R00145